I0713128

Perceivers

#1

MIND SECRETS

by

Jane Killick

Elly Books

Mind Secrets
Perceivers #1

by

Jane Killick

Published by Elly Books

ISBN: 978-1-908340-19-1

Third Edition
Copyright © Jane Killick 2016

Previously published as Perceivers copyright © 2011
and under the author name Chris Reynolds copyright © 2012

ellybooks.com

ONE

THE carpet stank of rubber and stale coffee. He didn't know how long he'd been lying face down, but it was long enough for the pattern of scratchy fibres to embed itself in his cheek. Blinking himself to consciousness in the fluorescent light, he saw the carpet was dark brown and ran the length of a corridor of glass doors that led into dark offices. He tried to remember how he got there. He tried to remember why he had passed out. But the only thing in his mind was a pressing headache.

He drew up his knees and pulled himself to a sitting position, fighting the sudden dizziness that came over him. He leant back against the flimsy partition wall which wobbled under his slight teenage weight and allowed his mind to clear. Breathing deep, he relaxed his whole body, except for a tension in his right wrist that spread down through his hand and all the way up his forearm. Looking down, he saw — gripped tightly in his fist — the smooth plastic handle of a kitchen knife, its wide stainless steel blade glinting silver.

He didn't know why he had a knife. Just as he didn't know where the building was or what he was doing there. He tried hard to think back to before he had woken up on the floor, but reaching for the memories was like grasping at smoke. Every time he tried to remember, his thoughts drifted away into nothing. He tried to think about ordinary things: about his family, his home, his past … but he couldn't remember them. Looking inside his mind was like looking into a darkness, as black as a night with no moon or stars.

"Michael?" a woman's voice called from somewhere in the building.

He tensed. His name, it seemed, was Michael.

She called again, close enough to be heard, but far enough away to sound ghostly. "Michael, please come back!"

The voice seemed familiar, but it scared him. Michael looked at the knife in his hand and wondered if she was the reason he held onto it so tightly.

Michael staggered to his feet, reaching out for support from the partition wall, until he stood up straight. At the end of the corridor, a fire escape sign with the green symbol of a running man pointed to an emergency exit. Michael decided to take it.

The fire door was locked with a metal safety bar across the middle. He pushed it, the lock sprung free and the door opened onto a concrete landing. He stepped through, as fire alarms wailed around him, and looked down at a stairwell that spiralled flight after flight for at least ten storeys.

Michael let the door shut behind him and started running down, the incessant alarm bell echoing off the hard grey walls and stairs around him. It was easy at first, his feet cascaded down the stairs with the light touch of a dancer, but his muscles soon tired and he found himself touching the handrail as he went. Halfway down one flight, he misjudged a step and grabbed onto the handrail to stop himself falling head over heels to the bottom. He slowed a little and concentrated more as he kept going, so the only things he was aware of were his feet, the stairs and the agonising wail of the fire bell.

He didn't see the red-faced man until he reached the bottom of one flight of stairs and turned at the same time as the man climbed onto the landing from the flight below. He was at least in his forties, slightly overweight and out of breath from climbing several sets of stairs. He wore a black suit with an open-necked white shirt, so he obviously wasn't a fireman.

"Hello, Michael," said the man.

Michael flinched at the use of his name. He felt the smoothness of the knife handle in his fist, held out of sight behind his leg.

The man pressed a finger to a communication device sticking out of his ear. "This is Agent Cooper," he said. "The kid's on the fire stairs, between floors three and four."

Michael took a step forward, but Agent Cooper sidestepped to block his path. "You're not going anywhere," said Cooper.

Michael pulled out the knife and held the blade in front of him, scared to hell that he might have to use it.

"Give that to me," said Cooper, presenting the palm of his hand.

"No," said Michael, the blade wavering nervously in front of him.

"Don't be stupid," said Cooper. "My men are in the building, there's no escape."

A noise above made Michael jump. It was another fire door opening and the sound of several pairs of shoes striking the concrete surface. He flicked his gaze up to see.

Cooper took his opportunity and reached for the knife. The flash of his black suit against the concrete grey at the corner of Michael's eye made him jump back. Just in time, as Cooper grabbed only air.

"Why don't you surrender to me?" said Cooper. "There's nowhere else to go, you know that."

"No." Michael shook his head. The same instinct that told him to hold onto the knife, told him he mustn't surrender to Cooper, no matter what.

But if he was going to escape, he had to do it soon, because he could hear the footsteps above closing in.

The fire escape was wide enough to evacuate a building of least ten storeys and Cooper was only one man standing in his way. He was near to the handrail, which meant there was a gap between his body and the outer wall. Not a big one, but if Michael was quick, he could slip through.

He made a break for it.

Cooper — quicker and more agile than he looked — lunged for Michael. Cooper's shoulder rammed into his chest and slammed him back against the wall, as Michael swung the blade wildly like a sword. Michael cried out as his spine hit concrete, but his knife arm was still free. He thrust it forward, aiming for the open target of Cooper's flabby belly. Cooper sucked in his stomach, releasing the pressure on Michael enough for him to break free.

He'd only taken one step before Cooper grabbed the collar of his shirt and pulled him back. Michael whirled around, swiping with his blade. Cooper ducked as the knife narrowly missed slicing into his forehead. He caught Michael's wrist mid-air before the knife could swing back. Michael lashed out with his other arm, punching at Cooper with his closed fist, but Cooper stopped him before Michael's knuckles could hit home, grabbing his forearm and holding onto it.

The two were in deadlock: Michael's arms held strongly in Cooper's grip; the knife hovering sideways between them, its blade threatening to go in either direction as they jostled for position.

"Drop the knife, Michael, don't be stupid," said Cooper, his red face centimetres from Michael, staring at him with determined eyes.

Michael held tight to the knife handle, even as his wrist was squeezed and the tendons inside weakened. Cooper was strong, stronger than him. He was larger and heavier too. The only way to defeat him was for Michael to use that advantage against him.

Michael suddenly shifted sideways. Cooper was pressing so hard that he collapsed under his own body weight. Stumbling forward, he pushed the knife away from him. Michael screamed as his own wrist was forced back and the tip of the blade plunged into his opposite arm. Pain ignited in his muscle and burnt up to his shoulder and down to his hand.

Cooper let go, stepping back as he realised what he had done.

Michael staggered back too, staring at the knife — which he still held — sticking out of his own arm, blood oozing from around the wound.

"Let's stop this now," said Cooper, looking genuinely shocked. "Come with me and we can fix your arm."

"*No!*" cried Michael. He pulled out the knife — stifling a scream as a second, searing pain spread from the wound — and held it out towards Cooper. "Stay back."

The blade dripped with blood onto the concrete floor between them. The bleeding from Michael's arm became worse without the blade inside it and ran a warm trickle past his elbow to his fingertips.

"Sir!" called a man from above — the owner of one pair of footsteps — now only a flight away.

Cooper looked up, and that was his mistake.

In that moment of distraction, Michael took his chance. He surged forward, aiming for the space between Cooper and the handrail, just large enough for his body to pass. Cooper wasn't distracted for long enough and leapt to close the gap. His ample belly blocked the way, but Michael wouldn't be stopped and thrust the knife forward. The point plunged through Cooper's shirt and into his flesh as the man cried out, his horrified scream echoing around the bare walls of the stairwell.

Michael let go of the knife and staggered backwards. Cooper slumped against the handrail, staring at the handle sticking out of his belly as his white shirt flooded with the red of his blood. He looked at Michael, his eyes glassy with shock, as his body collapsed underneath him.

"Sir!" cried the man above.

The voice jolted Michael into action. He turned and ran, the fatigue in his leg muscles forgotten as he raced down the steps, flight after flight, until he reached the fire door at the bottom. He pushed the bar lock and virtually fell out into the street.

He tasted the freedom of the cool night air, but footsteps still pursued him. So he kept running, clutching his injured arm as blood seeped between his fingers, fearing that whatever reason he had for running from Cooper, he must also run because he was a murderer.

TWO

MICHAEL stopped a short distance from the hospital entrance. Bright white light spilled out of the sliding glass doors ahead, offering a refuge from the dark of the night. He hesitated. The throbbing in his arm where the knife had sunk its blade pleaded for attention, but he feared that walking through the Accident and Emergency doors would draw attention of a different kind. If Cooper's men were still hunting him, they would check with local hospitals for a teenage boy who'd been stabbed in the arm.

A nurse in short-sleeved blue uniform dress, shivering in the night breeze, stood drawing on the butt of a cigarette by the entrance. She let out a final plume of smoke, dropped the butt and ground it into the tarmac with the toe of her shoe. He wondered why a woman with medical training was smoking when she must know what it was doing to her body.

She noticed him watching and gave him a smile. "Are you all right, love?"

Michael averted his eyes and looked to the ground where he saw a browning spot of blood had soaked into one of his trainers. "Yeah, I'm fine," he said, turning to walk away.

She hurried a few steps to join him, bringing the lingering smell of smoke on her clothes and breath. "You don't look fine," she said, gazing pointedly at the blood-encrusted sleeve of his shirt.

"It's stopped bleeding now," said Michael, "so actually I don't need any help."

"It could get infected," said the nurse. "At least let me clean it up for you."

She had a warm smile, it was cold outside and he had nowhere else to go, so he let her guide him inside the hospital.

A blast of air from heaters above the door greeted him as he walked into the reception area of A&E. The lights were so bright he actually squinted a bit until his eyes grew accustomed to them. Only a few people were there, dotted about on plastic chairs which were screwed to the floor in rows. An elderly couple on the back row with their coats buttoned up, a man with a bloodied bandaged hand sitting on the end of a row tapping his toe obsessively in front of him and a pair of teenagers at the front. A medical orderly in white tunic and trousers walked past at a casual pace. It was not the hustle and bustle he had expected. It was, perhaps, a quiet night.

The nurse, who Michael saw wore a name badge that said J. Hobson, took him to the front reception desk where a woman looked up from her computer.

"Linda, I'm taking this lad straight through to the cubicles, okay?" said Nurse Hobson.

The receptionist shrugged and typed something on her computer.

Hobson turned to the left and led Michael past the two teenagers sitting in the front row of the waiting area. The boy clutched his right arm close to his chest as if it would fall off if he let go. He was younger than Michael, maybe fourteen years old, pock-marked black skin, stringy hair and suspicious eyes.

"Oi!" he shouted at Hobson as she approached. "I was next."

The girl he was with nudged his good arm and hushed him to be quiet. She was a little older, with flawless brown skin and shiny black hair that fell in waves to her shoulders.

The nurse kept walking.

"I was talking to you, *Nurse Janice Hobson*," said the boy.

The nurse flinched at hearing her name. Michael could only assume the boy knew her first name from outside of the hospital because her badge had only given her initial. "Wait your turn," she told him, giving him one cursory look before turning to walk off.

But the boy got up and stood in front of her. A couple of inches shorter than her, and still clutching his arm, he lifted his nose high to suggest he was superior. "*I've* been waiting ages, so why does *he* get seen to as soon as he walks in?"

Michael stepped back, not wanting to be a part of the argument. He glanced behind and saw Linda on reception had one eye on what was going on while dialling a number on the phone in front of her.

"You need an X-ray," Hobson told the boy. "When someone is free to take you down to the X-ray department, you'll get one and not before."

"You think I'm an annoying, ungrateful teenager, don't you?" said the boy.

Nurse Hobson's face flushed.

The girl, still sitting down, kicked out her foot and jabbed the boy in the ankle. "Jack, stop it!"

Michael wasn't sure what was going on. He glanced behind and saw a security guard at the reception desk talking to Linda. The man didn't look like he could secure very much with his grey hair, glasses and gross belly that hung over the belt of his trousers.

The boy seemed not to notice, or to care. "You don't think people like me should be treated on the NHS, do you?" he said.

The red in her face turned from embarrassment to anger. "My God," she breathed. "You're a perceiver."

The girl got up and grabbed the boy's elbow. "Jack, shut up!"

The security guard was suddenly there, his hands on his hips, his fat belly sticking out in front of him, flaunting the authority his uniform gave him. "Problem, Nurse Hobson?"

"No," said the girl before the nurse could reply. "We can sit and wait to be taken to X-ray, can't we, Jack?"

Jack looked like he was about to say something in reply, but the girl tugged at his arm. She sat down herself and didn't let go of his elbow until he reluctantly sat down beside her.

"Thank you, Charles," said Hobson. "I think we are fine now."

"Very good," said the guard. "I'll be just over here if you need me." He retreated back to the reception desk. He leant the side of his body against it, not taking his eyes off the two teenagers.

Hobson resumed walking. Michael followed behind, not sure exactly what had just happened.

"You're not a perceiver are you?" asked the nurse as they walked.

Michael wasn't sure what a perceiver was, but he decided to say that he wasn't one. "No."

"Good," she said. "I hate perceivers. The little mind reading bastards."

MICHAEL didn't know what to say when Nurse Hobson asked him about his medical history. As far as he could remember, he had no history at all, let alone a medical one.

She looked up from her clipboard, twirling her pen between her middle and index finger, and gave him the same warm smile she had used when she first saw him outside of the hospital. "Name?" she said.

"Michael," he said.

"Michael…?"

She prompted for a surname, but he couldn't think of one that fitted. Was he called Smith or Jones or Papadopoulos? He didn't know.

"What about your parents? We could contact them to tell them you're safe."

He tried to remember. He closed his eyes and thought of the concept of mother and father, hoping to find an image inside his memory, but his mind was empty.

When he opened his eyes again, the cubicle was blurry from the moisture that had formed there. He wiped the dampness from his eyes, determined not for it to turn to tears, and gripped hard to the edge of the mattress where he sat, feeling the slippery plastic that lay beneath the sheet.

Hobson must have seen his distress, because she put the clipboard and pen aside. "Maybe we can fill that in later," she said.

After slapping on a pair of latex gloves, she selected a pair of scissors from her tray and cut into the sleeve of his shirt, removing all the fabric from his arm apart from the bloodied piece stuck to his wound. "What happened to you, then? In a fight were you?"

"No," he lied. "I…" He thought back to his encounter with Cooper on the stairs, remembering the pain as the knife plunged into his arm. "I … stabbed myself."

"You stabbed *yourself*?" said Hobson with a smile. "That's a new one."

"I didn't mean to," said Michael. "It was an accident."

"I see," said Hobson. She didn't seem to believe him, but she also didn't press the matter any further as she dabbed water-soaked pads onto his shirt to soften the congealed blood.

She chatted about the weather, in that typical British fashion, as she gently removed the last of the fabric from Michael's wound, cleaned up around it, spread on some anaesthetic gel and closed it with five stitches. Michael bore the pain. It made him feel alive, it made him feel real. Even though his earliest memory was only a few hours old.

There were other things about life he remembered. He knew that it was a British trait to talk about the weather with strangers, he knew that smoking could damage a person's health, he knew not to admit to the nurse that he had been stabbed in a fight. It was strange, like he had everything he needed to exist in the world, without any of the background.

"What do you know about amnesia?" he asked, as Nurse Hobson tied off the last stitch and snipped the thread free with her scissors.

"Amnesia?" she said, surprised.

"It's when someone loses their memory," said Michael.

"I know what it is," she said, "I was wondering why you were asking."

"No reason," said Michael.

"I see." She said it in the same way she had when he told her that he had stabbed himself, like she didn't believe him. "It's rare. It can happen when someone has gone through a trauma, or if they've had a bump on the head. Have you had a bump on the head?"

"No," said Michael. He had woken with a headache, but there was no bruising or blood on his skull.

"Well, it's usually only temporary. Unless it's a serious brain injury, people get their memories back gradually over a few days or weeks." She snapped off her latex gloves and laid them on top of the mess of bloodied cleansing wipes on her equipment tray. "I just need to get the doctor to sign off on this, I won't be a moment," she said.

She swished aside the curtain and went out to find the doctor. As she swished it shut again behind her, Michael worried that he had said too much. The last thing he needed was to be hospitalised by a doctor concerned he had some sort of brain injury. He had been in the hospital long enough, he decided, and needed to go.

On the examination bed next to him was his bloodied shirt, or what was left of it after the nurse had cut off the sleeve. His torso was naked and, although he wasn't cold in the warmth of the hospital, that wouldn't be the case if he went outside.

He hopped off the bed, just as the curtain was pulled open. He thought it would be the doctor come to examine his head, but instead it was the girl from the waiting area.

"You're Michael, aren't you?" she said.

"Yes." He crossed his palms over his chest, embarrassed that he was half naked in front of her. Not as if they covered up much.

The girl bit her bottom lip to disguise her amusement, getting reddish brown lipstick on her teeth. In the harsh light of the examination cubicle, he saw she wore subtle make-up to create the impression of flawless skin. A line of black drawn under each eye emphasised her wide brown irises, which didn't so much look *at* him, as look *into* him.

She brought out a scrunched up bundle of light blue fabric from behind her back. "You might want this," she said, handing it over.

Michael took the bundle. It was soft, made out of artificial woollen fibre. He unfolded it to see it was a long-sleeved jumper about his size. "Where did you get this?" It looked too big to belong to the thin girl.

"From a couple of cubicles down," she said.

"You stole it?" said Michael, trying to figure out why a girl he didn't know would be stealing clothes for him.

"The man won't be needing it," she said. "He died ten minutes ago."

Startled, he dropped the jumper on the bed. His hands felt dirty from touching something worn by a dead man and he wiped them on his trousers.

The girl giggled. She looked up and down his naked torso, adding to his embarrassment. "You don't want to go out like that," she said. "And you'll need to go soon if you don't want the men to catch you."

"Men?" A chill passed through him and he shivered in the warmth of the hospital air.

"They've been walking through the hospital looking for a stab victim called 'Michael'. They're pretending like they're police, but they're not police."

Michael looked at his blood-stained shirt with only one sleeve scrunched up on the bed and, next to it, the dead man's jumper. He had no choice, he grabbed the jumper and put it on. The wool felt soft and warming against his skin.

"How do you know all this?" he asked.

"I'm a perceiver," she said, as if it was obvious.

"What's that?" said Michael.

Her penetrating gaze surveyed his face and looked into his eyes, so deep that it made him feel uncomfortable. "You really don't know, do you?" she said.

A noise of voices — deep, men's voices — startled them both. The girl turned and snatched a quick look through the curtain. "They're checking the cubicles now," she said as she turned back. "You haven't got long."

"Why are you doing this?" said Michael.

"Let's say I know what it's like to be hunted by people who don't understand you."

Michael joined her at the curtain and peered out. He took a deep breath as he saw the back of a man in a grey suit standing at the foot of a cubicle two spaces down, apparently talking to whoever was in there.

He turned back to the girl, knowing she was right. "Thank you…" He was going to use her name, but realised he didn't know what it was.

"Jennifer," she said.

"Thank you, Jennifer."

He took another look out of the curtain and, while the man in the grey suit still had his back to him, he slipped out into the main part of the hospital. As quietly as he could, he retraced the way he had come, fearing at any moment he would hear the sound of pursuing men's footsteps. But with his head down, resisting the urge to run, he walked through the waiting area without turning a suspicious head, out through the double doors and into the night.

THREE

MICHAEL wandered the streets until the sun lifted itself above the buildings and spilled its orange light onto the pavement. It chased away the chill of the night and warmed the surface of his skin. But inside he remained cold and hungry. He passed cafes opening their doors to early morning customers. They enticed him with smells of cooking sausages and bacon, but he could only stare through the windows. He had no money.

The streets swelled with people venturing out into the rush hour. Workers on early shifts in cleaner and shop assistant uniforms gradually gave way to office workers in suits and smart shoes. There were children in school uniform: boys in grey blazers with red trim and girls in black jackets and dark blue checked skirts giggling in groups of three and four. The people jumped on buses or caught taxis or rushed across pedestrian crossings. All with somewhere to be. Michael had nowhere to be. He just walked. Like a ghost walking among the living.

After a couple of hours, the traffic thinned and the schoolchildren, businessmen and women gave way to young mothers with pushchairs and the elderly. Michael kept walking, and the more he walked, the more people looked at him. An old man gave him a sideways glance while pretending to fiddle with his glasses. A woman adjusting the display of shampoo in a shop window stared at him as he walked past, then hurriedly looked away when he stared back. A toddler in a buggy pointed at him and shouted, "Teenager!" before his mother grabbed his hand and stuffed it back inside. One elderly woman with a large shopping bag even crossed the road to avoid him.

Michael stopped to look at his reflection in a shop window. Perhaps there was something on his face. Perhaps his arm was bleeding again. But something else reflected in the glass caught his attention. The same word, in mirror writing, that the toddler had called him: *teenager*.

Michael turned and saw it was part of a poster encased behind transparent plastic on the side of a bus shelter.

Is your teenager a perceiver? it read. *Get them tested at school! It's quick, painless — and absolutely free!*

Another poster, printed on ordinary paper and taped to a lamp-post, read: *Get Teenagers Out of Your Head!* Then, underneath, in smaller letters: *Brought to you by Action Against Mind Invasion.*

A radio blaring out of the open window of a hairdressers carried the words of a newsreader, '*… are denying claims that up to five per cent of teenagers are perceivers …*'.

People stared at him because he was a teenager. Like Nurse Hobson, the population feared perceivers were seeing into their minds and reading their private thoughts. They knew that all perceivers were teenagers and didn't seem to care that not all teenagers were perceivers. So they continued to stare at him, to steer their children away from him and to cross the road to avoid him.

MICHAEL slept that night on a park bench. A fitful sleep, disturbed by sounds of wildlife in the trees, the loud voices of people walking home from the pub and the fear of being attacked. Huddled up to preserve his own body heat, he was small, vulnerable and alone. The night breeze leached away his warmth and he woke with the dampness of dew soaking through his jumper.

The days that followed passed in a stream of unmarked time. Time was a concept other people used to order their lives. For him, there was no lunchtime, no dinnertime and no bedtime. Just lightness passing into darkness and the constant search for food, shelter and warmth. He walked and he stopped, walked and stopped, wandering the streets like a vagrant.

No, not like a vagrant. He was a vagrant. A homeless person, a tramp, a bum.

Over the days that passed, he came to realise Nurse Hobson was wrong. His memories didn't come back. Each day he woke hoping that he would remember something of his former life, and each day he was disappointed. He wondered, if perceivers really could read minds, maybe they could see into the memories that he seemed to have forgotten.

IN the evenings, Michael got into a habit of sitting on a wall opposite a chip shop. Even though the smell of batter frying in oil drifted across the road and clawed at his hungry stomach, the wall gave him a vantage point where he could watch the customers. Sometimes they stood outside and ate their chips before dropping the wrapper in the rubbish bin, from where Michael could retrieve it and eat the scraps of crispy bits left in the bottom. If he was lucky, they would leave whole pieces of fish in the wrapper. He tried to eat them slowly, to savour their taste, but usually he couldn't stop himself and desperately gobbled them down.

It was early one evening as he sat with his bum soaking up the cold from the brickwork beneath him, that he saw Jack. He might not have noticed him if it wasn't for the white of Jack's plaster cast, caught in the light shining through the plate glass window of the chip shop. The boy didn't go in for chips, he walked straight past, presumably on his way to somewhere else. In the moments that he watched him, there was no mistaking the straggly hair and pock-marked face of the boy from the hospital.

Suddenly excited, Michael hopped off the wall. He thought about shouting after Jack, but it was Jennifer he had a connection with, not him, so he decided to follow at a discreet distance.

It was a strategy that nearly caused him to lose sight of his target as, up ahead, Jack jogged over the road at a pedestrian crossing just as the lights were changing. The red man was already lit up by the time Michael got to the kerb and the traffic started up again. Frustrated, Michael saw Jack getting further away as cars sped past, making it impossible to cross. Eventually the green man appeared, cars obediently stopped and Michael dashed across the road.

Moving faster so as not to risk losing him, Michael saw Jack turn off the path towards a large red brick building. As solidly built as a house, but as large as a barn, it was enclosed in its grounds well away from other buildings. As Jack went inside, Michael wondered if he should follow him or wait for him to come back out again. It was then he saw the wooden noticeboard by the road which revealed the building to be a community hall. Pinned to it was a printed notice which advertised a drop-in centre for teenagers every evening of the week except Wednesday and Sunday. Michael assumed, whatever day of the week it was, it wasn't Wednesday or Sunday. For the second time in ten minutes, he decided to follow.

The hall was dimly lit, full of music and teenage chatter echoing off the wooden floor and the high ceiling. It smelt of sweaty bodies and the musk of old buildings. All along the back wall were child-like paintings created with broad brush-strokes and bright, primary colours. Up one end was a more sober collection of notices with dates of choir rehearsals, a reminder of a price increase for Wednesday's yoga class, and a thank you for those who helped to raise £104.26 for the local hospice on bingo night. The place didn't belong to teenagers, they were merely guests five nights a week.

In the centre of the board, half-covering an old newspaper article about the community playgroup, was a hand-written notice: *Teenage drop-in centre closes at 10pm sharp! No hanging around outside after hours.*

At least, it used to say that, but someone had joined up the bottom of the 'h' in the word 'hanging' to turn it into 'banging', then in a different pen someone had crossed out 'around' and written 'your girlfriend'. So it now read: *No banging your girlfriend outside after hours.* Stupid, but it made Michael smile.

He looked around in the semi-darkness. There were groups of teenagers huddled together, talking over the beat of the music from the sound system. Others sat at the side, staring at their phones and occasionally tapping the screen. None of them were Jack.

Something white caught the beam of a spotlight at the back of the hall. It was Jack's plaster cast, emerging — attached to its owner — from the men's toilets. Jack strode down the length of the hall and through a door at the other end.

Michael walked up to the door. It was closed. He didn't know what was on the other side, it might be private. Michael decided he didn't care, gripped the handle and turned.

A conversation stopped mid-sentence. Five teenagers sitting on chairs in a rough circle turned to look at him. One of the five was Jack, and next to him sat Jennifer.

The room was small and sparse. Plain, white-painted walls with desks of light beech around the edge. It had one very small window high up on the exterior wall.

"Oi!" yelled the teenager at the back. He was older than the others, large and muscular with a crop of shocking blond hair. "Ain't you ever heard of knocking?"

Michael instantly felt he had made the wrong move.

"Hey, it's that skank from the hospital," said Jack.

"Oh yes," said the girl, her face softening into a smile. "Hello Michael."

"Uh … hello," Michael managed.

"Still wearing that jumper, I see," said Jennifer.

Michael looked down at the jumper he'd been wearing ever since she gave it to him, now a grubby version of its original light blue. "Yeah," he said.

"Who gives a ferret's nipples about his soddin' jumper?" said Jack.

"Do you always have to be so polite?" said Jennifer.

"Not with norms," said Jack.

Michael could almost taste the hostility in the air. "I'm sorry," he said, turning away from the four pairs of unfriendly eyes staring at him, "I didn't realise you were in here."

He backed out, pulling the door shut behind him. But Jennifer stood and caught the door before it closed. "Ignore that lot," she said. "What do you want?"

"It's nothing," said Michael.

"I can perceive it's not nothing." She looked deep into his eyes and Michael felt a connection between them. Simultaneously intrusive and caring.

"Jen, get out of his head and get back in the circle," the blond one called over.

"He wants something pretty damn bad, Otis."

"So?" said Otis. "Get rid of the skank and sit down."

Otis's tongue was not as sharp as Jack's, but his large muscular frame and deep, fully broken voice commanded more authority.

Jennifer didn't seem to care. "I won't be long." She hustled Michael out of the door. They were back in the main hall with its cliques of teenagers and loud music. A peel of giggles erupted from a group of girls standing little more than a metre away.

"Let's go somewhere quieter," said Jennifer.

She led Michael past the noticeboard, with its instruction about banging girlfriends, down the length of the hall and towards the toilets. Michael thought they were going to stop in the corner, but Jennifer headed straight for the women's loos. She pushed open the door with a hard slap of her palm. Michael hesitated, knowing he shouldn't go in there, then followed.

A short girl with hooped earrings who washing her hands at the sink, looked startled when she saw Michael. She stopped rubbing her hands under the tap and the stream of water ran uselessly past her fingers. Jennifer returned a smile as if everything was normal. The girl shook her hands dry, wiped them on the seat of her jeans and hurried out.

Jennifer checked the cubicles and confirmed that she and Michael were alone. She leant up against the main door with all her body weight so no one else could come in.

"What's so important?" she asked.

Michael was suddenly embarrassed. Seeing Jack in the street and following him was a spur of the moment decision. He hadn't thought of what he was going to say. A cascade of words rolled through his head, myriad possible explanations. All of them sounded lame. "I … this is so hard." He took a breath and slowly, in a string of bumbling and confused sentences, told her about his amnesia. "I was wondering … could you look into my mind? Can you see — I mean, *perceive* — my memories? Who I am? My family? My home?"

Jennifer looked doubtful. Michael's moment of hope slipped away. "Perceivers aren't mind readers," she said. "I know that that's what people say, but it's not entirely true. I perceive feelings and emotions, I pick up on thoughts occasionally — strong ones, especially. But to look into someone's head and see memories they have forgotten …?" She finished off her sentence with a shake of her head.

Despair descended. His only idea in days of living on the streets — dismissed with one shake of her head.

Jennifer must have perceived what he was feeling because she responded with a sympathetic smile. "Well, maybe I could try," she said. "I can't promise … but it wouldn't hurt to try."

All went quiet apart from the steady beat of the music leaking through from the hall. The smile slipped from Jennifer's lips. Michael waited. Nothing happened. "What do I do?"

"Do nothing."

Her face became serious and still. She leant into him. So close that he could feel her soft breathing on his cheek. Almost as intimate as a kiss. Anticipation rose inside of him. His heart quickened. He caught a hint of the perfumed soap she used to wash with. Saw the neat black line of eye pencil under each lower lid and the way mascara elongated her black eyelashes. Desire tingled through his body. As soon as he felt it, he knew she would feel it too; perceive it in him. He had to force it away. He focussed on the dark area of his mind where he had no memories. He tried to think of the time before waking up in the corridor, before running, before meeting Jennifer.

Her stare was intense. She looked into his eyes. Deep. Penetrating. Probing. Through the cornea, past the iris and beyond the pupil. Until she was inside his mind. He couldn't feel her, but he knew she had to be in there. The subtlety in her stare showed she was thinking about everything she perceived. Like a tiny flashing light on a computer, each byte of information sending a flicker across her eyes. Her breath shallow in concentration. Body absorbed in stillness. Her singular perception, sharp and focussed, stretching out the seconds into minutes.

Until her eyes softened and she withdrew. Back through the pupil, the iris, the cornea. Her breathing deepened. She blinked her mascaraed eyelashes and their connection was severed. She leant back against the door and her body relaxed.

A mixture of nerves and excitement trembled inside him. "Well?" he said.

"Strange," said Jennifer. She seemed distracted, not quite there. Like a person emerging from a dream. "There's so little of you, it's like perceiving a baby."

"But did you see my memories? Do you know who I am? Where I live?"

"No."

Michael deflated. His legs hardly had the strength to keep him upright any more. He staggered backwards and felt his bum hit the rim of a sink. He perched on it. "God!" he cursed. He turned and kicked at the wall. Plaster came away from the brickwork and scattered to the floor in pieces. He kicked the bits to the other side of the room. "God! God! God!"

His face was hot with frustration. He turned on the cold tap with such force that it sent water spraying onto his trousers. He cupped his hands and splashed it onto his face until his skin, his hair and jumper were dripping wet.

"I'm sorry," said Jennifer. "There's a nothingness inside of you. Like someone sucked out your memories."

"Am I brain damaged?" said Michael. The thought — suddenly in his head — scared him.

"I don't know. I've never perceived anything like you."

Jennifer flinched at a sound on the other side of the door. Michael heard it too. The smashing of glass.

Then another.

Screams erupted from behind the door. The frightened, high-pitched screams of teenage girls.

Jennifer's eyes widened. She turned and dashed out the door.

Michael followed her into the screaming.

The door opened onto an orange glow. People were running. Shouting. Flames leapt from half a dozen places. A glass bottle sailed through an already-smashed window. The flaming rag in its neck arched across the hall and struck the back wall. Glass shattered. Liquid spurted in all directions and ignited with a *whompf* of flame.

Petrol bombs had exploded throughout the hall and they were still coming.

FOUR

FIRE consumed the hall. It feasted on its wooden floors. Devoured curtains at the window. Licked at paper pinned to the noticeboard. The children's paintings blackened, their corners withered in the heat and started to burn.

The half-dozen seats of fire where petrol bombs had exploded were merging into one, carried by the accelerant which had burst from smashed glass bottles.

Michael ran. He dodged the flames which pawed at his trouser legs. Their heat was fierce and each breath sucked hot air into his lungs. But the fire hadn't entirely taken hold of the building yet. His escape route was clear. He ran through the main door and out into the open.

He breathed deep and savoured the clean air. Around him, other teenagers were standing with shocked faces, staring back at the burning hall. A girl was crying and being comforted by a friend. Michael turned and saw what they saw. The fire flickered orange through four smashed windows and an open door. A boy ran out, screaming in terror, flames flapping around the sleeve of his sweatshirt. An adult ran past Michael and engulfed the boy with a jacket. Pushed him to the ground and smothered the flames.

"Are you all right?" said the adult.

The boy nodded, his face streaked with sooty tears.

The adult — a man with thinning hair — stood. "Everyone back from the building." He waved his arms like he was shooing a herd of cattle. "Back!"

The teenagers moved a few steps away from the burning hall, Michael among them.

The man pulled a phone from his pocket and dialled. He put it to his ear and asked for the fire service.

"Oi!"

Michael looked up and saw Otis and Jack picking their way through the crowd towards him.

"Where's Jennifer?" said Otis.

"She came out before me," said Michael.

"She's not here," said Otis.

"Are you sure?" Michael looked around at the ragtag collection of teenagers. He couldn't see her.

"I told you," said Jack. "She must've gone back for her stuff."

"We're gonna have to go in and get her," said Otis. He took a gulp from the bottle of water in his hand.

"Are you mad?" Michael looked at the building, its fiery glow now lighting up the night. "You need to wait for the firemen."

"She could be dead by then," said Otis.

Jack shot Michael an accusatory glance. "He should go, he's the one who left her in there."

"Hey!" said Michael. "I thought I followed her out, remember?"

"ForChrissake!" Otis glared at both of them. "Are we gonna argue or are we gonna get Jennifer?"

"I'll go," said Michael. Somehow, he knew what to do. Like he had known talking about the weather was a British trait, the knowledge was inside of him. He thrust his hand towards Jack. "Give me your T-shirt."

"What?"

"My jumper's the wrong material. Give me your damn T-shirt." Michael presented his open hand again.

"Do it," said Otis.

Grumbling, Jack took off his T-shirt — pulling it awkwardly over his plaster cast — and handed it to Michael.

"I'll need that." Michael grabbed the bottle of water from Otis's hand and poured it over the shirt. The water expanded the fibres in the material, making a crude smoke filter. Michael took a last, deep breath of clean air, put the material over his mouth and nose and headed back inside the hall.

What wasn't fire was smoke. It hung in black clouds from the ceiling so thick that it was impossible to see more than a metre in front of him. The heat was searing. His sweat did nothing to cool him. Michael knew he was potentially walking into his own grave, but he walked anyway.

He made a conscious effort to remember each step as he hopped from one tiny piece of non-burning floor to another. He trod a winding path towards the door to the back room, his breathing laboured through the wet T-shirt as his lungs sought to find the oxygen in the air.

The door to the back room was closed. Michael reached for the handle.

He let go. "Argh!" It was burning hot. The fire had heated the metal like the ring on a hob. He pulled the T-shirt from his face, wrapped the dry end around his hand and used it like an oven glove to open the door.

Jennifer was inside. Stamping on a burning shoulder bag on the floor, trying to beat out the flames.

The fire wasn't as severe in the isolated room. The closed door had protected it from the main blaze. There was a fire in the corner under the tiny window — now smashed — but the area where Jennifer stood was free of flame and the air was almost clear.

Michael grabbed Jennifer's hand. She kept stamping on the bag, hopelessly extinguishing one part as another started to burn.

"Leave it!" shouted Michael over the crackling of the blazing building. The open door was sucking the heat and smoke into the back room. Jennifer's little haven from the flames was about to be engulfed.

Michael's next breath was tainted with smoke. He coughed it back out again. His lungs urged him to take in more air, but he fought the instinct until the T-shirt was back over his mouth. The material had almost dried out from the heat and the filter was becoming ineffective. If they didn't leave now, he felt sure they would die in there.

Jennifer stopped stamping. Whether it was because she perceived the desperation in him or saw the urgency in his eyes, Michael was not sure. But whatever the reason, she abandoned the bag to the flames. She stood and watched for a second as they multiplied across its surface.

"We need to go," said Michael.

She nodded. Together, they turned towards the door.

Hell stood between them and the way out. A mixture of fire and darkness. The smoke was so strong now, it stung Michael's eyes. Water welled inside them and blurred what little he could see of their escape route.

Jennifer coughed beside him. He pulled her close and put the other end of the T-shirt over her nose and mouth. She held it there.

Hand in hand, they stepped out into the hall. Michael retraced the winding path to the door, picking his way through from memory because he couldn't see. Stumbling through lack of oxygen, the surface of his skin burning with the heat, he looked desperately for the door.

It appeared. Like a magic door in a children's story book. One moment, they were staggering blind, clinging onto each other to keep each other safe from the flames, and the next they were looking at their way out.

Michael lurched for it. Tripping on the doorstep, he collapsed on all fours and felt the stony tarmac of the path under his hands and knees. He took a large lungful of fresh night air and coughed it out again. He retched from the bottom of his stomach and felt it rasp his throat. He spat something vile onto the pavement. It was green and black. But he was out. The heat and the crackle of the fire was behind him.

Beside him, Jennifer coughed too. Hands reached down to pick her up. Otis and Jack took her away.

Michael crawled to a patch of grass where he sat back to look at the hall. The blaze had started to take over the roof. Soon, the whole building would be ashes.

Someone asked if he was all right. Michael nodded. Someone else passed him a bottle of water. He took it with a 'thank you' and sipped. It washed some of the fire out of his throat, but he could still taste the soot.

Then Otis was back. Standing above him like a pale, blond giant. He offered his hand. Michael took it and Otis pulled him to his feet. "Look, thanks, man," said Otis. Michael glanced behind where Jennifer was sitting with Jack on the wall of the front garden of a nearby house.

"You're welcome," said Michael. What he did was stupid and he could have been killed, but even he had to admit he probably saved Jennifer's life.

"Jen says you, er … got nowhere to stay," said Otis.

"That's right," said Michael. He hadn't said anything to her. She must have perceived it when she looked into his mind.

"I was thinking …" Otis shoved his hands in his jeans pockets and looked away as if he was embarrassed to say it. "If you want … you could stay with us."

"Really?" The offer took a moment to sink in. Michael didn't know whether to feel excited, relieved, or just grateful.

Sirens howled. They both looked up. Two fire engines came racing round the corner, red and blue lights mingling with the orange of the blaze. Michael realised Otis had been right. If they'd waited for the firemen to arrive, Jennifer would probably be dead.

"I'd rather not be here when the police arrive," said Michael.

Otis sighed. He looked out into the distance from where more sirens were screaming. "Me neither," he said.

FIVE

OTIS and Jennifer lived in a squat in Hackney, north east London, about a ten minute walk from the burning remains of the drop-in centre. Jack came with them, even though he actually lived with his family a few streets away.

It was a one-bedroom flat in a council block, one of many in the area behind the High Street. Access to the building was supposed to be via a swipe card and secure code at the front, but the wire mesh gate that locked off the fire escape was broken and, with a little perseverance, Jennifer was able to use her fingernails to prise it open. Michael followed Otis and the others up a flight of concrete stairs to the front door which Otis unlocked with a key.

It opened directly into a messy living room that smelt of stale air. Everything about it was old and tired. The wallpaper, which looked like it had been designed in the last century, peeled at the edges. A sofa and two armchairs sagged with the weight of years of use, while the true state of the table against the back wall was disguised with a cloth slung over the top. The floor was covered in junk. An empty pizza box, several mugs with the remains of coffee in the bottom, a pile of paper in the corner, a dirty green suitcase and a couple of abandoned cigarette ends.

"Got a T-shirt I can borrow?" said Jack as soon as he walked in. "I'm bloody freezin'." He was naked from the waist up apart from the plaster cast and had been shivering throughout the walk.

"Bedroom," said Otis.

Jack trooped off through a door at the back.

"Make sure it's an old one!" Otis called after him.

Otis sat on the sofa with Jennifer. Michael chose the least-worn of the two armchairs. They said nothing for a while, silent in their own contemplation. Michael kept thinking about the fire.

"Do you know what happened?" he said eventually.

"Some kid saw a group of adults run off," said Otis.

"Not exactly a surprise," said Jennifer.

"The kid said they had scarves over their faces and their hoods up. Smashed the windows first, lit some petrol bombs then chucked them in," said Otis.

"Did they know about us?" said Jennifer.

"That there was a bunch of perceivers meeting in the back?" Otis shook his head. "Doubt it. It's a teenage drop-in centre. They were probably targeting teenagers, thinking they'd scare the snot out of a few 'ceivers while they were at it. We're supposed to be five per cent, right?"

"You're all perceivers then?" said Michael. "You, Jennifer and Jack?" He'd suspected it, but he wasn't sure.

"Does that bother you?" said Otis.

"No," he said. But he had to admit he felt self-conscious being around them. He understood they were reading his thoughts and feelings, he just wasn't sure how much.

Jennifer leant her head back against the sofa and closed her eyes. "God," she said, like the weight of everything that had happened was suddenly coming down on her. "Do they hate us that much?"

"It's more fear than hate," said Otis.

Jennifer opened her eyes again and looked straight at him. "Being frightened makes them want to burn children? Jack said a boy got petrol on his arm. It spilled out of a bottle as it flew past."

"I heard," said Otis. "Caught fire as he ran out."

"They could have killed that boy," said Jennifer, her voice trembling. "They could have killed all of us." Michael saw the tears forming in her eyes, but she held them back.

"They could have killed you," Otis said. "Why did you go back, Jen?"

"My bag," said Jennifer. "It had everything in it. My phone. Everything. I had to get it. It was stupid, I know. I wasn't thinking."

"I'll get you a new phone," said Otis.

"It wasn't the skanking bit of tech, it was what was in it!" said Jennifer. "Contacts for the other perceiver groups. Passwords. Aliases. All of it. I don't believe I deleted our online backups! After the other group got their stuff hacked, I thought it was safer. I don't believe I could've been so stupid."

"You're not stupid," said Otis, gently wiping a strand of her hair from her cheek. "I've got some of the details, we should be able to get it all back eventually."

Jennifer clearly wasn't in a mood to be soothed, and batted his hand away from her face. "Eventually? If we're gonna fight this thing, Otis, we need that information now."

The bedroom door banged open and Jack emerged wearing a black and white striped T-shirt two sizes too big for him. "What d'ya reckon?" he said, twirling in a clumsy imitation of a catwalk model.

"Is that all you can think about?" said Jennifer, accusingly.

"I perceive you're upset, Jen. I thought I'd lighten the mood."

"Maybe some of us don't want it to be lightened." She got up from the sofa and rushed off to the back of the flat.

"Where are you going?" Otis called after her.

"Shower," said Jennifer. "I smell like skanking Guy Fawkes."

MICHAEL went in the shower after Jennifer had finished. She had used most of the hot water, but the cleansing sensation was still glorious. It washed the whole week from his skin. The soot of the fire turned the water black as it swirled down the plug hole. Then he lathered his whole body with soap and let the white bubbles strip away the grime of sleeping rough. When, at last, he stepped out of the shower, he no longer smelt like a mouldy sock. He wrapped himself in a towel and started to believe he was a civilised person again.

Otis made up a bed of sorts for him on the sofa. There weren't any spare bedclothes in the flat, so he offered Michael a couple of coats to throw over the top of him. After sleeping on a cold, hard park bench, someone else's lounge, a sofa and some old coats were luxury.

Jack cobbled together the cushions from the two armchairs and made a place for himself on the floor. He was used to it, apparently. He didn't say explicitly, but Michael suspected Jack preferred the company of other perceivers to his own family and slept on Otis and Jennifer's floor quite often.

Michael closed his eyes and his body sank into the warm softness of the sofa. Days of half-snatched sleep and endless wandering pulled him into unconsciousness. He slept deeper and longer than he had in days.

MICHAEL woke with a start to the sound of a fist banging on wood. He prised open his eyes to see the dawn light struggling into the flat through the window.

Someone knocked loudly on the front door. "Nathaniel?" a muffled woman's voice called from outside. "Nathaniel!"

There was a click and artificial light flooded the room. Michael squinted to see Otis standing outside the bedroom door near the light switch. He wore an unflattering pair of maroon pyjama bottoms.

Thud, thud, thud!

"Nathaniel, open up! I know you're in there."

Otis staggered, half-asleep, towards the door. He tripped over the corner of Jack's bedding. He swore.

The woman kept knocking.

"All right, all right, keep your wig on!" Otis complained.

He stopped at the front door and laid his palms out flat on its wooden surface.

Jennifer emerged from the bedroom. Her hair was a tangled mess. She wore a short cotton nightshirt that only just covered the cheeks of her bum. Michael, now fully awake, couldn't help but stare at her naked shapely legs as she walked by.

"I'm 'ceiving one person," said Otis to Jennifer as she approached. "Agreed?"

She nodded. "One person."

"Okay."

Otis opened the door and the knocking abruptly stopped.

Standing outside was a short black woman in a knee-length coat, a silk scarf and a determined expression. "Where's Nathaniel?"

She pushed past Otis.

"Excuse me!" Caught by surprise, he didn't have a chance to stop her. He followed her into the lounge. "Who the hell are you?"

"I know Nathaniel comes here. I followed him once." She walked around the room, looking everywhere. She went into the kitchen and came out again. She looked behind the sofa and the television.

Michael covered his body by struggling into one of the coats he'd been using as a blanket and got off the sofa. "Who's Nathaniel?" he said. But no one answered. They were absorbed watching the woman rampage through the flat.

She pulled the crumpled duvet off the makeshift bed on the floor. Michael expected her to uncover Jack's sleeping body, but all there was underneath were two armchair cushions.

"What have you done with him?" she demanded.

"We ain't done nothing," said Otis.

The sound of a toilet flushing made everyone turn their heads to the bathroom. The flushing subsided and there was the click of a sliding bolt as it was unlocked. The door opened to reveal Jack standing in the doorway in his underpants.

"What the ferret's scrotum's going on?" he said blinking into the light, looking around at the four of them standing before him. His eyes settled on the woman. They widened in surprise. "Mum?"

"Nathaniel Jackson, where have you been? I've been ringing and ringing!"

"Mum, what are you doing here?"

"I came to find you — to tell you, you got an appointment."

"Appointment?" Jack shook his head in confusion. "When did this happen?"

"Yesterday. Isn't it wonderful?"

Jack steadied himself with a hand on the bathroom doorframe. The colour drained from his face.

Michael shot a glance at Jennifer and Otis to see if they understood what was going on. They looked as shocked as Jack did.

"Mum, why didn't you tell me?"

"I didn't want to get your hopes up."

"My hopes?" He laughed. An ironic laugh. A frightened laugh. "At least a month, you said. We'd talk about it, you said."

"I thought we'd decided it was for the best."

"You decided!" said Jack.

She gave him a reassuring smile. "You'll feel different about it tomorrow. Tomorrow, you'll be normal."

"You don't get it!" He brushed by his mother and dropped himself onto the armchair cushions. He curled his knees up to his chest and looked back at her. "I don't want to be normal."

"Well," said Mrs Jackson. "It's all booked now. Why don't you get dressed, eh? We can talk about it on the walk home."

Jack was like a lost little urchin boy sitting near-naked on his ragamuffin bed, staring up at his mother. He shifted his gaze to Jennifer and then to Otis, as if asking for help.

"You don't have to do this," said Otis.

Mrs Jackson stepped forward, blocking her son's view of his friend. "I'm sorry, but it's already booked."

Otis turned on her, his face angry. "Hey! This is none of your business."

"I'm his mother!"

"It's his decision," said Otis.

"Shut up!" screamed Jack. His words cut through their argument as sharply as turning off a radio. He scrambled through the bedclothes and pulled out his borrowed T-shirt and trousers. "I'll go for the damn appointment."

He got dressed in silence. The disagreement hung in the room, but Jack seemed to have made his decision. He put on his trainers with stoic determination and tied the laces like a person getting ready to leave, not like someone playing for time.

When he stood up, fully clothed and ready to go, Otis came up to him. "Are you sure about this?" he said.

"I knew this day was coming," said Jack, resolved. "They're coming for all of us in the end, aren't they?"

"Not if you help us stop it," said Otis.

Jack looked across at his mother. She still had her coat on and stood with her arms folded. "I can't."

Jennifer came up to Jack, wrapped her arms around him and gave him a long, gentle squeeze. "I'll miss you," she said. "But we'll keep in touch, yeah? I'll text you when I get my new phone."

"Come on, Nathaniel," said Mrs Jackson.

Jennifer withdrew her arms from Jack and stood back. Jack straightened his T-shirt and, with a nod, indicated to his mother he was ready to leave.

He kept his head down as Mrs Jackson led him from the flat. He avoided looking at Otis or Jennifer as he passed them. He didn't say anything. He allowed his mum to open the front door for him, they walked through and she closed it again; pushing it shut with a gentle click of the catch.

"Bitch!" said Otis.

"Did you 'ceive him?" said Jennifer. "He's so scared."

Michael looked from one to the other, wishing to hell he was in the perceivers club. "What's going on? What's this appointment?"

"He's going to have the cure," said Jennifer.

"Cure?" said Michael.

Otis paced around the room. His anger, barely controlled, thumped down into the floorboards. "They're going to take everything he is and throw it away." His rage seethed from every syllable. "They're going to turn him into a norm."

"But you said he was going to be cured," said Michael.

"Of perception," said Jennifer. "It's a cure for perceivers."

SIX

Natasha Hill looked directly into the camera. She'd chosen an electric blue blouse to read the news that evening and two pearl earrings large enough to poke out from her shoulder-length blonde hair.

"Waiting lists for clinics have soared since it was announced the procedure to cure teenage perceivers will be available on the NHS. Doctors say they're getting more calls from desperate parents every day. Our Health Correspondent, Toby Pearce is outside a cure clinic for us now…"

The shot cut to Toby: looking into camera, a light breeze wisping at his thin hair. Behind him, a concrete building with a temporary sign reading Cure Clinic attached to the door.

"Yes, Natasha. Ten teenagers were cured at this clinic today, but doctors I've been speaking to say demand is so great, they could have seen ten times that many. I'm with Marjorie Schaffer and her daughter Evy…"

The camera widened the shot. Marjorie — mid-thirties, trendy in T-shirt and jeans — stood proudly next to Evy — not much more than thirteen, clasping onto her mother's arm like a three-year-old.

"Marjorie, you brought your daughter here to be cured today … How did you feel when you got the appointment?"

Toby directed his fluffy microphone at the mother.

"So relieved. When we got that phone call to say we had a place — well, we knew this was going to be a fresh start for our family. I feel sorry for the other parents. To be living with a perceiver in the house, not knowing how long it's going to be like that … I mean, I know how hard it is."

"Evy, if I can turn to you …"

Fluffy microphone angled to the daughter.

"… How does it feel to have been cured?"

Quietly: "Okay."

"Were you frightened?"

Looks up to Mum for guidance. Mum smiles. Evy shrugs. "Gave me an injection, I woke up in the recovery room. Now I can't perceive anymore …"

MICHAEL dried his hands on the bathroom towel which was a bit smelly and needed a wash. The sound of the toilet flushing subsided from a gush to a gurgle of the cistern refilling. It allowed the murmur of voices in the lounge to be heard. Michael opened the bathroom door a crack.

"… we should start meeting again." Jennifer's voice.

"Where?" Otis's voice. "The community centre's a pile of ashes."

"Here."

"I don't think so. Adults torched the last place we met. I don't fancy being asleep when they burn down the flat."

"Groups are gathering across the country, we can't sit around doing nothing, especially now Jack is gone."

"Okay, here. I've got stuff this afternoon, so they can come this morning. But we find a new place for next time."

"Otis," said Jennifer. Her voice lowered to a whisper — the words so quiet, Michael couldn't make them out.

Otis responded with more whispers.

Michael guessed he'd been discovered. Perceivers didn't have to see him to know he was eavesdropping.

He flushed the toilet again — to pretend he'd only just fin-ished — and walked into the lounge, trying to act natural.

"Hi, Michael," said Jennifer.

"You off out today?" said Otis.

"I suppose," said Michael.

"Good," said Otis. "I mean, that's fine. See ya later."

Michael usually went out during the day, it didn't feel comfortable for him to be around the others too much. Usually Otis said nothing about it, but on that particular day it seemed he was unwelcome. Which was fine, he knew he wasn't one of them. He was an outsider among outsiders, a squatter in someone else's squat, a norm among perceivers.

He went to the park. He often went to the park. The wide open spaces allowed him to see any police officers out on patrol from far away and avoid them. Not as if he got the impression that the few he saw were hunting for the murderer of Agent Cooper, but he couldn't be sure.

It also gave him space to think and try to remember details about his life. He spent hours sitting on a park bench with his eyes closed, thinking himself back beyond the moment he found himself in the corridor. Or, trying to think beyond it. Because all he encountered was darkness. An endless nothing. He replayed the sound of the woman's voice who had called his name and tried to remember who she was, but he kept coming up against the blackness. He tried so hard it hurt, but then — frustrated — his eyes would snap open and he would find himself staring at the only reality he knew.

That day in the park, he saw a group of boys playing football. They were school-age teenagers and split into two teams in red and blue football kits. He stopped to watch a little distance where a smattering of parents were gathered on the touchline. Occasionally they shouted, "Come on my son!", "Pass the ball!" and "Put it in the net!"

One boy drew Michael's attention. He was a lanky black teenager with pock-marked skin and wearing a red football strip. He played with impressive dexterity. He dodged his opposite number on the blue team, intercepted the ball with his inner right foot, dribbled it for two steps and passed it to a stocky white boy in red. Cheers erupted from the parents… which turned to groans as the white boy shot for goal, the ball struck the post and bounced back onto the field. The black boy slowed to a walk and gave his teammate a commiserating slap on the back.

There was something familiar about him. For a moment, Michael thought he was watching someone from his lost past. His heart leapt with excitement.

And then he realised.

The boy he was watching was Jack.

Free of his plaster cast, with shorter hair, and showing unexpected athleticism, it was definitely him.

Michael wanted to go up to him. To ask Jack what happened, to find out if he was all right. But the game continued on the pitch. And he noticed, for the first time, that one of the parents on the touchline was Jack's mother.

Eventually, the referee blew his whistle and the players sagged to a stop. Jack jogged off the field and collected a water bottle from his waiting mother. He swigged some round his mouth and spat it out on the grass. He took a second sip, which he drank, then wandered away from the others to a large sycamore tree. The gentle sunlight filtering through its yellowing autumn leaves cast a mottled shadow on Jack as he leant against the trunk and extended his leg behind him in a calf stretch.

Michael cast a glance back at Mrs Jackson. She was engrossed chatting to the referee.

He approached Jack, who appeared not to notice. Jack swapped legs and stretched the other calf.

"Hello, Jack," said Michael.

Jack stopped stretching and stood up straight. "Do I know you?"

"It's me, Michael."

Jack returned a blank stare. His cheeks were flushed from exercise, but they were the only living features on an otherwise dead expression.

"I was with Otis and Jennifer, remember? I was the one who rescued her from the fire?"

"Oh yeah," said Jack. The tiniest hint of recognition flickered across his face. "I'm not supposed to talk to you."

"Why not?"

But Jack was already turning away.

"Wait! Jack!" Michael pulled at his shoulder and twisted him back. "Can't you just tell me how you are?"

Jack looked at the hand on his shoulder like it was a hairy tarantula crawling on his skin. He flicked Michael's fingers off him. "My name's Nathaniel," he said.

"Okay, Nathaniel — what happened? Why haven't you called Otis or Jennifer? Aren't you guys friends anymore?"

"I've been cured," said Jack simply.

"Cured of your friendship?" Michael searched Jack's face for the boy he remembered. The boy who screamed injustice in the hospital when he thought someone was queue-jumping, the boy who stood up to his mother and said he didn't want to be normal.

"Thank you for your concern," Jack said with precise politeness. "I'm much better now."

Michael was still trying to reconcile his memory of Jack with the boy who was standing in front of him when the sound of Mrs Jackson's voice drifted across the park. "Nathaniel!"

She waved at her son from the touchline.

"Excuse me," said Jack. "I have to go."

He turned and walked away without giving Michael a second glance.

Michael took several steps backwards until he felt the solid trunk of the tree at his back. He let it take his body weight as thoughts spiralled through his mind. So that was the cure, he thought. It had taken a strident, vivacious boy and emptied him of his spirit.

Like Michael had been emptied of his memories.

Looking into Jack's face had been like looking into his own mind — the harder he stared, the more he saw only blankness.

SEVEN

"I'VE seen Jack!" Michael cried as he entered the flat.

Otis looked up from where he was sitting sprawled out on the furthest armchair, tapping away at his phone.

Jennifer put down the kettle halfway through making herself a cup of coffee. "Is he all right?" she asked. She came out of the kitchen to join Michael in the lounge.

"He was…" Michael tried to think of the right word. "… different."

"But he was all right?"

Michael didn't know what to say. The way Jennifer was looking at him, it was like she wanted him to say 'yes'. To tell her that Father Christmas exists, there's gold at the end of the rainbow and everyone's going to live happily ever after. Michael didn't believe in any of those things and so he said nothing.

Otis was the one to break the silence. "He'd had the cure."

"That's what he said," said Michael.

Otis got out of his seat and discarded his phone on the cushion behind him. "Seem withdrawn? Unemotional? Robotic?"

"Yeah," said Michael.

"Like they'd taken part of his soul and thrown it in the rubbish?"

Jennifer turned on Otis, accusation in her eyes. "It can't be that bad."

She turned to Michael. "It wasn't that bad?"

But Otis's description wasn't far off.

As Jennifer looked deeper into Michael, she must have perceived his thoughts because she didn't ask him again. She just sat down hard on the sofa, like she had no strength left to stand anymore. "We should have stopped him, Otis."

"How? He's underage. We'd only have the police coming down on us."

Frustration was rising inside Michael. This was how it often went with Jennifer and Otis. They'd talk about things and he wouldn't understand. "Are you going to tell me more about this cure or what?"

"You're such a skank sometimes, Michael," said Otis. "How come you don't know this stuff?"

"Amnesia," prompted Jennifer.

"Convenient!" Otis sighed. "What d'ya wanna know? I mean, you saw it. It takes away perception. It's supposed to turn a perceiver into a norm, but it's like taking eyes from a sighted person or ears from a hearing person. We experience life through 'ceiving. When it's gone it's like we're suddenly blind or deaf. Jack ain't the first I've known who's been cured. They're lobotomised. Like little robots programmed to pass exams and join the chess club."

And play football in matching strips, be polite and obey their mother, Michael thought. "How does it work?"

"Injection. As far as we know. For some reason it has to be given by specially-trained doctors at a special clinic." Otis gave him a disapproving look. "Not as if you couldn't have found out all this by looking it up your skanking self."

He bent down and snatched up his phone from the chair. He spent a few moments typing something and chucked it over to Michael.

Michael — taken by surprise — lifted his hands to catch it. The device bounced off his wrist and turned in the air. He fumbled for it and managed to grab hold before it fell to the floor. He turned it sideways and watched the video which Otis had started to play on the screen.

> *Soft, classical music drifted over images of a stone-clad building with the sign* Perceivers' Clinic *on the door. The shot closed in and the door opened to allow in the camera. The shot followed through into a brightly lit waiting area with a smiling doctor in a crisp white coat and several teenagers and their parents looking excited.*
>
> *A calm voiceover: "The cure is a simple, quick and painless procedure that can be given to any teenager showing symptoms of perception. Just a little injection and your child becomes normal again."*
>
> *The shot changed to a bunch of teenage girls playing basketball.*
>
> *Then changed again to show one of the girls standing on the courtside, speaking to an interviewer out of shot. "I feel soooo much better." She had long flowing hair as soft as a shampoo advert and a smile as white as a toothpaste commercial. "It's just like being a normal kid. I've been able to join the basketball club and concentrate on my school work. I wouldn't ever want to go back to the way I was…"*

The video continued, but Michael had seen enough. He passed it back to Otis.

"I'm presuming Jack wasn't acting like that?" said Otis.

"No," said Michael.

"Propaganda's everywhere," said Jennifer. "We're trying to tell people the truth, but they keep shutting down our websites."

"Jennifer's in touch with 'ceivers all over the country," said Otis. "Maybe we can do something to stop it, if they don't cure us all first."

Michael sat on the chair opposite Jennifer. "What else does this cure actually do?" he asked.

Jennifer didn't answer him immediately. She rested her elbows on her knees, clasped her hands together, sat her chin on top and looked at him. Looked into him. After a moment, her expression changed. A smile suggested she had found what was looking for. "You think you've had the cure," she said.

It was the one thing that had dominated Michael's thoughts since leaving the park.

Otis laughed. "Michael? A perceiver?"

"Why not?" said Michael.

"I've 'ceived you, Michael mate. I'm telling you, you're a norm."

Michael turned away from Otis's mocking laugh, hoping to get more sense out of Jennifer. "Is it so ridiculous? The cure affects your brain, right? Could it affect memory?"

She shook her head. "They remember. They just can't perceive anymore. It's what's so cruel. Knowing what you once were and real-ising you can never be that person again."

"But Jack forgot stuff," said Michael. "When I asked about you two, he looked at me blankly."

"He remembers," said Jennifer. "He's moved on, that's all. The cured don't hang around with perceivers. They turn their backs on us."

"But…"

The conversation wasn't going the way Michael had imagined it would. They hadn't looked into Jack's eyes like he had. Michael wasn't a perceiver — at least, not anymore — but he wasn't wrong about recognising something of himself in the boy who insisted his name was 'Nathaniel'.

"Are you sure it does all that with one injection?"

"Using specialist doctors and the specialist clinics," said Jennifer.

"Doesn't sound like a big deal," said Michael.

"It ain't like we haven't thought of this stuff before," said Otis.

"And?" said Michael.

"And nothing," Otis replied. "The few of the cured we've talked to only remember the injection. Then they wake up in a recovery room."

"So you don't actually know what goes on inside clinics." An idea was forming in Michael's head. An exciting idea. Generating a plan as he spoke.

Otis nodded, like he was perceiving Michael's thoughts as quickly as he was having them. "If you want to find out, why don't you go into one of the clinics?" said Michael.

"No!" Jennifer stood up and backed away from the others, shaking her head. "No way, Otis. I'm not going near one of those places. I'm not."

"Not you," said Michael. "Me."

Jennifer looked at him, uncomprehending. "But you're not a perceiver."

"Exactly," said Michael. His mind was racing ahead of theirs. It was exhilarating. "Either I've always been a norm or I've already had the cure. Either way, it can't hurt me."

"As far as we know," said Jennifer. "You've seen what happened to Jack. What will it do to a norm?"

Michael didn't know. He hoped he wouldn't have to find out. "I need to understand what happened to my memories... to get them back."

Otis scoffed. "You might as well climb Mount Everest to learn about knitting!"

That wasn't fair. "Even if I don't find out anything about my own situation, I might find out something about the clinics that can help you."

"Why do you care?" said Otis. "You're not one of us."

"But I'm sleeping on your sofa," said Michael. "Maybe I don't want to be homeless."

Otis put his head to one side and looked into him, like a dog trying to understand a human. It was unnerving. Not like when Jennifer perceived him. He felt the prickle of hairs on his arms as his skin developed goose pimples. Only for a moment. Then Otis righted his head again and Michael's skin relaxed.

"I'll take that as an answer for now," said Otis. He strolled around the room and went back to his armchair. He sat and spread his legs wide. He rested his elbows on his knees and leant forward. "So … memory-challenged norm-boy — what's your plan?"

EIGHT

OTIS drove Michael out to the countryside in his ugly, dented hatchback and left him to walk the last mile to the cure clinic on his own. The authorities had set up the cure clinic for one day in a building usually used by a private healthcare company. How Otis had managed to set Michael up with an appointment at such short notice, he didn't ask. There were a lot of things to do with Otis he didn't ask about. It felt safer that way.

At the front desk, a short, wide woman squeezed into a trouser suit one size too small for her, took Michael's picture, his name, fingerprints and contact details. Michael lied. He used the false name Otis had given him, handed over the bogus ID and appointment card he had brought with him and trotted out a fake address and contact number. She noted it all down in her computer without comment. Michael tried not to show he was relieved to get through the first part of the plan.

She asked him to sit in the waiting room of plush furnishings, springy carpet and neutrally wallpapered walls. It was already full of other teenagers, some with their parents — most with just the one, others with a pair — all sitting with stark faces around the edge. Not exactly the excited group which had been portrayed on the promotional video. Michael hadn't brought anyone to play parent and he realised it made him stand out from the others, so he kept his head down and avoided making eye contact with anyone. Fortunately, no one seemed interested in him. If they weren't playing with their phones, they were looking at their own feet and occasionally making hushed comments to their parents.

The woman, whose buxom chest strained the top button of her one-size-too-small jacket, sat at a desk at the head of the room like an exam invigilator, watching the children in her care with a stern face. If one of them — especially one of the younger ones — looked directly at her, she would smile. But otherwise, she spent her time staring blankly ahead or typing the odd thing on her computer. She was the one in control. With one word from her, a teenager would be called and off they would disappear to be cured.

Michael's plan was to pose as a patient, ask as many questions as he could, snoop around as much as possible and get out without having the treatment. He'd tried asking the woman in the bulging jacket, but all she did was hand him a leaflet and told him to sit and wait.

The mother of the girl sitting two chairs away shifted uncomfortably on her seat. "Do you think there's a toilet close by?" she whispered to her daughter, one of the youngest ones there. Probably thirteen, with braces on her teeth and long ginger hair running in a plait down her back.

"Mum! Again?" said the girl.

"I'll ask." The woman, ginger-haired like her daughter and surprisingly tall when she stood on her high heels, went over to the desk at the front.

The girl shifted up the couple of spare seats next to Michael. "I think she's more nervous than me," she said.

"Really." Michael tried to sound disinterested. He'd chosen to sit on that chair especially because there were free seats on either side of him. Now one of them was occupied by the girl.

The woman at the desk directed the girl's mother into the corridor. The mother nodded a 'thank you' and was out of the room.

The girl leant in close to him. "I know you're not a perceiver," she whispered.

Michael stared at the girl in shock. He suspended his breathing as he waited for the tiniest sign of what she was going to do next. He thought about running.

"Don't worry." The girl smiled. "I won't say anything."

He glanced around at the room to see if anyone else had heard. They seemed oblivious.

"How did you …?"

"I haven't been cured yet," she said.

Of course. Everyone under the age of eighteen in that room was a perceiver, apart from him. It only took one of them to be curious enough to look closer. He felt such a skank. Quickly in and out was the plan, mingling with non-perceiving adults so he wouldn't be noticed. He hadn't counted on the waiting. The long, interminable waiting.

"So, what you doing here?" said the girl.

"I'm standing in for my brother," said Michael, keeping his voice low. "He didn't want to come."

"Liar."

Of course she could tell he was lying. Another one of those irritating tricks perceivers had.

Michael looked up at the fat woman. She was staring out of the window where the trees of the landscaped grounds were bowing gently in the breeze. He wished she would look at her computer screen, see his name, call him to the front and get him away from the prying girl. But the woman continued to stare with hardly a blink.

"My name's Elaine," said the girl.

"Eric," said Michael, remembering to use his false name.

Elaine raised her eyebrows. "Hello, 'Eric.'"

Of course, she probably perceived that was a lie as well.

"It must be great to be born normal," she said.

"I suppose," said Michael. He really didn't want to talk to her.

"No hiding. No going through the diagnosis thing…"

Michael was suddenly interested. "'Diagnosis thing'?"

"Didn't they come to your school?" said Elaine. "Ask you questions? Speak to your parents and teachers?"

"No."

"Lucky."

"I didn't think you had to be diagnosed," said Michael. "I mean, didn't you already know you were a perceiver?"

"I wasn't going to tell anybody, was I?" said Elaine. "When your friends find out, they don't talk to you. You get banned from the athletics squad because they think you're cheating. The teachers refuse to teach you. The woman over the road even told my mum to keep me indoors. Said I was…" She trailed off. As she became more agitated, her voice got louder and a couple of kids were looking up from their phones. "It'll all be over after today."

Elaine seemed relieved. Almost as if she were looking forward to it. He wished he could perceive what she was really feeling because, after everything Otis and Jennifer had told him, her reaction didn't seem to make sense. "You want the cure?" he asked.

But he didn't get a reply. The door opened and her mother entered, wiping her hands on a piece of tissue. "Oh, here she is," said Elaine. "Bonsai Bladder herself."

She sat down beside her daughter, apparently not noticing she had shifted seats, and started to complain about the state of the hand driers in the women's toilets.

It put an end to their conversation.

Only ten minutes later, the fat woman called Elaine forward. Michael feared for her. She seemed a nice girl. She had been true to her word and not given him away. So he wondered, as she headed for the door, what sort of person she would be by the time the day was over.

IT was another half an hour before the buxom woman called Michael to the front. The sound of his false name sent butterflies leaping and dancing in his stomach. He made a point of noting where she was taking him as she led him into the corridor. If he had to make a quick getaway, he wanted to be sure he knew the way out.

At the entrance to the corridor stood a beefy man in a white coat. He had a pen in his top pocket and every semblance of being a doctor. But the way he stood — his feet exactly hip distance apart, his hands clasped neatly behind his back — made him look more like a sentry. As Michael passed him, the man kept his eyes front, apparently not interested. Although, Michael suspected, the beefy man was aware of everything.

The woman stopped beside a laminated sign which read: *Treatment Room #1*. It had been stuck over the top of a plaque which must have indicated what the room was usually used for. She knocked. There was a muffled, "Come in!" and they went inside.

Its clean and clinical walls were in contrast to the plush, hotel-like feel of the waiting room. Vinyl easy-clean floor, seamless white decoration, functional desk, chairs and examination bed. All presided over by a man in a crisp, white nurse's tunic buttoned to the neck. He was in his late twenties: his hair, nails and posture as neat as his uniform. He stood up as Michael came in, gave him a reassuring smile, then nodded to the woman to leave them to it.

"Sit down, please," said the nurse. He glanced at the piece of paper in his hand. "Eric, isn't it?"

"Yes," said Michael. He sat. "I want to know more about the cure."

"It's very simple," said the nurse, taking a seat by the side of the desk. "We get you to hop up on the bed, I call in the doctor and we give you a little injection. Then we take you through to the recovery room. And that's it."

The same story Michael had seen in the propaganda films. "It can't be that simple."

"Really, Eric, there's nothing to be afraid of."

Michael obviously wasn't going to get any more than the party line out of the nurse. He was going to have to play along until the very last minute before making a break for it.

Out of the corner of his eye he saw a collection of hypodermic needles sealed in individual sterile plastic wrapping on top of a stack of plastic admin trays. In the tray beneath, sat a collection of glass vials containing some sort of liquid. That's what, if he wasn't careful, was going to be injected into his arm.

"So, Eric, I just need to check a few details," said the nurse, consulting the computer screen in front of him. "Your name is Eric Hughes?"

"Yes."

"You live at …" He hesitated, distracted somehow by something he saw in Michael's face. "Sorry … You live at number 32 Maple Avenue."

"Yes."

"You go to school … Your school is …" He stopped. He was staring at Michael now. An intense, penetrating stare. Almost like Otis when he was trying to perceive something deep inside him. It was unnerving. Uncomfortable. Michael turned away. But the nurse reached forward, grabbed Michael's face and jerked it back to look at him. Michael tried to shake himself free, but the nurse kept a vice-like grip on his cheeks.

"You're not a perceiver," he said.

He let go of Michael's face, but Michael didn't move. He was too stunned. There was no way the nurse could have known that. *No way.* Adults didn't look into people's heads and read their secrets.

Only teenagers. Only perceivers. Adults weren't perceivers, all the propaganda said so.

The nurse got up and went to the other side of the desk where there was some sort of intercom. He pressed a button. "Can you get Doctor Page to come in here?"

Michael wasn't waiting around for some doctor to examine him. He had to run now and figure out what the hell was going on later. He made a bolt for the door.

The nurse, caught by surprise, shouted after him. But Michael was already in the corridor and running.

The beefy man at the entrance was alerted to the noise. He turned and his large body filled the corridor. Michael reversed, but the nurse had come out of the treatment room behind him. He was trapped between the two. Michael spied another door off to the side and dived for it. Grasping the handle, he tried to turn it, but it didn't budge. The door was locked. Panicking, he wrestled with the handle, knowing he didn't have the strength to force the lock, but not knowing what else to do.

Large, beefy hands grabbed his shoulders. They pulled him away and the door handle slipped from his fingers. The man turned Michael's body to face the nurse.

"What do you want done with him, sir?" he said.

Sir? What person in a white coat ever called a nurse *sir*?

"Back in there," said the nurse. He stood aside and Michael found himself staring back at the treatment room he had run from.

The man's strong hands pushed him, and Michael went sprawling inside. His body crashed against the desk. The vials in the admin tray tinkled as they knocked together.

The door closed and Michael heard the sound of a key turning in the lock. He tried the handle just in case. It wasn't going to open. "Shit!"

He looked around the room. There was a window. One of those long, rectangular windows that opened from the bottom and angled outwards. He tried the handle. That, too, was locked. He could try to break the glass, but it was double glazed. The only way to smash it would be to break the vacuum seal between the two panes. He frantically looked for a small, sharp object. He pulled open drawers, knocked books off shelves; desperate for something like a screwdriver or a drill bit. Not exactly standard equipment for a medical treatment room.

He reached for one of the hypodermics. The needle was thin and fragile, but he prayed it was enough. He ripped off the packaging. Just as he heard a key being placed in the door. Too late to get out the window. But he could use the needle as a makeshift weapon. He hid it behind his back.

The key turned. At the last second, he thought to reach for one of the vials in the admin tray and secrete it in his pocket.

The beefy man entered followed by the nurse and, behind them, a woman in a white coat. She really did look like a doctor. Tall and slim and neat, with long brown hair pinned back from her face, a bold blue blouse and straight black trousers under her doctor's garb. Her eyes widened when she saw Michael. A startled stare, like she was looking at the impossible.

Michael wondered if she, too, perceived he was a norm.

"There he is, Doctor Page," said the nurse, pointing at Michael.

"Thank you, Alan," said Doctor Page, her voice soft and preoccupied. Still staring at Michael. "Leave us, please."

"What?" said the nurse.

"Thank you for bringing this to my attention," she clarified. "I will deal with this."

"Ma'am," said the beefy man. "I wouldn't recommend…"

"It's fine, really," said Doctor Page. "Just take the hypodermic needle he's hiding behind his back and I will be fine."

Michael stood as the beefy man came forward, reached for his arm and prised the needle from his fingers. There was no way the doctor could have seen it was there. Even if she saw he was concealing his hand, she couldn't have known what was in it.

"If you're sure …" said the nurse.

Doctor Page nodded.

The nurse grabbed the admin trays — with their hypodermics and vials of curative liquid — and exited, taking the beefy man with him.

The door closed and Michael stood alone with Doctor Page. He stood beneath her gaze. A scared kid without a weapon, without a plan or a way to escape. What happened next was going to be up to her.

And then she did the most unexpected thing. She hugged him.

She engulfed him in her arms and drew him close. He felt her breasts press against his chest as she gently squeezed him. So close he could smell the musk of her perfume. Michael — confused and uncomfortable — stiffened against her embrace. Until she finally let go and he was able to pull away.

"My God, Michael. What are you doing here?"

She knew his name. His real name. Did she perceive it? He didn't know how to respond. It was still her move.

"Did they take your picture, Michael?"

"Picture?"

"Yes. Did they check you in? Did they take your details?"

"Uh … yeah," he managed.

"My God, Michael," she said again. "Why? Don't you know all that stuff goes straight to Cooper?"

"Cooper?" The name chilled him. Michael flashed back to the man slumped on the fire exit stairs with a kitchen knife in his stomach. "He's alive?"

"We have to get you out of here."

There was a knock at the door. Doctor Page was so startled, she visibly jumped. For a second, Michael thought she looked just as scared as he was.

"Doctor Page?" called a voice from outside. It was the beefy man. "Are you all right?"

"Yes! Just a minute!" She looked at Michael. Looked into him. Her eyes gently unpeeling layers from his mind. "It's so good to know you're okay, Michael, but I wish to God you hadn't come."

"You know me?" The realisation struck him with the force of an electric shock. "My name? My life?"

But the beefy man was knocking again.

"Yes, yes!" said Doctor Page. She took Michael's hand and propelled him to the door. She opened it to find the beefy man standing there, his body filling the doorframe. "It was a simple mistake," she told him. "This boy's already been cured. Must have got turned around in the system. He was so confused, poor lamb, he didn't realise. I'll take him back to recovery."

"I'll do that for you," said the beefy man. "You have more important things to do."

"No, no. It's all right. I'm going that way, anyway." She squeezed past him. The man stood aside to allow her through. Michael tagged along behind, his hand still in hers, like a small child being helped across the road. Then they were in the corridor again, the beefy man behind them and a clear path ahead.

"Do you know your way out?" Doctor Page whispered.

"Yes, but …?"

"No time for questions," she said. "Cooper'll be on his way, if he's not here already. I want you to get out and keep going. I'll cover for you here as much as I can, but it won't be long before someone realises."

She let go of Michael's hand and stopped walking. He felt her touch his back and give it a little nudge: a signal for him to keep going. He took a couple of steps then glanced behind. She had already turned away from him and was walking in the opposite direction.

He breathed deep. He was back on the plan: get out now; think about it later.

The way back to the entrance was unimpeded by other people. He walked with confidence, giving the impression he had every right to be there. He held his breath as he walked past the buxom woman at the head of the waiting area. She didn't so much as look up from her computer.

Emerging outside through the main entrance onto a landscaped gravel area, he realised how far away he was from his agreed rendezvous point with Otis. The main road lay some one hundred metres down a thin, gravel drive edged with trees and shrubs and he had at least a ten minute walk after that. Not exactly prescription for a quick getaway.

In those seconds that he paused, he heard footsteps on the gravel behind him. His heart beat faster, but as he turned, he saw that it was Elaine and her mum, their ginger hair bright in the autumn sunshine. He sighed with relief.

"Hi, Elaine!" he said, trying to sound all bright and cheery.

"Oh, hello," said Elaine, that vacant stare on her face that reminded him of Jack.

"I just called my dad and he's stuck in traffic," Michael lied. "He doesn't think he can pick me up. Couldn't give me a lift, could you? Just to a bus stop or something?"

Elaine, now cured and unable to perceive his lie, looked up to her mother. "Mum, can we give Eric a lift?"

Her mother looked across at Michael. "Oh, hello again," she said. "I suppose we could."

He walked with them to an adjacent car park, a square of black tarmac layered with the yellow and red of fallen leaves from the overhanging trees. Elaine's mum's car was a light blue Renault which had seen better days, but was roomy enough. He got into the back seat. Elaine offered to sit in back with him and they made their way slowly up the thin, gravel drive.

"It's so strange." Elaine looked across at Michael. "It's like you're here, but you're not here."

"What do you mean?" said Michael.

"I can see you, but I can't feel you."

"You mean, you can't perceive me?"

She thought about it for a moment. "I can't perceive anything. It's weird."

"Do you remember what happened?"

"Mum held my hand while the doctor gave me an injection."

"Anything else?"

"The recovery room." She smiled. "They gave me chocolate."

Her mum called out from the driver's seat. "I've enrolled Elaine in a new school. Isn't that right, 'Laine?"

"I can make new friends," said Elaine. "No one will ever know I was a perceiver." Then she stopped talking and gazed out of the window. There was something serene about her. Disoriented, but oddly happy. Looking at her, it was difficult for Michael to believe what Otis had said, that the cure had taken part of her soul and thrown it in the rubbish.

The car braked suddenly. "Bloody hell!" gasped Elaine's mum. The tyres skidded on the gravel and the car jolted them against the seatbelts with a sudden stop.

A large black car had turned into the driveway as they neared the entrance which was only wide enough for one vehicle. They'd come to a stop centimetres from the other car's front bumper.

"Don't these people look where they're going?!" said Elaine's mum. She sat there resolutely and made some gestures out the window. After a few moments, the other car backed down. It reversed slowly out onto the road.

Elaine's mum put her car into gear and, with the scattering of stones from her wheels, continued out of the driveway.

Michael looked out of the side window at the offending car as they passed — it was large, imposing, sleek and black. He caught a glimpse of its front seat passenger: He was a middle-aged man with a full head of dark hair, dressed in a suit. He had his elbow resting at the base of the window while he gazed out at the scenery.

With a chill, Michael recognised him.

It was Cooper.

Even though he knew who it was, Michael continued to stare. A moment too long. Cooper turned his attention from the scenery towards him. Their eyes locked.

Michael ducked down into the footwell, out of sight of the window. Too late, he feared.

"What you doing down there?" said Elaine.

Michael kept quiet. He held his breath. And hoped.

Above him, he heard the tick-tock of the car's indicators. A rev of the engine. He held onto the back seat as the Renault jolted forward and sped away from the clinic.

NINE

MICHAEL threw open the passenger door of Otis's ugly, dented hatchback. "We need to go."

Otis — caught by surprise — jolted in the driver's seat, almost dropping his phone. "Jesus!"

Michael hopped in and shut the door. "We need to go now!"

"What happened?"

"Go now, ask questions later."

Otis started up the engine, put the car into gear and pulled out of the lay-by onto the main road. Michael swung his head round to look out of the back window. There was no sign of Cooper's sleek, black car.

"Is someone following you?" said Otis.

"I don't think so."

Michael sat round to face front and allowed himself a relieved sigh. The road ahead was clear. The speedometer on Otis's dashboard pushed sixty.

He braked sharply at the approach to a roundabout. They swung round to the third exit. He put his foot down as soon as they turned off onto the dual carriageway.

"So what happened?" said Otis.

Michael checked behind him again to make sure Cooper wasn't there, then he explained everything.

"This nurse *perceived* you?"

"Yeah," said Michael.

"Not possible."

"He looked into me. Like you and Jennifer sometimes do."

"Adults aren't 'ceivers."

"You can't know that for sure."

Otis glanced in his rear-view mirror and slipped into the left hand lane. "No one had it before us teenagers. That's why they hate us. Among perceivers, I'm about the oldest there is. It couldn't have existed before that, people would've noticed."

"Are you sure? Because this nurse … he must be about ten years older than you — and he had it. I'm telling you, he really had it. You can perceive me if you don't believe me."

"I perceive you believe it, Michael mate, but there's no way it's true."

"I think it is," said Michael. "I think they're lying to you."

Otis looked at him. For as long as he could possibly keep his eyes off the road. Like he was really wondering if it was possible. Then he turned away, reached forward and switched on the radio. Music blared out of the speakers. Loud and raucous. He turned it up. The base shook the car in a steady rhythm that blocked out the sound of the tyres rumbling over the road, and chased away difficult thoughts.

OTIS entered the flat and threw his keys into the kitchen. They hit the back wall and dropped onto the worktop below. Michael followed him in and closed the door.

Jennifer jumped up off the sofa, turning off the TV with the remote as she did so. "Well?" she said, approaching Michael. Her eyes looked intently at him. He knew she was trying to perceive him before he had a chance to tell her. "Did they…?"

"…cure me of something I don't have?" said Michael. "No."

She seemed relieved. She sat back down on the sofa. Otis joined her. He put his arm around her shoulders. She allowed it to rest there, but didn't sink into his affection. "So," she said, "what happened?"

He told her what he had told Otis. She sat, open-mouthed, listening to it all.

"What do you think, Jen?" said Otis. "Adult perceivers — is it possible?"

"Yesterday and I would've said no, but today…?" She let her doubt fade away.

Jennifer pulled her phone from her pocket. "We need to tell people."

Otis reached across her and spread his hand over the screen. "No."

"We can't fight this together, Otis, if we don't share information."

"We don't know anything for sure."

"Then how are we gonna find out? You can't send Michael back in there — and we can't go without risking being cured."

Something triggered in Michael's mind. He'd been so focussed on escaping Cooper, he hadn't thought about anything else. "I almost forgot." He delved into his pocket and pulled out the vial of liquid he'd taken from the nurse's desk. It was warm from being close to his skin. He handed it to Otis.

"What is it?" he said.

"That," said Michael, "is the cure."

Otis's eyes widened. He turned the glass tube around in his hand. "This?"

It was about ten centimetres in length with a rubber stopper on one end and clear liquid inside. On the outside was a label that read: *CLINIC #1. 50ml. Serial no. 537986B*

"Let's see," said Jennifer. She took it from him and held it up to the light. The liquid sparkled with purity. "It's so small."

"But powerful enough to change your life," said Otis.

"What are we going to do with it?" said Jennifer.

"We should get it analysed," said Otis.

"How are we going to do that?" she asked.

"I know someone." He grabbed it back from her.

"Who?" Jennifer asked.

"No one you know." Otis looked at his watch. "I'll be a couple of hours." He got off the sofa.

"You're going now?" she called after him.

"You know what they say," said Otis, halfway to reclaim his keys from the kitchen. "Strike while the women are hot!" He tossed his keys into the air and caught them again. He gave her a cheeky smile as he went out of the door.

Where Did Perceivers Come From?

The short answer is, nobody knows. One day teenagers were those young people who hung around on street corners looking glum, then four years ago we found out they were looking into our minds.

We found out. It's almost certain they existed before then. As Professor Olong of the University of Birmingham says: 'It seems likely these children were Perceivers before their teenage years. The research we've been able to do so far suggests they were capable of perception in a limited form before puberty. Probably misunderstood as instinct, or the ability to read body language. While the children themselves kept quiet about the truth for fear of being singled out as abnormal.' *[www.dailynews.co.uk/ science/olong]*

As for why perception appeared all of a sudden, the reasons are still unclear. 'More research needs to be done,' says Olong. 'But it seems to me that something in our environment must have triggered this change. For a fifth of teenagers to suddenly have this condition, it cannot be a coincidence.'

Page **[1]** [2] [3] >>>next

MORE FROM AAMI

Claudia Angel-heart's Blog

Is Your Teenager a Perceiver?

Living with a Perceiver

How to Get Your Teenager a Cure Clinic Appointment

'Perceivers are from Outer Space' Theory Dismissed

Supporters, Links and Affiliates...

JOIN AAMI

TEN

JENNIFER stood in the kitchen, her back resting against the worktop while reading something on her phone.

"Hi, Michael," she said without looking up.

Michael stepped into the kitchen. It smelt of the curry Otis had cooked last night. The pans he put in soak were still in the sink, the bubbles from the washing up liquid no longer on the surface, just an orange goo floating in the water. A kettle on the side rumbled loudly as it boiled.

"What are you doing?" he asked her.

"Nothing." Her eyes stayed focussed on the phone.

"You're always on that thing."

"Need to keep in touch with other perceivers."

"Why?"

"I ask myself that sometimes." She pressed a couple of buttons and held up the screen to him. "Some kid's been told he can't sit his exams because he might perceive the answers off other pupils."

Michael hadn't time to see the screen before she'd whipped it away again, tapped another button, and flashed a different screen. "A girl wants to know if she should go to her cure clinic appointment. What the skank are we supposed to do?" She tossed the phone down on the worktop. It bounced to rest by the toaster.

"What about your perceivers network?" said Michael.

"We text and post and chat. Anytime someone suggests doing something, it all breaks down into stupid arguments. No one knows what to do."

The kettle shuddered to the boil.

"Fancy a coffee?" said Jennifer.

"Not for me," said Michael.

She grabbed a single mug from the draining board and took the coffee jar from the cupboard. Michael enjoyed watching her coffee routine. She seemed at home doing it.

She shook a spoon from the draining board and unscrewed the coffee jar. She tipped the jar towards Michael so he saw the brown grains inside. "Sure?"

"Don't like the stuff," said Michael. "Not tea neither. Even with three sugars. Bleh!"

She took a spoonful of granules, dropped it in the mug with the clink of metal on china and poured water from the kettle. The coffee fizzed a little and sent a plume of its distinctive smell into the air. "I remember the first time I had coffee," she said. "My dad used to drink it all the time. The smell would come wafting out of the kitchen. I kept asking to have some and he kept saying I was too young. When he finally caved in and made me a cup, it tasted horrible. Strong and bitter. But I drank it anyway. I wanted to be grown up, I suppose."

She stirred her drink and dropped the spoon into the sink, where it plopped into one of the pans and sunk to the bottom of the cold curry water.

"I never heard you speak about your dad before," said Michael.

Jennifer sniffed, bringing herself out of her nostalgic haze. "Yeah, well … Dad wanted a normal little girl."

She picked up her mug, stuffed her phone into her pocket and made her way to the lounge. Michael followed and sat in the chair opposite her. "I … didn't exactly tell Otis everything," he said eventually.

"I know," said Jennifer.

Michael's eyes narrowed. "Do you have to perceive me all the time?"

"Sorry," said Jennifer. "Your thoughts are loud, I can't help it."

Michael composed himself. "The doctor at the clinic … she knew me."

"What do you mean, 'knew you'?"

"Knew my name. She hugged me! Said she was glad I was okay."

"Who was she? Did you ask her where you're from and what happened to you?"

"Didn't get a chance. Her name was Doctor Page, that's all I know."

"First name?"

"No."

Jennifer frowned. She pulled out her phone and tapped her index finger across the screen. She nodded at the display. "Doctor Page, cure clinic — there you are."

She handed the device to Michael. She'd pulled up several reports. All fairly bland and uninformative. They were blogs from parents or patients who mentioned her in passing: *"My son was treated by Doctor Page, a pleasant woman whose bedside manner … Doctor Page said my mum could hold my hand while she gave me the injection …"* and so on.

"I suppose it proves she works there," said Michael, passing back Jennifer's phone.

She perused it a little longer. Frowned again. "Hmm. No biographical details. No photo. No first name. Weird, though, that she should be working there."

"Yeah, weird." He thought about it for a moment. Everything he'd experienced at the clinic was still a jumble. Like a mixed up jigsaw puzzle he didn't know how to put together.

"There's something else, isn't there?" said Jennifer.

"You're perceiving me again."

"But I won't know what it is until you tell me."

Michael sighed. "Cooper was there."

"Cooper?" she said. "The man-you-ran-away-from-Cooper?"

"Yeah."

"What's he got to do with the cure clinic?"

"I don't know!" said Michael in frustration. "The doctor said all the details get sent to him. Our names, pictures and addresses…"

"Someone's keeping records of all the perceivers that go for the cure?"

Michael shrugged. "Apparently."

Jennifer tapped her nails on the back of her phone. "Something's going on in those clinics they're not telling us about."

"That's my theory," said Michael. "But how do we find out? I can't go back there. Neither can you or Otis without the risk of being cured."

"Maybe we can come at it from a different angle," said Jennifer.

"Like what?"

"Otis isn't the only one who knows people, you know." She grinned.

JENNIFER had done one week's work experience at *The Daily News* while she was still at school. She'd got to know a reporter there called Sian Jones. Sian was one of its recent intake of internet-savvy reporters who recognised the days of rushing to get a story ready for the morning edition were part of history. 'Up to the minute' was the latest buzzword and she was the epitome of it. Smart, yet fashionable, full of energy and ready to go at a moment's notice, she was all-London. Thriving in a grimy, ethnically diverse city, unfazed by its pollution and crowded streets, like she was born into it. Only the occasional hint of her accent suggested that she was born and brought up in Wales.

Sian worked at the newspaper offices on Gray's Inn Road and suggested meeting Jennifer and Michael in an American-style diner a few streets away.

"You can't have a private meeting in a building full of journalists," she explained as she sat down with them in an enclosed booth in the corner of the restaurant. "Even if you book a private room, nosy people will watch you walk into it."

Jennifer had become more than just a work experience girl when she had worked alongside Sian back in her schooldays. They had been sent to report on a salacious murder case at the Old Bailey and, over a lunchtime sandwich, Jennifer admitted that she knew the man in the dock was guilty. She had perceived it from him. Sian, rather than being scared or shocked by what she had done, had been excited and wanted to run a story on the potential uses of perception. It came to nothing because her editor wasn't interested, but it meant she remembered Jennifer when she rang to ask for her help.

Sian had steak and chips, and a tea. Jennifer went for coffee and chicken salad. Michael wanted everything he saw in the mouth-watering pictures on the menu, but settled for Coke and a burger, despite not having any money. He hoped Jennifer was going to foot the bill, otherwise he was going to have to eat and run. He'd done that once when he was living rough. The cafe owner had chased him for two streets before Michael finally lost him. He didn't want to do that again.

"I've been doing some research into cure clinics, as it happens," said Sian, for an opening gambit.

"Are you working on a story?" said Jennifer.

"That's the idea," said Sian. "My editor has a different opinion."

"We think there's more going on than they're telling us," said Jennifer.

"Interesting," said Sian. She leant back to allow the waitress to put a mug of tea down in front of her. It was a pale, milky-looking liquid with the teabag still bobbing about on the top. Jennifer's coffee smelt as strong as it was black. Michael's Coke was half full of ice. He shivered. It was a dull and overcast day outside and he didn't see the point of being cooled down any further.

"If the cure's just an injection, why does it take specialist nurses to administer it?" said Jennifer, keeping her voice low. "If it's so important for all perceivers to be cured, why are there so few clinics? And why do they operate only one day in the week and move on?"

"All good questions," said Sian, twirling the teabag around in her mug with her spoon and giving it a squeeze before dropping it on the table. It sat there abandoned, scrunched up and steaming like something left by a dog on a cold winter morning.

"Answers?" said Jennifer.

"Difficult to come by," said Sian.

Michael wasn't impressed. All that way across London to talk to a woman who, apparently, knew little more than they did.

"What I can tell you," said the journalist, "is that the clinics aren't run by the Department of Health."

"I thought …" began Jennifer.

"So did I. But I've been doing some digging. It's Department of Health on the posters and the signs and the adverts, all right, but the running of the actual clinics is contracted out to a private company: Panoplia Healthcare."

She looked at Jennifer, as if waiting for a response. Then she glanced across at Michael. Michael shrugged his shoulders.

"It's a subsidiary of Advanced Medical Investments which is owned by …?" Sian waited for them to finish the sentence.

Jennifer shook her head.

"Ransom Incorporated," Sian concluded. "Headed by Brian Ransom."

"The pill guy?" said Jennifer.

"The pill guy, exactly," said Sian. She sipped her tea.

"Who?" said Michael.

"Brian Ransom supplies vitamin pills to pregnant women for free," said Jennifer.

"What's he do that for?" said Michael.

"To ensure that every baby born in this country gets the best start in life," said Sian. "Or so he claims. Had something to do with his wife desperately wanting a child and having to undergo IVF, or something. He made a personal fortune out of that flu vaccine his company developed, so he could afford it at the time."

"They thought those vitamin pills caused perception at one stage, didn't they?" said Jennifer.

"That was a storm in a teacup." Sian sipped from her mug. "Turns out some perceivers were born before the pills came out."

"Otis is one of those," said Jennifer.

"Plus, they analysed the pills and discovered they contained…" The journalist paused for dramatic effect. "Vitamins! Not exactly headline news: *Vitamin Pills Contain Vitamins Shock!*"

The waitress arrived with their food. Michael's burger and chips smelt amazing. It was almost enough to wipe away his concern about paying the bill. He sprinkled salt on his chips, picked up one with his fingers and bit into it. It was piping hot, but he ate it anyway, sucking in cool air between his teeth in an attempt to avoid burning his mouth.

"Basically," said Sian, spearing one of her own chips with a fork, "Ransom's your man if you want to know more about the cure clinics. I've been trying to get an interview with him for ages, but he seems to have gone to ground. Odd for a man who was all over the news when he launched the great vitamin pill giveaway."

"He's rich," said Jennifer. "I suppose he doesn't need the publicity."

"Or doesn't want it," added Sian. "Turns out the cure clinics aren't the only contract he's got from the government. He recently picked up a big order to supply flu vaccines to GP surgeries across the country. Since the patent ran out on his original vaccine, he's had a tough time maintaining his share of the market. The Health Minister — in the longest and most boring document I think I've ever read — said, despite the increased cost to the NHS of buying the vaccines from Ransom, it would save the country money in the long run by securing the jobs of British workers."

Michael's eyes had started to glaze over with all the talk about politics. "What does that mean?"

"It means, his company's not as flush with cash as it first appears. It's only being propped up by government contracts."

"Why's that important?" said Michael.

"Dunno," said Sian. "Interesting though, isn't it?" She bit down on a chip and chewed with self-satisfaction.

And then it was time for swapsies. It was a condition for their meet. The journalist gave something to them and they gave her information in return. Michael told her about the cure clinic. He said nothing about Cooper and Doctor Page, but he did mention the nurse he thought was a perceiver. Sian's eyebrows rose at that piece of information and she made a note on her phone.

When they had finished, Sian put her phone in her bag. "I was curious when you phoned," she said to Jennifer. "I wondered what happened to the smart work experience student I remembered, so I looked you up on the internet. I thought maybe there would be something about you winning a journalism prize or something. But there's nothing like that. The only place I found you was on a missing persons' list. Several missing persons' lists, actually."

"What do you mean?" said Jennifer.

"Your parents have reported you missing. They say you ran away six months ago."

Jennifer went pale. "You had no right to poke your nose into my business."

"Your parents are really worried about you."

"You didn't call them?"

"No," said Sian. "But I think you should."

Jennifer sat with her mouth open, eyes wide, breathing faster than normal.

"They've left messages all over the web," Sian continued. "They really care about you."

"Yeah? Well, they've got a funny way of showing it." Jennifer stood up. Her chair scraped noisily against the hard floor. "Excuse me." She turned away and headed for the back of the diner. Michael watched her disappear into the women's toilets.

Sian called over the waitress and asked for the bill.

The journalist paid for everyone's lunch with her credit card, much to Michael's relief. "Thanks," he said. "For the food."

"Don't forget to pay me back when you get that interview with Ransom." She put her credit card away in her purse and pulled out a business card. She handed it to Michael. "It's quaint and old-fashioned, but my editor insisted we had some printed. Contact me when you get that scoop."

She looked up. Jennifer was coming back from the toilets.

"Look," said Sian. "I know Jennifer won't listen to me, but she might to you. There's a charity called Missing People that can get in touch with her parents for her. She doesn't have to say where she is, only that she's alive and well."

Sian took the card from Michael, turned it over and scribbled a number on the back. He secreted it in the back pocket of his jeans just as Jennifer returned to the table.

"I've been thinking," Jennifer announced, not bothering to sit down. "We should keep this relationship strictly professional."

"Absolutely," said Sian.

"So we don't talk about personal stuff?"

"Agreed."

"And that bit of information you found out about me — you're not going to do anything about it, are you?"

"Not if you don't want me to," said Sian. "I protect my sources."

"Good," said Jennifer. "Thank you for your time, Miss Jones. We'll see how far we get with Brian Ransom and let you know. Come on, Michael."

Surprised at her authoritative tone, he got to his feet and followed her out of the diner.

Jennifer was silent as they went to catch the bus. They climbed up to the top deck where she gazed through the window, her breath gently steaming up the glass. Michael watched her, realising how little he knew about her. Ironic that while he was trying to remember his past, she was running away from hers.

ELEVEN

MICHAEL woke to the bleep of a reversing lorry and the sound of inconsiderate dustmen shouting to each other as they emptied the bins from outside the flats. He squinted at the clock on the microwave in the kitchen to see what ungodly time of the morning it was. All he saw were blurred green numbers. He decided it was too early to get up and he leant his head back on the arm of the sofa where he'd been sleeping.

It was then he noticed the rectangular black object on the table in front of him. It was Otis's phone. For some reason, he hadn't taken it with him when he'd gone to bed that night. Michael picked it up and tried to figure out how to use it. He thought back to the code he had seen Otis use to unlock it. After a couple of tries, he found the correct four digits and opened the internet browser to run a search on Brian Ransom:

Ransom's picture made him look more laid back than business-like. Rather than wearing a suit, he wore a jumper with a red and black checked pattern like someone about to step onto the golf course. His black hair was wavy and a bit longer than the standard cut for a man and his smile was wide and grinning, almost cheeky. Not the sort of look one would expect from the CEO of a multi-million-pound corporation.

Michael flicked through the links at the bottom of his bio. Sian Jones had been right, most detailed his early career — from computer game whiz-kid to vitamin pill philanthropist — and gave precious little information about his recent years. There was, however, an old *Daily News* article by Sian Jones herself:

last time a treatment was launched fully fledged onto the market in this way."

The answer may lie in the personal fortune of Brian Ransom, known by many as The Pill Guy for his vitamin pill giveaway to pregnant women. The head of Ransom Incorporated, who has consistently featured in the top ten of The Times's rich list, is widely regarded as one of the few men who could fund such research. Furthermore, his personal relationship with Prime Minister John Pankhurst (Ransom was one of the main financial contributors to his last election campaign) is likely to be behind the quick adoption of cure clinics by The Department of Health.

Ransom has been no stranger to Number 10 this past year. His visits to Downing Street are a matter of public record, but attempts to interview him about it have been constantly turned down by his people at Ransom Incorporated …

Jennifer had had the same problem. She'd been constantly on her phone trying to get Ransom to agree to talk to her. She even tried turning up at his offices claiming to have an appointment, but the receptionist had been immune to her girlish charm and turned her away.

Michael scrolled back up the article and clicked on the link to The Pill Guy. It took him to another article about Ransom's pill giveaway. This one, however, had video. Michael clicked:

Ransom stood in some sort of factory, with his arm round the waist of a heavily pregnant woman. He was neater and a little older than he had been in his photograph: his black hair was cropped at collar length and he was dressed in an expensive dark suit and tie. The woman smiled at his side.

"When Mary and I embarked on the adventure of having a baby," he announced to the camera. "We were lucky. We had money to buy the best care and the best doctors—"

Loud guitar music burst from Michael's hands. He jumped in surprise and dropped the phone. It rolled to the floor where it continued to blare raucous guitar riffs — Otis's ringing tone.

Otis — blurry-eyed and wearing only pyjama bottoms — staggered out of the bedroom.

Michael picked up the phone and held it aloft. "It's ringing," he said.

Otis gave him a *that's-skanking-obvious* stare and grabbed it off him.

"Hello?" He put the phone to his ear and walked to the kitchen where he talked to the caller in hushed tones.

Jennifer came out of the bedroom in her short nightshirt and disappeared into the bathroom.

Otis finished his call, went back into the bedroom and emerged fully clothed. He knocked on the bathroom door. "Jen?"

"Yeah?" she shouted from inside.

"Something's come up, I gotta go out. Won't be back till late this afternoon."

"Okay," she replied, and the sound coming from the bathroom changed to that of the shower running.

"What's come up?" said Michael.

"Analysis on the cure's done," said Otis.

"What's in it?"

"Dunno. Gotta pick it up."

"Can I come?"

"No!"

"Come on, Otis, you wouldn't have had it to analyse if it weren't for me."

"It's a three-hour round trip to collect an envelope. It ain't a day out at skankin' Alton Towers."

"I can keep you company," said Michael.

Otis gave Michael the most filthy look. Like he was his little brother begging to play games with the big boys. "Okay, if you must. You've got two minutes to get dressed." He tutted to himself. "Norms!"

FOR the second time in a week, Michael sat in the passenger seat next to Otis as he drove out of London. It was a pleasant change to look at the city from the safety and warmth of the car. He could observe the passing grey, crowded streets without people staring at him and wondering if he was a perceiver.

Otis took the Blackwall Tunnel to get to the south side of the River Thames. Descending into the concrete tube was unnerving for someone who — as far as Michael remembered — had never been in it before. Artificial lights in the tunnel roof softened the transition from daylight to underground, but he and Otis were still enclosed deep beneath the surface, with tonnes of earth and millions of litres of water above them.

Traffic crawled to a stop.

Otis turned on the radio. A pop station was playing the latest bland number by a female vocalist Michael didn't know the name of. It faded out and the urgent beat of a news jingle crashed on top of it.

"It's 10 o'clock. Good morning, I'm Rob Flintoff. At least two teenagers have been killed and many more injured in a fight at a school in Essex. It's thought the cause is perceiver-related. George Aziz has more…"

Another man's voice: "It was just after eight o'clock this morning that the fight broke out at Mountbatten High School in Romford. It's believed several teenagers who had been diagnosed with perception were taunting other children about secrets they had pulled from their minds. When a

*group of normal teenagers tried to intervene, a fight broke
out. Police believe as many as fifty teenagers were involved
at its height. Paramedics took twelve to hospital where two
were pronounced dead on arrival. They are a thirteen-year-
old girl and a fifteen-year-old boy. Their names are expected
to be released later today."*

"My God, it's getting worse," said Otis.

"The news?" said Michael.

"If those two dead kids turn out to be norms, they're gonna blame
us." He pulled his phone from his pocket.

"What are you doing?"

"Texting Jen."

The car in front of them eased forward. Otis pocketed his phone
and put the car into gear. They crawled along.

"Fancy listening to some decent music?" said Otis.

"Yeah."

He leant over and switched from the radio to a pre-recorded track.
Soft rock guitar flowed from the speakers. Soon they were out of the
tunnel and into overcast daylight.

Michael became lost in the music. The guttural vocals drifted up
and down with a melody that was both familiar and moving. The
people and the streets and the cars went by the window, while the
lyrics told a story about lost love.

"You're singing," said Otis.

"Was I?" said Michael, embarrassed. "Sorry. I'll shut up."

"I'm surprised, that's all," said Otis.

"That I can sing?"

"That you remember the lyrics."

"So?"

"This track is five years old," said Otis. "If you remember the lyrics,
maybe you can remember other stuff."

Michael got excited. But as soon as he was conscious of the song lyrics, they fell out of his mind. In a panic, he tried the thing he used to do in the park, to think himself back to before he ran from the office building. The place where his memory should be was still dark and empty. He listened to the song again and tried to remember where he had heard it. He couldn't.

"God," said Otis as the track played. "Five years ago."

"Five years ago, what?" said Michael.

"Five years ago, I was … nothing … doesn't matter." Otis reached forward and turned up the volume. It caught the last few chords of the song and then there was a moment of quiet before the heavy guitars of the next track crashed through and chased away the reflective mood with their adrenaline-thumping vibe.

Otis kept the music loud as they drove down the A2 out of London and across the border into Kent. At the outskirts of Chatham, Otis turned off the main road into an industrial estate. It was full of modern, glass office buildings and anonymous cubed warehouses interspersed with small sections of landscaped greenery and acres of black, tarmac car parks. It took a while to find a space, but eventually Otis squeezed in on the end of a row of other cars.

Otis, with the confidence of someone who knows where he's going, led Michael to a large building with a sign above the entrance, announcing: *Randall Miller and Parnell Research Labs*. They went in through the rotary doors to a spacious reception area with comfortable seating, several large palms in pots and a fish tank. The reception desk itself was a large semi-circular affair with one woman sat behind it. If Randall Miller and Parnell intended to impress visitors when they walked in, they had succeeded.

Otis approached the desk and said hello to the receptionist. She was immaculate. Smart black jacket with the collar of her white blouse lying crisply on her shoulders. Hair tied back neatly at the back of her head. Flawless make-up. Perfect nails painted a subtle pink. Michael wondered how long it took her to get ready in the morning. She gave Otis a corporate, welcoming smile.

"Hi," said Otis. "Doctor Smith's left a package here for me."

She looked puzzled. "I don't think so."

"Are you sure? He said he'd leave it at reception."

"I'll call him," she said. Otis tried to stop her, but the receptionist had already picked up the phone.

"Doctor Smith? There's a young gentleman out here said he's come to pick up a package? … Yes, that's right … I'll tell him." She put the phone down and gave Otis another one of her corporate smiles. "He'll be right out. Why don't you take a seat?"

Otis looked like he absolutely didn't want to take a seat, but he still wandered over to the comfy chairs as instructed. Michael tagged along and actually sat on them, while Otis hovered beside him nervously, with his hands in the back pockets of his jeans.

Michael watched the fish. They swam in a tank about the length of Otis's car, lit from above by a soft blue light. They were beautiful, luscious colours. Some yellow, some striped white and black, a few orange ones, a shoal of small blue ones. All living in one tiny little world. He didn't know whether to envy their simple, carefree lives or pity them for being trapped in the tank with nothing to do all day except swim.

A man in a lab coat came out of a side door behind reception and walked towards them. Otis was fiddling with his phone and didn't notice.

"Hello, Oliver," said the man.

Otis twizzled round. "Dad," he said instinctively.

Dad?

It was hard to see the resemblance between the teenager and the man. The man, who had to be Doctor Smith, must have been pushing fifty. He was balding and, if he'd ever had Otis's shocking blond hair, then grey had long ago chased it away. He wasn't overweight, but neither did he have the muscular frame Otis had. He wore a pair of dark-rimmed glasses, while Otis had naked eyes. But, as Michael looked closer, he realised there was something similar in their faces.

"We can talk in the boardroom," said Doctor Smith.

Otis shuffled his feet nervously. "It's okay, I'll just take the envelope."

"Sign in, Oliver," said Doctor Smith, dismissing his son's protest. "You can bring your friend if you want."

Otis didn't argue anymore. He gave his father an annoyed look, then went back to the desk where the receptionist provided him with a pen. Michael signed in after him. He saw that Otis had scrawled O. Smith into the book, confirming that he and the scientist were father and son. Michael used the same false name he had used at the clinic.

"Oliver?" whispered Michael as they followed Dr Smith through the side door.

"Shut up," said Otis.

The boardroom was only a couple of doors down the corridor. It was a rectangular room dominated by a long wooden table with a dozen chairs placed around the edge and a neutral beige decor that was as corporately neat as the receptionist.

Doctor Smith flicked the catch on the door so they wouldn't be disturbed. He pulled out two chairs for them to sit in. Otis gave him a suspicious glance, then sat down next to Michael. He shifted on his seat like a nervous child sent to the head teacher's office.

"How are you, Oliver?"

"What's this about, Dad?"

"Still living in that filthy squat?"

"Dad!"

Doctor Smith turned to Michael. "And who are you? Involved in one of Oliver's scams, I suppose."

Michael leant back from the coldness of the man's disapproving eyes. "Just a friend."

"If you're a friend, can you get him to call his mother a bit more often. And tell him a visit at Christmas wouldn't come amiss either."

"Dad!" Otis stood up. "We came for the results, not an interrogation. If you haven't got them, then I might as well go."

"For goodness' sake, Oliver, sit down. I did the analysis." Doctor Smith pulled a folded piece of paper from the pocket of his lab coat and laid it out on the table in front of them. Otis sat back down and perused the piece of paper. Michael looked over his shoulder to see it was a printout, listing a series of chemical names and percentages. It wasn't the exciting result he was anticipating. Just a lot of scientific gobbledygook.

"What does it mean?" said Otis.

Doctor Smith reached into his lab coat again and pulled out a glass vial which appeared to be the one Michael had taken from the cure clinic. "I suppose it would be pointless to ask how you got hold of this?"

"Pointless," agreed Otis.

"You're certain this is the drug injected into perceivers to cure them?"

"Certain," said Michael. "Why?"

"Because it's not what I expected."

"What is it?" said Otis.

"It's Midazolam," said Doctor Smith. He folded his arms and sat back in his chair, as if that explained everything.

Michael looked across at Otis. He seemed just as lost as he was.

"What the hell's that?" said Otis.

"It's a sedative." Doctor Smith was smiling, pleased with himself.

"It puts you to sleep?" said Otis.

"Depends how much you inject," said Doctor Smith. "Could put you to sleep. Could make you drowsy. It's often used by dentists to treat nervous patients or to carry out lengthy procedures. It makes patients relaxed or sleepy. Most people don't remember the treatment they had when they were under. Useful, if you're having root canal."

Michael sat forward in his chair. "It destroys memories?"

"Patients only forget what happened while under the influence of the drug," said the doctor. "It won't make you forget your ex-girl-friend. Sadly."

Otis looked confused. "That's the cure? A sedative?"

"The cure, I don't know about," said Doctor Smith. "But that drug is Midazolam."

Otis turned to Michael. "You took the wrong drug."

"I didn't!" said Michael.

"You must've. Going to sleep don't do nothing to 'ceivers."

"It was the only stuff in the treatment room," said Michael.

Otis turned on his father. "Then you made a mistake."

Doctor Smith picked up the vial and looked at it. "I tested the stuff you gave me."

Michael took the vial from him and turned it over to read the label. It said: *CLINIC #1. 50ml. Serial no. 537986B.* It was the same vial, now with only a dribble left in the bottom. "This is what I took. It's what they were injecting into perceivers, I swear."

"What if," said Doctor Smith. "They *are* using that drug, but *that* drug isn't the cure."

"What do you mean?" said Otis.

"The teenagers get injected with Midazolam," he replied. "It makes them drowsy and compliant, then the doctors at the clinic carry out a second procedure. It's that second procedure that actually cures them of perception."

Michael sat, dumbfounded, letting the words sink in. It made sense. The injection was a smokescreen. Whatever the cure was, it was something the doctors wanted to keep secret. That was why the injections couldn't be given by ordinary doctors in ordinary hospitals and GP surgeries. It's why there were so few clinics. It was easier to keep the secret the fewer people knew about it.

It also meant they were no closer to finding out what the cure really was.

Otis picked up the printout, thanked his father and headed for the door. Michael was about to follow him when Doctor Smith pulled him back. Michael tensed at his grasp. He looked at the man's fingers digging into his arm. It scared him a little, but the man didn't look like he was going to hurt him.

"How is he? Honestly?" asked Doctor Smith, his voice quiet so Otis wouldn't hear.

"Otis?" Michael didn't know what to say. He shared a flat with the teenager, but he didn't really know him. "He's all right. I think."

Otis's voice came booming down the corridor. "Michael, are you coming or what?"

"Yeah," Michael called back. He went to go, but Doctor Smith was still holding his arm.

"He knows he can come to me if he's in trouble, doesn't he?" said Doctor Smith. "He knows me and his mother worry about him?"

Michael looked at the man's face. He wondered what had happened to keep the two of them apart. "He's a perceiver," he said. "I'm sure he knows."

TWELVE

"**SO**," said Michael as they got into Otis's car, "are we going straight back to London, *Oliver*?"

"Don't call me that," said Otis.

Michael grinned at his discomfort. "Why not? It's your name isn't it?"

"If you really want to know, my name is Oliver Terrence Ian Smith. My initials spell Otis — and that's what you're gonna call me, unless you want my fist to rearrange your face."

Otis started up the car. They drove out of Chatham, back to the A2 and towards London. Music blared out of the car stereo, most of it by a band called The White Rhinos. Otis tapped the steering wheel with the fingers of one hand and, after a while, started to sing along. Michael found some of the lyrics were in his head. He joined in. Much of the journey back was spent singing.

They got to the flat to find Jennifer sitting on the sofa reading a book on her phone. She put it aside when they entered.

"You wanna beer, Mike mate?" said Otis, going into the kitchen.

He'd never offered Michael a beer before. Otis kept a few cans in the fridge, but Michael always thought it was better to leave them alone. "Sure."

"My mouth's so dry, it feels like my tongue's licked a camel's arse," said Otis.

Jennifer came over to them. "Did you guys hear the news?"

"No," said Otis, passing a can of beer to Michael. He yanked back the ring pull and it opened with a *fitz*.

"We were listening to The White Rhinos," said Michael.

They both spontaneously broke into the chorus of one of the tracks: "*My wounded baby, don't you turn away from me!*" They burst into laughter as if it were the funniest thing they'd ever heard.

But Jennifer wasn't laughing. "Can't you perceive I'm being serious? They named the two teenagers who died in the school fight. They were norms."

"Oh," said Otis.

"And that's not the end of it." She went back to the lounge and turned on the TV. Using her phone, she streamed video footage onto the screen:

Prime Minister John Pankhurst stood outside 10 Downing Street, surrounded by microphones in fluffy covers. He wore a dark suit and a white shirt, but his normal bright tie was replaced with one of deep brown with a light blue stripe. It was windy outside and, as he brushed his unnaturally brown hair from his face, it was possible to see its grey roots.

He adopted the remorseful face he used for tragic occasions. "I wanted to say on behalf of the country, how saddened I am by the playground violence in Romford in Essex. My sympathies go out to the families of the children who died and my prayers are with those who were injured. This is a tragedy that I am determined should not happen again.

*The hatred and fear generated in this country by perceivers
is unacceptable. It is driving a wedge between communities.
Our schools have become battlegrounds. Families are being
torn apart. This situation cannot be allowed to continue.*

*"My government and I have, therefore, decided to bring
in a series of measures to ensure the law abiding citizens
of this country are protected from perceivers. The cure that
is currently being offered to people on a voluntary basis
will now be made compulsory. To help facilitate this, I will
be increasing the number of clinics where treatment can
be received and putting more resources into training staff
to service these clinics. In addition, testing in schools will
become more widespread and comprehensive. It is my belief
that, if we all work together, this country can once again be
free of perception — and communities, schools and families
will be able to resume their lives, free of fear and hatred."*

*The Prime Minister's face froze in an expression of feigned
concern.*

Jennifer had pressed pause.

"Bastard," she said.

Otis put his arm around her. She relaxed into his body and allowed
her head to rest on his chest. She clung onto his waist like a lost child.
He touched her hair, but it seemed to do nothing to comfort her.

Michael turned away, feeling he was intruding on a private
moment. They were perceivers. He was a norm. They were the ones
who had just been named as the national enemy. Whatever he might
have been in the past, he couldn't share in their fear. Jennifer and
Otis had woken up that morning as free citizens. They would go to
bed that night more or less as wanted criminals.

THIRTEEN

Gavin Swankler crossed his legs on the red sofa and turned to camera. "Welcome back to Sunday Morning with Gavin Swankler. Joining me on the sofa is the Chair of Action Against Mind Invasion, Claudia Angelheart…"

The image cut to a wide shot to show Claudia Angelheart, whose excessive make-up looked clown-like under studio lights. She nodded and smiled at him.

"… And, of course, Dave Malik MP is still here."

There was a close-up of a man in a formal brown suit on the sofa next to Angelheart. He didn't seem to be aware that he was on camera and was looking off in a completely different direction.

"Mrs Angelheart, you're going to help us review the papers later, but first I have to ask — do you think we're winning the fight against perceivers?"

"No, Gavin, I don't…"

The camera moved in close on Angelheart:

"...I commend the Prime Minister's tough stance against perceivers, I really do, but what exactly has he done since he told us he would take definitive action?"

"If I could just say—" Malik butted in. "The Prime Minister has gone to great lengths..."

In the wide shot it was possible to see Angelheart put her hand on Malik's knee. "Excuse me, dear, but you've already been interviewed. This is my turn, if you don't mind."

Malik looked affronted.

Angelheart removed her hand as if she had touched something unpleasant, and turned to Gavin with a smile. "As I was saying, the Prime Minister has failed to act on his promises. We were told we would get more clinics — where are they? We were promised more trained staff to fill them — where are they? I can't tell you, Gavin, how many hours I'm at my computer replying to parents who are at the end of their tether trying to get their teenagers cured. Promises aren't good enough, we need action from the government now. If not, I fear that people are desperate enough to take matters into their own hands..."

MICHAEL looked out of the window of the cafe at the head offices of Ransom Incorporated. The vast block of concrete and glass stood tall and powerful. Even sitting across the street, cradling a glass of iced lemonade, it seemed to dominate.

"Stop staring," said Jennifer.

Michael blinked away and looked across the table. Steam rose from Jennifer's coffee cup and curled up in front of her face. The strong, black bitterness of her drink eclipsed the smell of food from the people eating lunch around them. Most appeared to be office workers out for a quick bite before returning to business.

Jennifer could almost be one of them. She was dressed in the suit Otis had picked out for her. Her dark navy jacket and skirt were set off with a white collarless top and a silver necklace that sparkled its tiny cut glass pendant as she turned under the light. The clothes were a little big for her, but they made her look smart and presentable, if a little young to be wearing them.

Michael also had on a suit. It was the most uncomfortable thing he remembered ever wearing. Otis had insisted he wear a tie. The cloth around his neck felt so tight it almost choked the breath out of him. The trousers were loose fitting and made of some sort of polyester-type material that had none of the comfort of his usual jeans. The smooth, nylon lining of the jacket rustled when he moved and caused static which gave him a jolt any time he touched metal. How men spent their whole working lives dressed like that without going insane mystified him.

Jennifer looked up from her coffee. Michael turned to see what she was looking at. Otis entered, looking quite the part in a black suit with subtle brown stripes and a white open-necked shirt. With his hair brushed neatly in a side parting, he looked a different man.

"Got them," whispered Otis as he sat down next to Jennifer. He reached covertly under the table and placed something on Michael's lap. Michael's fingers found the smooth, flat, rectangular shape of a security pass, with its metal clasp at the top. He took a peek. A ghastly photo of his own face stared back at him. Above it, written in red, were the words: *Ransom Incorporated*.

Step one of Otis's plan was complete. The passes had been copied from one Otis had stolen earlier that day from an employee he passed in the street. It didn't take him long to rustle up new ones with photos and false names.

"Ready?" said Otis.

"Yes," said Jennifer.

"Your friend better be right about this Ransom character," he said.

"She is."

They pinned the fake passes to their lapels, left the cafe and crossed the road.

Otis, Michael and Jennifer weaved themselves in among the suited office staff coming and going on their lunch break; whirling in the revolving doors at the entrance with blank expressions, like adults who didn't want to get on the fairground ride in the first place.

Their disguise worked! No one paid any attention to three people dressed — like everyone else — in suits with security passes pinned to their lapels.

Beyond the revolving door was a large reception desk. As grand and imposing as the building itself. Projecting power. Emphasising how small and insignificant Michael was compared to the corporation. Beside it was the security barrier: two metal arches seven foot high, topped with a red and a green light, and flanked by two security guards in brown uniforms with black ties.

Michael's stomach cramped.

He watched a suited man carry a mug of takeaway coffee through the arch. The green light lit up and the security guards paid him no attention. This was the most difficult obstacle. According to Otis, the security passes included a computerised electronic chip which was detected by the arches. A green light meant the person was security cleared and could enter. A red light meant the opposite.

Michael self-consciously adjusted the pass on his lapel and hung back while Otis and Jennifer went on ahead of him. Not that he doubted Otis's ability to copy the chip, he just wanted to make sure it worked. He put his hands in his trouser pocket and crossed his fingers where no one could see them.

Otis walked through first. A green light. Approved.

A few steps behind, Jennifer followed. A red light.

Michael tensed. She shot a giveaway worried look behind at Michael. But the guard looked bored and didn't say anything. He waved to her to try again. Jennifer took two steps backwards. She waited for a signal from him. He waved her forward. A green light! Michael let out the breath he'd been holding.

Michael's turn. Step, step, slowly, step. Under the arch. Green light. Relief! He walked into the inner sanctum of the building.

Otis and Jennifer waited a distance from the lifts until one arrived and the crowd of suits in front of them crammed themselves into the metal box. The three of them watched as the lift doors closed again and took the suits away. Only then, when things were much quieter, did they step forward and press the button.

A second lift was there in seconds. Two metal jaws parted and allowed more grey-faced adults to tumble out onto the ground floor. Otis, Jennifer and Michael stepped into the emptied lift alone. Otis reached for the panel of buttons and hit the top number. A moment. The doors glided shut, enclosing them within the four metal walls. Then the lift jolted and started its ascent. Red electronic figures on the display above the doors counted up: *1 ... 2 ... 3 ...*, each number ratcheting up Michael's nervousness.

Jennifer giggled. Nerves.

"Jen ..." Otis gave her a stern look.

"When the red light went on," said Jennifer, "I thought that was it."

"Arches don't always detect the chip properly," said Otis. "It's a glitch."

Otis focussed on the display: *4 ... 5 ... 6 ...*

"Are you sure we need to go to the top floor?" said Jennifer.

"All CEOs are on the top floor," he said.

"Are you sure?"

Jennifer didn't get an answer to her question because the lift jolted again. The display rested on *12*.

Michael felt a nervous cramp in his stomach.

Doors parted to reveal ...

... a wall with a number twelve on it.

The three of them stepped out into an ordinary corridor.

Déjà vu struck Michael as sudden and painful as a bee sting. He staggered and fell sideways, putting his hand out on the wall to steady himself.

"Michael?" Jennifer's voice quiet, but urgent.

"I know this place," he said.

The brown carpet, the fluorescent lights, the partition walls and their glass doors that led into offices. Except, this time, the offices were not dark, but bright and occupied by office workers.

"What place?" said Jennifer.

"We shouldn't have come here," said Michael. "It's the first place I remember. The place I ran away from."

Otis took Michael roughly by the arm. "Sort yourself out," he whispered in his ear, "you'll get us noticed."

Michael made a conscious effort to feel the solid floor at his feet and concentrate on every detail of that corridor that differed from the one he remembered. From the ringing of telephones and the indistinct chatter of workers, to the daylight spilling through the doors and the fact that this corridor seemed to be higher up than the one he remembered.

"You okay?" said Jennifer.

"I think so," said Michael.

"You better be," said Otis.

If nervous was what he'd felt inside the lift, then what he felt following Otis down the corridor was a hell of a lot worse. He was supposed to be there to help Otis and Jennifer find out about the cure clinics, not delve into his own past. It was what he wanted to know — of course! More than anything! — But he hadn't been prepared to enter a carbon copy of the corridor; and the fear of walking along it grew with each step.

One of the office workers stepped out from behind a glass door and blocked their path. "Can I help you?" She wore a flowery blouse and a pair of black-rimmed glasses which made her eyes look wider as she glared suspiciously at them.

"Uh … yes actually," said Jennifer, leaning out from behind Otis to give the woman a friendly smile. "We've got an appointment with Mr Ransom."

"Really?" said the woman, doubtfully. She didn't smile back.

"Yes." Jennifer lifted the ID badge on her lapel and angled it towards her. "This is the right way, isn't it?"

The woman narrowed her gaze and looked Jennifer up and down. "That's right," she said begrudgingly. "It's the large office at the end. You can't miss it."

"Thanks." Jennifer moved past Otis and took the lead, striding up the corridor before the woman had a chance to question her again.

Michael risked a look back in her direction as they passed. She stood in the doorway, watching them for a moment, then went back inside her office.

At the end of the corridor was an ordinary office door. It was wedged open, allowing a little peek into a carpeted room. A dark blue Perspex sign embossed with white lettering read: *Mr Brian Ransom*.

Otis looked back at the others before taking a tentative step inside. Jennifer and Michael followed.

Inside was a kind of antechamber. A small, ordinary office with rudimentary furniture. A desk of light beech, cluttered with computer, printer, phone and a stack of papers. Probably an office for Ransom's personal assistant. There was a chair, but no one sitting in it. No one home.

But, like walking into an Egyptian pharaoh's tomb, it was what lay beyond the antechamber that was amazing.

Behind the desk was a wall, four metres long, made entirely of glass. Even the door, apart from its brass handle and hinges, was made of glass. And, beyond that, a large executive office. Big bold furniture exuded status: from the large solid oak desk to the stout black leather chair that sat behind it. A sprawling sofa and armchair, also in black leather, set around a squat oak coffee table to allow for laid back meetings. At the far end, the London skyline could be seen through a giant window that ran the length of the office, including the distinctive dark glass cigar-shaped building everyone called *The Gherkin*. It was a breath-taking view.

The executive office, too, was empty.

"Ransom's not here," said Otis.

"Obviously!" said Jennifer.

There was a hint of concern on Otis's face, but he dismissed it with a nod. "Probably at lunch. He'll be back soon. We'll wait."

Otis reached for the handle of the glass door.

"You're not going in?" Michael said, his stomach starting to twist again.

"Best place to wait," said Otis. He turned the handle and led them inside.

The first thing Michael noticed was the feeling of space. Not just because the office was large, but because the glass window made it seem part of London. Michael approached and stared out at the rooftop view. Ancient and modern buildings were squeezed, higgledy-piggledy, in between each other; their brick, concrete and stone shapes standing tall and short against the off-white cloud of the autumn sky.

Otis paced the office, impatient and nervous.

Jennifer sat in the armchair. She laid back into the cushions without inhibitions. "Otis, will you sit down? You'll wear out the carpet."

Otis sighed and did what she asked, perching his buttocks on the edge of the sofa, as if he knew he didn't really belong there.

"Whose brilliant idea was it to come at lunchtime?" said Jennifer. It was a rhetorical question, as all three of them knew it was Otis who came up with the plan.

"Easier to blend in," said Otis. "More people coming and going."

"Including, apparently, Brian Ransom," said Jennifer.

Michael turned away from the skyline and rested his back on the windowsill. "Why was I here?" he said. "Why is my first memory before I ran, being in these offices?"

"Are you sure?" said Jennifer. "Offices can look pretty much the same."

"Not that corridor," said Michael. "This means … I don't know what it means."

"It means we can add a few more questions to the list we want to ask him," said Jennifer. She sighed, got up from the armchair and walked over to Ransom's desk.

"Jennifer, leave that alone," said Otis.

"I'm just taking a look." She sat on the executive chair. Its sophisticated suspension bounced under her body weight.

"Jen, they'll chuck us out for snooping."

"Three teenagers with forged security passes in the boss's office?" she snorted. "Likelihood is, they're gonna chuck us out anyway. I think we should have a snoop around first."

The desk was neat with computer, keyboard and old-fashioned bound A4 diary laid out precisely as if ready for inspection. Only a coffee mug with a few millimetres of cold, brown liquid left in the bottom and a framed family photograph beside the computer monitor suggested the desk belonged to a real person.

Michael watched as Jennifer struck the space bar of the computer keyboard and the monitor flickered into life. It asked for a password to log on.

"Hmm," said Jennifer, doubtfully. She turned her attention to the diary and flicked through page after page. "Meeting … meeting … doctor's appointment … meeting." She shut the diary. "God, could this guy be more boring?"

She moved on to a stack of drawers under the desk. She pulled the handle of the first one. It rattled against a lock and wouldn't open. But the second slid open without objection. Inside was a collection of cardboard files. Jennifer pulled out the files and slapped them on the table. She leant forward to look, but something else caught her eye. She reached for the framed family photograph on the desk and pulled it close. She studied it.

Michael didn't understand. It was just a photo. A man, a woman and a child of about thirteen, presumably their son. He recognised the man as Ransom from his publicity photo. Otherwise, it was an unremarkable picture of people smiling into the camera.

Jennifer turned to Michael. She looked at him with the intensity of a perceiver. He felt her burrowing. Then she turned back to the photo.

"What is it, Jen?" said Otis, approaching.

"Michael, is this you?" She pointed to the boy in the photograph.

Michael went cold. The boy in the picture stared back at him like the image in a warped mirror. A little chubbier than him, a little happier than him, face a little more boyish than his, hair a little shorter than his — but still familiar. In every real sense, the boy's features — eyes, lips, wide-bridged nose, the shape of his chin and ears — were the same.

Otis leant over the desk and snatched the photo from Jennifer.

"Hey!" said Michael. Wanting the picture for himself. Wanting to look closer. Wanting to hide it.

But Otis saw. His gaze flicked from Michael to the picture and back again. He didn't say anything. He didn't need to. They all knew what it meant.

The office door opened. Jennifer gasped. Otis turned to look. Michael ducked down behind the desk.

"What's going on in here?" A female voice. Angry. Part of him wanted to peek out over the desk, but common sense told him to stay where he was, to crunch up his body until it was the smallest it could be.

"We were looking for Mr Ransom." Jennifer's voice.

"Yeah, Mr Ransom," Otis chimed in.

"Well, he's not here," said the woman, stern like a schoolteacher.

"Which is why we'd thought we'd wait," said Jennifer, just a hint of nervousness underneath her fake naivety.

"I'm going to call security to escort you out. All three of you," said the woman.

Michael tensed. Held his breath. Closed his eyes to pretend he wasn't there.

"Yes, I know there's another one of you hiding behind the desk," she said. "Come out now."

Michael didn't want to. He wanted to stay hidden.

"I can get security to drag you out."

He let out the breath he was holding. There was no use pretending any more. He uncurled his body and stood up, revealing himself to the woman. And seeing her for the first time.

She was tall, slim and neat, with long brown hair pinned back behind her ears. She wore a crisp blouse of navy blue with white pinstripes, and straight black trousers. Her familiar face quickened his heart. He looked into her eyes and she looked into his and recognition passed between them.

"Doctor Page," said Michael.

Jennifer spun round to look at him. "Doctor Page? From the clinic?"

Unbelievable. But unmistakable.

"Michael," breathed Page. "God, Michael! What are you doing here?"

She turned to a panel of switches on the wall beside the door and flicked the top row with one swipe of her hand. The windows went suddenly dark, like someone had turned off the day. In an instant, the glass was black. The London skyline and the antechamber were hidden and the office was instantly bathed in artificial light from halogen bulbs blazing from the ceiling.

"What did you do?" said Jennifer.

"Wow," said Otis. "It's that special glass, Jen. The stuff with liquid crystal inside it that turns black when electric current runs through it."

Page ignored him. "You shouldn't have come," she said.

"We have questions for Mr Ransom," said Jennifer.

"Naïve little children. Just because you're perceivers, you think you can come in here and take whatever you want?"

Otis stepped forward. The fact that she had correctly identified them as perceivers clearly wasn't lost on him. "What the skank's going on? Who the hell are you?"

He stood directly in front of her. In her heels, she easily matched his height, but he had the bulk and power to physically outrank her. It did nothing to intimidate her. "I'm Rachel Page. Brian Ransom's assistant."

"No." Michael came out from behind the desk. "You're Doctor Page. You work at the clinic."

"Oh, Michael." She sidestepped Otis and went up to Michael. She looked into him. "You don't remember me at all, do you?"

He only remembered the clinic and the way she had hugged him.

"Hey!" Otis put his hand on Page's shoulder and spun her back to face him. "I asked you what's going on."

Then — suddenly — Otis let go of her shoulder. Like she was diseased. He stepped away, his face ashen. "God," he said to himself. "Oh my God."

"Otis?" said Jennifer.

"Can't you 'ceive it, Jen? She's a perceiver. An adult perceiver."

"That's not possible," said Jennifer, concentrating on the woman, her expression blank as she looked into her mind. Then she dropped her head and looked away. Her hand felt for the desk to support her. "It can't be right …"

"So you know," said Page. "Had to happen one day, I suppose. I hope I can rely on your discretion."

"Lady, you can't rely on skank," said Otis. "Not till we get some answers."

She turned on him. "You haven't got a clue, have you? Not a damn clue. You bring Michael in here? *In here?!* God! Do you know how hard we …?" She took a moment, calmed herself. "Look, we need to get you out."

"No," said Michael, finding courage from somewhere beneath his confusion. "Otis is right. We came for answers. We're not leaving until we get them."

She looked directly at him. Her face softened. Like she genuinely cared, as she had seemed to care back at the clinic. But he still didn't understand why. "Michael, I'd like to tell you, but it's to protect you, do you understand that?"

"No."

"I perceive your confusion, but you have to leave. Believe me when I say you can't be found here." She turned to Otis and Jennifer, her arms flung out to her sides, leaving her body wide open. "Perceive me. Both of you. I'm telling the truth."

They stared. With that deep, probing stare Michael had seen so often.

"Otis," said Jennifer.

"Shut up, Jen."

"But I think she's right."

Otis sighed. "Okay, lady. I'm listening."

"Did anyone notice you come in?" Her manner business-like now.

"No." Otis flashed his badge at her. "Security passes, see?"

"Hang on," said Jennifer. "There was that woman in the corridor."

"What woman?" said Page.

"Um … I dunno, she had ugly glasses."

"Flowery blouse?" suggested Page.

"Yeah," said Jennifer.

"Marian!" said Page under her breath. "Terrific. Chances are she was straight onto Cooper."

"Cooper?" Michael's stomach cramped. The image of the man standing before him on the fire escape flashed in his mind.

"Who's Cooper?" said Otis.

But Page was at the phone on Ransom's desk, dialling a number. She held up one single finger in a signal for them to be quiet. They obeyed.

"Hi, Ann, it's Rachel," said Page, adopting a smile and a matter-of-fact pleasantness in her voice. "Yeah, I'm well thanks … Look, don't suppose you know anything about Bill Cooper coming today do you? Someone said he's coming to see Brian, but there's nothing in his diary … Yeah, thanks, if you could." Her eyes flicked to the others. Her foot tapping. Impatient. A distorted voice muttered through the receiver at her ear and her false smile returned. "Great. Thanks, Ann. You're a diamond."

Page put the receiver down. "Bloody marvellous. He's already in the sodding building."

"Cooper's here?" said Michael, panic rising.

"Yeah." Page reached for the door. "I'll stay here and stall him as much as I can. Think you can find your own way out?"

"Yeah," said Otis. But he stopped beside her at the door and looked into her face. "This isn't a ploy to get rid of us, is it?"

"If I can perceive Michael's fear for the man, I'm sure you can—"

Michael felt himself blush. Cooper scared him, and everyone in that room could feel it.

"—You've already acknowledged I'm telling the truth," said Page. "The question is, are you going to act on what you perceive or are you going to hang around here waiting to be caught?"

Otis turned away from her, his decision made, and walked through the door. Jennifer followed.

Michael hesitated. He looked up at the woman. He wished he understood. "Doctor Page …?"

She put a gentle finger on his lips to silence him. "Go, Michael. Please. Or it all will have been for nothing." She held the door open. He didn't want to go. But he didn't want to get caught either.

Reluctantly, he passed through the glass door, into the antechamber and back into the corridor.

It was surreal. Panic inside of him, but calm all around him. The office continued as if there was no danger, no urgency. A man in a suit, carrying a sugary doughnut on a plate, opened a door leading into one of the offices off the corridor without even noticing them.

Otis and Jennifer had several metres head start on Michael and were almost at the lifts. Jennifer turned and waved for him to hurry up. Michael quickened his pace.

Otis jabbed at the button to call the lift as Michael got there, and then they were forced to wait.

Waiting for the lift when every muscle inside of him was geared up to run was almost painful. His body was flooded with adrenaline, but his brain told him to wait. Looking up at the number above the door as it counted; *4… 5… 6…* Getting closer to them, but ever so slowly. Otis jabbed at the button, but the lift made no concessions to his impatience. If anything, it seemed to count even slower, as if to spite them; *7… 8… 9…*

10… 11… and *12.*

Cramping in his stomach as he stared at the lift doors, willing them to open. The faint jolt as, behind those dull, grey, metallic doors, the lift adjusted itself to be level with the floor. The tiniest whir of motors and the doors opened. Revealing, first a chunky black man in a suit and tie, then a tall white man in carbon copy uniform. Behind them, a slightly overweight, dark-haired white man in a black suit and open-necked white shirt. He and Michael locked eyes. It was Michael who recognised him first.

"Cooper!" he said in a terrified whisper.

Cooper's weary eyes widened in recognition. He pushed his way past the other men.

The adrenaline in Michael's body burst into action. He turned and ran. He didn't see Cooper get out of the lift, but he knew he was there.

Otis's heavy footsteps thumping behind him. "Which way?"

Michael knew which way.

He glanced back as he ran.

Jennifer was a couple of metres behind. Running wildly on high heels. The chunky black man and the tall white man closing on her, with Cooper behind.

"Jennifer!" Michael shouted.

Jennifer kicked off her shoes. One after another flew behind her. Bare feet quickened on carpet. But the men — longer legs, no broken rhythm — were at her back. Chunky black hands grabbed her jacket.

Jennifer screamed. "*No!*"

She struggled, trying to wrestle herself free from the material. But masculine white hands grabbed her shoulder before she got her jacket off and held onto her.

"Jen!" Otis moved to go back for her, but Michael reached for his arm. He didn't have the strength to stop him, but it was enough to make Otis think twice. Either he perceived Michael's fear of the men, or he realised he couldn't help Jennifer without being caught himself.

Jennifer wriggled. Arms and legs lashing out at the men, but they were stronger and kept firm hold of her.

Cooper was trapped behind them. Shouting at them to get out of the way. He pushed past the men and their struggling prey.

"Come on!" Michael tugged at Otis's sleeve.

A moment of hesitation and Otis continued to run down the corridor. Michael joined him, heading for the fire escape.

"Otis!" Jennifer shouted. "Michael!"

Her desperate cries were like knives plunging into him. Michael tried to block them out, knowing if all three of them were caught, it would be game over.

Michael slammed his palms against the bar of the fire escape door. It swung open. The fire alarm wailed.

Onto the concrete landing and down the spiralling flights of stairs, running for their lives as the fire alarm wailed around them.

FOURTEEN

THE smell of urine hung in the subway. With every breath, Michael was conscious of breathing it in. The narrow passage under the dual carriageway was damp and cold with the constant rumble of traffic on the road above, vibrating through the tunnel walls that curved around him and Otis.

Michael had slept in a place like this, once. When he was homeless. He remembered how the damp from the floor soaked through the cardboard he lay on. How the cold seeped through his clothes. And how it was regarded by many as a public toilet. He remembered watching a tramp unzipping his trousers right in front of him and exposing himself and peeing up the wall with no regard to anyone else around him.

He had promised himself he'd never go back to a place like that. And yet, there he was, sitting on the damp floor, resting his back on the damp wall and feeling the heat of his body leach through the shirt, trousers and jacket of his suit.

Otis paced in front of him. The heel of his smart, sensible shoes struck the concrete with repeated hollow clacks that echoed around the subway. His suit hung off him; the jacket crumpled, shirt half hanging out of his waistband, the bottom of his trousers splashed with mud.

"We should've gone back for her," he said. He pulled his hair back from his face, his fingers tugging so hard on the blond strands that they stretched the skin taut on his forehead.

"They would have caught us too," said Michael.

"You don't know that."

But he did. Three fully grown men and an office building full of other adults? They would've had no chance. They did the only thing they could have done. They ran.

Otis stopped pacing and slammed his back against the opposite wall. "Shit!" he said to the world in general. "Shit, shit, shit!" His cries reverberated around the tube of the subway until their echo dissipated into nothing.

All Michael could think of was Jennifer's terrified face as she struggled in the hands of Cooper's men. Her desperate cries for help and how they had turned their backs on her to save their own skin.

"I suppose you're pleased," said Otis.

"What do you mean?"

"You lured us there."

Otis's body had almost recovered from their run, but his face was still red in anger.

"I what?! No!"

Otis reached into the inside of his jacket. He pulled out something flat and rectangular and chucked it towards Michael. In reflex, he lifted his hands to catch it. A sharp corner struck his palm — "Ow!" — and the object fell into his lap.

It was face down, but Michael knew instantly what it was. A piece of smooth hardboard framed by a silverish, metal border: it was the photo from Ransom's desk.

He turned it over and looked at the unfathomable picture of Ransom, a woman — his wife? — and a boy with Michael's face.

"Want to explain that?" said Otis.

Michael wished he could. But he had no memory of the picture having been taken. No memory of the lush garden in which they stood, with its bright greens vibrant in the summer sun. No memory of the woman who stood behind the boy (his younger self?) with a hand on his shoulder. "I can't," he said.

"Or won't. Looks skankin' obvious to me. You're Ransom's son. Aren't you?"

The statement shot a shiver down Michael's spine. From the evidence of the photo, he suspected it was true, but his conscious mind dared not believe it.

"You don't know that."

"Look at it!" Otis pushed himself away from the opposite wall and leant over Michael. He tapped his index finger on the glass that covered the image. Michael could feel Otis's hot, angry breath on his face. It scared him. The teenager was bigger than him, stronger than him and fuelled with rage.

"I don't know what to tell you, Otis."

"Tell me why you lured us there. Did you want Jennifer to be caught, is that it?"

"No! Otis, believe me …"

Otis grabbed Michael's tie. He'd loosened it as he ran, but the piece of cloth was still tied round his neck, allowing Otis to pull him forward like a dog on a lead. "You're the one who said we should go."

"Only because Jennifer's journalist friend said—"

Otis yanked the tie again and Michael was pulled to his feet. The photo slipped from his lap and clattered to the ground.

Otis pulled the tie above Michael's head, forcing his body to reach taller than his height, his feet scrabbling to take his weight as the cloth dug into the back of his neck.

"What do they want with Jennifer?"

"I don't know," said Michael.

"What are they doing to her?"

"I don't know. Otis, can't you perceive I'm telling the truth?"

Otis glared at Michael. His eyes like spears thrusting into his mind. Michael stared back at him, with snatched nervous breaths. Until Otis's angry, revengeful expression turned to hopelessness and desperation.

He thrust Michael backwards and let go of the tie. Michael's body struck the wall behind, hard. "I'm sorry, Otis." He rubbed the back of his neck and felt the tingle of blood flow returning.

Otis grunted. He turned away and rested his palms against the other subway wall. He bent his head and stared at the ground.

Michael, desperate to say or do something helpful, thought about what Cooper would be doing with Jennifer. "If Cooper's looking for me, he'll probably question her."

"Yeah," said Otis.

A lorry rumbled overhead and spread its vibrations down the walls, into the concrete floor and up through Michael's shoes.

Otis sighed. "Figured as much." He sniffed and stood up straight. He turned back round to face Michael. "Means we can't go back to the flat."

"No."

"I've got a mate, owes me a favour. He'll put us up, no sweat." Otis delved into his trouser pocket and pulled out his phone. But before his index finger could tap at the screen, the whole pad lit up. Its rock guitar ringtone filled the subway, echoing back from the concrete walls.

Otis's eyes widened as he looked at the display. "It's Jennifer," he said.

Otis thumped the keypad and lifted it to his ear. "Jen? Are you all right? Where are you?"

But the delight on his face evaporated as he listened. "Mr Cooper," he said. "Yes, I know who you are."

MICHAEL sat in the passenger seat of Otis's car. The last time he had sat in that position, they had been singing. They weren't singing now.

Cooper had taken Jennifer's phone and used it to call Otis. He offered Otis a trade: Jennifer for Michael.

Michael could have said no. He could have run. But, truth was, it was his fault Jennifer had been taken. He was the one Cooper wanted, the man only took Jennifer because she was in the way. Anyway, he was tired of running. In all the weeks of sleeping on Otis's sofa, what had he learnt? That he might have been, in the past, a perceiver? That he might be Ransom's son? Nothing that he understood. Nothing that added up to anything. At least, if he submitted himself to Cooper, he might get some answers. And he could finally rest.

So he agreed to the trade.

It was to be made in the basement floor of a shoppers' car park in Edgware at 8am. Otis got there early. He wanted to stake out the place before Cooper and his men arrived, to make sure there were no surprises.

It was Sunday, almost three hours before the shops opened, and the place was near deserted. Only three cars had been left on the basement floor in the concrete gloom of the car park. Otis drove slowly around the edge, ignoring the demarcation lines of the marked bays by allowing his wheels to bump over them, perceiving every-thing around him. His eyes stared straight out ahead, but it was like he wasn't looking. Just feeling. Searching for the presence of other minds which would betray they were not alone.

In a total of three revolutions, he perceived no one. He concluded it was safe to park.

Otis turned the key in the ignition and the rumble of the engine shuddered to a stop. The background breeze of the car heating sys-tem ceased. A nervous silence hung in the car. Otis didn't unclick his seatbelt or open the door. He sat there for a moment, in thought.

"What d'you reckon this Cooper bloke wants with you?" he said eventually.

"I don't know," said Michael.

"Seems to want you pretty badly."

"Yeah."

"And you've got no clue?"

Michael shrugged.

"Got something to do with you being Ransom's son?"

"If I am Ransom's son."

"Still don't remember, huh?"

Michael shook his head.

"What do you think he'll do to you?"

Michael had tried not to think. If he wasn't already frightened enough by the man. Ever since he'd encountered him on the fire stairs, Cooper had been at the back of his mind. Like a wolf scratching at the door, refusing to go away. In the end, he had to let the creature in.

"You're scared, aren't you?" said Otis.

Shit scared. Like lying in the dark not sleeping scared. Getting up in the middle of the night to poo out last night's dinner scared. Sweaty palms, trembling hands scared. The wolf clawing inside his stomach.

"You can perceive that?" said Michael.

"Loud and very clear."

Of course. There was no hiding feelings from a perceiver.

Otis placed a hand on his shoulder. Michael shuddered at the touch, even though it was friendly. "Just wanted to say, Michael mate, that I appreciate it. I'm sure Jen does too."

"Yeah," said Michael. "What time is it?"

Otis peered round the steering wheel at the digital display on the dashboard. "Half seven."

"Half an hour," said Michael. Not long to wait. But, at the same time, an eternity.

"Come on," said Otis, pressing his thumb down on the seatbelt holder. With a click, it jumped out and the belt rolled off of his lap. "Let's get set up."

The cold of the morning struck Michael as he stepped out into the stark atmosphere of the car park. No sunlight ever fell there. Its concrete floor, ceiling and walls shut out all the heat from outside. The only evidence that the morning was waking up was a glimmer of daylight filtering down the ramp used by cars to get into the basement.

Michael was instructed to join Otis round the back of the car where they could huddle out of sight. Otis sat with his bum on the ground and his back rested against the bumper, every now and then poking his head out for a quick look at their surroundings. Michael squatted on his toes, not wanting to press his buttocks to the cold, hard floor.

Otis pulled a battered mobile phone from his pocket and laid it on the ground between them. Like the car, it kept a record of the time: 7.35am, it said. Five more minutes had gone past. Twenty-five to go.

Otis had chucked his normal phone in a river near the subway after Cooper's phone call, fearing Cooper could use it to trace their location and capture them without the need to go through with the agreed exchange. Otis had replaced it with a used phone from a second hand shop and loaded it up with the minimal amount of credit. He only planned to use it once.

The next fifteen minutes were the longest fifteen minutes in the world. Until the quiet was invaded by the distant sound of a car engine.

Michael's heart thumped like crazy. His body was ready to run, but his mind remembered the promise to Otis: that he would save Jennifer. And so he stayed there, adrenaline pumping, as he rested against the car bumper.

Otis peered out from behind the car. "Game on," he whispered.

The engine got louder, its mechanical growl echoing around the concrete cathedral of the car park. Michael turned to see a sleek, black car drive down the ramp. He recognised it as a BMW, the same large, imposing car he had seen Cooper in at the clinic.

It raced down the middle of the car park, then spun, its tyres screeching as it turned back to face the entrance. The car stopped, but its engine continued to growl as it waited patiently for its prey. Headlights glowed harsh and white, lighting up the whole car park, alighting on Otis's car and casting a shadow where both of them hid behind it.

Otis picked up the phone and dialled. Michael heard a muted ringing through the tiny speaker clasped to Otis's ear. A ringing that stopped and was replaced by the indistinct sound of a man's voice.

"Cooper," said Otis, "I take it that's you in the BMW." He paused, listening to the answer. "So, how's this gonna work?"

Otis listened for a few minutes. Argued. Negotiated. Then took the phone from his ear and hit the disconnect button. He nodded at Michael. "When they phone me back, that's the signal for you and I to walk to the middle of the car park. Cooper will bring Jennifer out and stand in front of the car. Then, at the same time, she walks towards me and you walk towards him."

Michael swallowed hard. The idea of sacrificing himself for Jennifer had seemed noble and brave when he agreed to it. Now it seemed terrifying. He attempted a smile. "Like in those old movies."

"Yeah," said Otis. "Like in those old movies."

The phone came to life in his hand. It chirped only one ring before Otis answered it. "Okay," was the only thing he said into it. Then he moved it away from his ear and muffled it against his chest. "Let's do it," he said to Michael.

Michael's knees complained as he stood up. Cold and stiff from squatting down behind the car, they ached like crazy. His legs trembled as he walked towards the centre of the car park with Otis clutching his arm like a boy scout helping an old lady across the road.

Up ahead, masked by the glare of the BMW's headlights, two figures stepped out of the rear door. One slightly overweight and masculine, the other small, female and delicate. As they stepped in front of the car, their bodies cast long shadows on the concrete floor.

Both parties stopped and faced each other. Michael tried to focus on Jennifer. He wanted to be sure she was all right. But she was silhouetted in the lights and he only saw her outline. He saw the outline of Cooper too, unmistakable from their other encounters. His left hand clutched Jennifer's elbow, his right clasped a phone to his ear.

"We're ready," said Otis into his own phone. Otis let go of Michael's arm. Michael looked back at him. For validation or encouragement or for him to call the whole thing off. Otis just nodded. "Go on, mate," he said.

Michael squinted into the bright headlights. He took a step forward. In front of him, Cooper's silhouette released Jennifer's elbow and pushed her gently in the small of her back. She stumbled forward one step.

"Good luck," Michael heard Otis say behind him.

Michael gathered his courage and took another step. Jennifer did the same. Like two chess pieces advancing towards each other one square at a time. Her footsteps were hesitant, unsure, unsteady. She stepped into Cooper's shadow and, in that moment, Michael saw her properly. She wore the same suit she'd used to get into the Ransom building. Somewhere along the way, she'd lost her jacket, but she still had the skirt and the white collarless top, now crumpled and slightly grubby. He caught a glimpse of her face. Blank, staring eyes. And then she stumbled sideways, back into the blazing light, and became a silhouette again.

"Jennifer?" It was Otis calling behind him. "Jen, it's okay. Come on."

"Otis?" Her voice tiny, hesitant.

"That's right. Walk to me."

Her steps quickened. As did Michael's. It was a long walk to the gallows, and — by God — he wanted it to be over.

At the halfway point, they met. Michael paused. They were close. Her musky, unwashed scent drifted over to him. Stale, but still alluring.

He saw bewildered confusion in her face. He wanted to reach out to her, to say it was all right. But she didn't so much as glance at him. She kept staring straight ahead towards Otis. Another step and she was behind him. Ahead was only Cooper, his face in shadow. Michael took a deep breath and forced his feet to keep walking.

A car engine roared behind him. He turned. Speeding down the ramp, headlights blazing, tyres screeching, came a white Peugeot.

Out the corner of his eye, he saw Otis run forward and grab Jennifer by the arm. She screamed as he yanked her towards him. Then they were both running, heading for his parked car, as the Peugeot revved.

Something grabbed Michael's arm. It was Cooper. He pulled Michael backwards, dragging his feet across the concrete.

The Peugeot braked suddenly with a shriek of burning rubber. A crack pierced the air. As loud as thunder.

Michael's whole body tensed.

Cooper tugged him to the ground. Michael landed on his hands and knees. Cooper pulled the belt of Michael's trousers and forced him to crawl on the grit and the dirt, behind Cooper's car.

Another crack, and a loud *ping* of metal against metal, ricocheting next to his ear. Instinctively, Michael ducked his head behind the BMW's front wheel. He knew, then, what the noises were. Gunshots. The first into the air, the second striking the body of the car.

"Let him go, Cooper!" a woman's voice called out into the emptiness.

Michael leant forward to look, but Cooper — still holding onto his belt — jerked him back.

He looked back at Cooper's face. The man was determined and full of concentration. As Cooper kept hold of Michael with one hand, he opened his jacket with the other, revealing the handle of a pistol sticking out of a gun holster strapped to his body. He pulled it out and pressed himself close to the body of the car.

"Is that you, Page?" Cooper shouted.

"Shut up and let him go," the woman shouted back. Michael recognised the voice now. Cooper was right, it was her.

"Not gonna happen, Page."

Gunfire. Michael ducked down even further. Glass shattered centimetres from his head. As the echo subsided, he dared himself to look. The windscreen of Cooper's sleek, black BMW was a craze of broken glass.

"You tell your man to stay inside," Page yelled. "I'll shoot him if I have to."

Michael saw, then — through the unshattered passenger window — one of Cooper's men sat at the wheel. It was the thin one from the offices. In his hand was a gun, chunky and powerful, like Cooper's. The man cast a look over to his boss. Something unspoken passed between them, because the thin man nodded and stayed in the driver's seat.

"What's your plan, Page?" Cooper shouted out. "Backup's on the way. You won't get out of here."

"Let me worry about that. Send Michael out."

"I knew you were behind this, Page. All you've done is prove it to me."

"Enough talking!"

A bullet cracked the air. The tyre by Michael's face exploded. It hissed with air leaking out of the bullet hole.

Cooper swore. He lifted both hands to his gun to steady his aim and fired. His body jerked at the recoil.

With both Cooper's hands on the gun, Michael was free. He jumped out from behind the car and ran. He looked for Otis and Jennifer but, half blinded by the crossing beams of the BMW's and Peugeot's headlights, he couldn't see them. He couldn't even see Otis's car.

"Michael! This way!" It was Page. Leaning out of the driver's window. Gun in one hand. Beckoning him with the other.

With nowhere else to run, he ran to her.

A shot rang out behind him.

Page's body jerked backwards. Blood spurted across the driver's window.

Screams!

From her and from his own mouth.

"Hold your fire!" bellowed Cooper. "You'll hit the boy!"

Michael — somehow still running — glanced back to see the thin man pointing the barrel of his gun out of a hole he'd knocked in the shattered glass of the windscreen.

Michael reached Page. She was slumped back in the driver's seat with her left hand clutching her right shoulder. Blood seeped through her fingers and ran down her arm. Her face was flushed with the sheen of sweat.

"My God," Michael breathed. He didn't know what to do.

"Get in," said Page.

"But …"

"Get in!"

Jolted out of his paralysis, he dived for the back door.

Climbing in, he was thrown back as the car lurched forward. He reached for the handle and slammed the door shut.

He saw they were speeding towards the ramp.

A glance behind. A split-second view of the BMW's headlights before the rear windscreen exploded! Shattered pebbles of glass spat across the back seat. Michael clasped his hands to his head as they rained down on top of him. His heart beating so fast now, it shook his entire body. Unless it was the fear making him tremble.

"I thought he said not to shoot!" said Michael, as he emerged from his arms.

"Cooper's crazy," said Page. "Better belt up and get your head down." She turned as she talked to him, taking her eyes away from where she was driving for a second. The car swerved to the left as its wheels hit the exit ramp and bumped against the wall. The impact jolted Michael sideways. Metal bodywork scraped against concrete as the

Peugeot revved its way up to the ground level. Daylight permeated the windows and a rush of fresh air blew through the broken rear screen. Michael tasted freedom.

His hands scrabbled for the seatbelt. He pulled it around his body and clicked it into place.

A ricocheting bullet bouncing off concrete behind him made him duck down. So he half lay, half sat on the back seat as the Peugeot sped down the quiet Sunday road.

"Are you sure you're okay to drive?" Michael shouted up front.

"Better than the alternative," said Page. The engine roared and she put more power onto the accelerator and weaved in and out of parked cars. Michael felt sick. From the adrenaline, the fear and the movement of the car. He gripped the edge of the seat, its plush cream leather scattered with pieces of glass, and feared it would also soon be full of the contents of his stomach. He fought the nausea. He needed a plan, not a pile of vomit.

"Have you got a phone?" he called out.

"What?" Page shouted back. Her mind, clearly on the road. Or — worse — clouded by blood loss.

"A phone!"

"In my bag. By your feet."

In the footwell, stuffed under the driver's seat, and partly camouflaged against the black carpet was a black leather handbag, its silver zip glinting in the light. He strained against the seatbelt to reach it. Unzipping it, he rummaged through tissues, receipts, pen, purse and glasses case to pull out a device no bigger than his palm. The screen lit up when he touched it, illuminating a picture of a fluffy dog playing with a ball.

He thought. He closed his eyes. But he didn't know anyone's number. Even if Otis still had his old phone, Michael had never memorised the number. Then he remembered the place where Otis had bought the second hand phone. He ran an internet search, found the number of the shop and dialled.

A ringing tone.

Michael looked behind. The BMW still following.

It kept ringing.

"They're gonna catch us," said Michael.

As he looked back, he saw Page's eyes reflected in the rear-view mirror. Pained, frightened, desperate. She lurched the steering wheel to the right. The seatbelt dug into Michael's ribs as he was thrown forward against it. He saw the traffic lights up ahead turn from amber to red. The Peugeot kept roaring. Through the red light, turning hard to the right, almost tipping over as it sped round the corner.

A car honked. But they made it through without hitting anything and were on a new road. A wide dual carriageway heading out of town.

No sign of Cooper behind. Trapped, no doubt, behind the red light.

"Phone Palace," mumbled a bored voice in his ear.

He'd almost forgotten the phone pressed to the side of his face. "Uh, yes," he said into it. "I came in with a friend of mine yesterday to buy a phone. I wrote down his number, but I seem to have got it wrong. I don't suppose you have a record of what it is, do you?"

"Erm…" said Mr Bored.

Michael drummed his fingers on the leather seat. Being chased by two gunmen in a car was the wrong time to have a conversation with someone who had all the time in the world.

"Two white boys?" said Mr Bored. "One, a big blond fella?"

"Yes!" He glanced out the back window. The stretch of Cooper-free road was lengthening behind them. "Do you have the number?"

"Erm… I'll check."

Michael sighed and rolled his eyes. This brilliant plan of his was taking too long.

A police siren wailed into the air. Not an unusual sound for London, but it was close and his body tensed.

"Hello?" said Mr Bored.

"Yes, hello," Michael said, rather too keenly.

"Got it. You got a pen?"

Michael rummaged in Page's handbag for a pen. The man rattled off a series of numbers. Michael wrote them on his hand.

"Shit!" said Page.

"What?" said Michael. But she didn't need to answer. Her worried eyes in the rear-view mirror said it all. Michael looked behind and saw what she saw — Cooper's BMW, red and blue lights flashing from a strip at the top of their windscreen as the siren wailed. Through the passenger window, the barrel of a handgun pointed towards them.

Michael disconnected the phone without a thank you.

A loud pop and the car shuddered like it had hit a pot hole. It swerved, but kept going. Bumping like they were driving over fist-sized stones.

"What was that?"

"I think they shot out a tyre," said Page. "We can't outrun them now."

Michael looked up ahead. The dual carriageway narrowed to one lane as it left the urban landscape towards suburbia. On either side were green fields. "Can you make it on foot?" he said.

"I can't make it on a flat tyre," said Page.

"Then park. Anywhere."

Half a plan was in his head. Crazy as hell, but better than nothing. He fumbled as he rushed to dial the number he'd written on his hand.

It rang.

He looked behind at the closing BMW. The phone kept ringing. "Come on, Otis!" His plan depended on Otis still having the phone and answering the skanking thing.

The Peugeot braked suddenly. A skid of tyres and it came to a halt. Not parked, just stopped.

Michael released himself from the seatbelt and jumped out of the car.

The ringing stopped. "Hello?"

"Otis?"

"Michael?"

"Thank God!"

The flashing lights of the BMW were almost on top of them. Page hadn't even opened her door.

"Do you know the dual carriageway that runs out of town near the car park with green fields either side?" Michael said into the phone.

He grabbed the handle of the driver's door and flung it open. Page sat inside: pale, sweaty and unmoving. Trails of blood from the bullet wound in her shoulder were drying down her right side.

"Come on!" Michael urged her.

"You go," said Page.

"Not without you. You're the one with the answers." He took her left arm and helped her out of the car. Her reluctance gave way to renewed effort and she allowed him to lead her to the side of the road where a slatted wooden fence marked the edge of the field. The BMW was almost upon them, slowing with the confidence of a hunter who knows its prey is almost in the bag.

Michael put his foot onto the bottom rung of the fence and swung his other leg over. He took Page's hand to help her.

Otis's distant, tinny voice shouted through the speaker of the phone. Michael lifted it to his ear. "Otis, on the left of the dual carriageway, there's a field. Pick us up at whatever the road is on the other side."

"Michael, what the—?"

"Hurry."

Michael terminated the call and pocketed the phone. He and Page were over the fence and in dewy grass up to their ankles. He ran — his hand still holding hers — pulling her behind him.

"Michael, I don't think I can."

"Run or get caught," he said. He tugged at her hand. She stumbled, but kept going. Finding energy from somewhere.

Behind, Cooper and the other man were out of the BMW and climbing over the fence. Michael's legs pushed on. He let go of Page's hand. He couldn't let her slow him down. "Try to keep up," he said. "They won't shoot you for fear of shooting me." He hoped.

The field was vast. A farmer's field, bumpy from ploughing, left fallow for the winter. His feet slipping on mud every fourth step, grass swishing at his ankles, soaking his socks with dew. And the opposite side, so far away. Green, almost to the horizon, where a line of trees spread their bare branches across the grey sky. Between them was the dark line browny black line of another fence and the tarmac of a road beyond. If it wasn't just wishful thinking.

Page gasped behind him, her uneven steps thudding down in the mud. Behind her, Cooper shouted at them to stop. But Michael kept on running, trying to put as much distance between him and Cooper as possible.

As they got closer, the black of the road became clearer. But it was empty. No Otis, no nobody.

He felt the ache in his lungs and legs as hope slipped away. But he kept running. Towards the fence, towards the road, like a marathon runner striving for the finishing line.

He crashed into the fence. As he swung his leg over, he saw Page's exhausted body staggering towards him. Closing fast was the thin man from the BMW; lean, fit and long-legged. Cooper brought up the rear, huffing and puffing in his suit.

Michael jumped over onto a grass verge by the road. "Come on!" He beckoned to Page.

The sound of a car engine caused Michael to turn. It was Otis's ugly, dented hatchback. A beautiful sight in a world of grey. New energy rose within him. He helped Page over the fence as the hatchback reached them and braked hard.

"You all right?" said Otis through the open driver's window. Beside him, in the passenger seat, was Jennifer.

"I am now," Michael panted.

He flung open the back door and pushed Page inside.

"You're not bringing her!" Otis protested.

But she was already in the back seat. Bloody, exhausted, and gasping.

A crash of something hitting wood made him turn. The thin man had made it to the fence. Red faced, breathing hard, with staring eyes. He lifted his gun with both hands and pointed it at Michael. His right index finger wrapped around the trigger.

"Stop," he said. "Or I'll shoot."

Michael bet his life it was a lie. He stepped into the car.

Cooper reached the fence and collapsed his unfit body on top of it. Eyes flashed from Michael, to the car, to the gun.

The thin man's arm muscles tensed, ready to fire.

"No!" shouted Cooper.

Michael's bum hit the back seat.

Cooper pushed the man sideways. His gun veered left and went off. Gunfire rang out across the field. Birds screeched.

"Drive! Drive!" shouted Michael, closing the door.

Otis's foot hit the accelerator. Tyres spun, gripping tarmac and propelling them forward.

Out the back window, Michael watched the figures of Cooper and the thin man recede into the distance. They were stuck in a field with no transport as their prey raced to freedom.

FIFTEEN

OTIS drove the car round the back of the office building and turned off the engine. It rumbled into nothing and left a ghostly silence.

They'd driven through a virtually deserted industrial estate, right to the last building where only Monday to Friday people worked. Lights were off, windows closed and doors locked in the Sunday morning quiet. There was no sign of Cooper and his men.

"What now?" said Michael.

Otis flipped the button of his seatbelt and got out of the car. The cold of the morning air flooded inside.

Michael got out too and watched Otis as he helped Jennifer out of the passenger door.

In the light of day, without the blinding brightness of headlights, she looked so fragile. She usually covered her thin body in a baggy coat and, without it, she looked almost skeletal. One bony knee stuck out of a hole in her tights where a ladder ran up to her thigh and down to her calf. The breeze lifted strands of her dishevelled hair in front of her face.

Otis took her hand and led her from the car. She leant on him, like an old woman.

"Jennifer, are you okay?" Michael asked as they walked past him.

She didn't answer. She didn't look. It was as if she didn't know he was there.

They stopped at the wall of the office building. Sheltered from the breeze, Otis allowed her to rest her back on the red brickwork. She let go of his hand and slid down the wall until she sat on the dirt of the ground, surrounded by cigarette butts abandoned by office smokers.

"Otis?" said Michael. "She's all right, isn't she?"

Otis turned to answer his question. His mouth opened, but no words came out. He shook his head and shrugged at the same time.

Michael looked at Jennifer again; sitting on the cold ground, huddled up like a hedgehog in winter. Small and lost. Otis squatted next to her, he brushed the strands of her black hair from her face. "What did they do to you?" he whispered softly.

She stared back at him with blank, glassy eyes.

"I'm going to take a look, okay?" said Otis.

Jennifer continued to stare. Not giving him permission, but not resisting him either.

The concern on Otis's face turned to concentration. Looking into her eyes at first. Then looking beyond them. Inside of her. Hard. Deep. The unmistakable, burrowing stare of a perceiver.

"My God," he breathed.

He stood. Backed away.

"What?" said Michael.

"Shit."

"What?"

"Shit! Shit! Shit!"

"What is it, Otis?"

Otis kicked the wall. Splinters of brick flew off and scattered to the ground. "Shit! Shit! Shiiiiit!" His cries dispersed in the wind. Carried away to where no one would hear them.

Otis spun and slammed his own back against the brickwork. His face was red. There were tears in his eyes.

Michael glanced at Jennifer beside him. She hadn't moved. Her expression still blank. Like a coma victim whose eyes are open, but whose mind is barely alive.

"Otis?" said Michael.

"She's been cured," he said. The tears in his eyes fell to his cheeks. He wiped them on his sleeve. He sniffed.

"Are you sure?"

"'Course I'm skankin' sure!" Otis spat back at him. "That's why they were willing to give her back to me. They turned her into a norm. They took my Jen away and turned her into a skankin' norm!"

More tears fell. Suddenly embarrassed, he pulled himself away from the wall and strode towards the car.

"Otis, you're not leaving her here?"

But it wasn't the driver's door he was heading for. He went round the other side and yanked open the back door. He dived in and came out dragging Page by the arms.

Her screams ripped through the air as he threw her body against the boot.

"Did you do this?" he shouted into her face.

"What?" She had to be confused and terrified.

"You work at the clinic. Did you do this to her?"

Page's eyes followed Otis's pointing finger to where Jennifer sat curled against the wall. "She's been cured?" said Page.

"Don't act like you don't know!" Otis slapped her across the face. She yelped in pain and shock. Her hand went to her cheek where a red mark was forming.

"Otis!" said Michael. "What are you doing? She saved me!"

Otis looked back with a narrow stare. "Saved you — sacrificed Jen."

"I didn't know," said Page. "I'm sorry, I really am."

"Don't lie to me, bitch!" He slapped her again. The sound of flesh on flesh rang out across the emptiness.

"I had nothing to do with it, perceive me."

Otis went quiet. He stared at her. Into her. Perceiving her.

He broke off eye contact and hung his head. "That doesn't make you innocent. You're involved in all this somehow."

"What are you going to do?" said Page.

"Why should I tell you?" said Otis. He abandoned her on the boot of the car and went back to leaning against the wall.

But it was a valid question.

Michael walked up to him. He spoke to him softly so the women couldn't hear. "We can't stay here."

"Don't you think I don't know that?" said Otis.

"And we can't go back to the squat."

"Are you going to stand here and state the obvious to me all day, Michael mate? Or are you actually going to have some ideas?"

Otis was the leader. He was the one who was supposed to have ideas. "You're not going to abandon Jennifer," said Michael.

"Don't be a fart."

"You abandoned Jack."

"That was different, that was …" Otis shook his head. "Jesus, I don't know! Cooper's seen my car, that'll be a target too."

"And Doctor Page?" Michael glanced back at where Otis had left her.

"What about her?"

"Wound looks pretty bad."

"Fine," said Otis. "We leave her here and call an ambulance."

"With a gunshot wound?" said Michael. "They'll notify police. Cooper'll find her." He shivered at the memory of his own near miss with Cooper's men at the hospital.

"Like I care!"

"But, Otis, she knows stuff. She knows about the clinics and the cure, and … she knows about me."

"What does that matter now?" He glanced down at Jennifer, curled up on the floor, dumb and apparently deaf to their conversation.

"It matters more than anything," said Michael. "Jennifer sacrificed herself to get information about what's going on. If we don't honour that, then it'll all have been for nothing."

Otis went quiet. It seemed Michael had struck a nerve.

"I think I need a doctor," Page called out from where she leant against the car boot. Her hand clutched her shoulder where fresh blood oozed through her fingers. Her wound had probably re-opened when Otis dragged her out the back seat. "Take me to a hospital and I'll tell you everything."

"So you can meet up with your friend Cooper?" Otis shouted back at her. "You think I'm stupid?"

"He's not my friend," said Page. "My friends don't shoot me." She slipped sideways on the boot as if she were about to faint. She let go of her wound, grabbed hold of the car and managed to stop herself. "If you won't take me to hospital, at least take me to a hotel."

Otis laughed. "A hotel? This ain't a holiday, sister."

"If it's about money, I can pay," she said, her breathing laboured, perhaps through pain, perhaps through blood loss. "Michael, have you still got my phone?"

Michael reached into his pocket where he had stashed it just before they ran across the field. He'd forgotten it was there. "It's not a bad idea, Otis. We could take a taxi; Cooper won't be looking for that."

"I dunno …"

"It's better than staying here."

"Fine," shrugged Otis. "Whatever."

"Michael, give me the phone," said Page.

He passed it over to her and, with cold trembling hands, she made the arrangements.

MICHAEL kicked open the hotel room door and helped Page inside. The fully grown woman — although slim — weighed heavy, with her good arm draped across his shoulders and his arm clasped around her back. The two of them made it down the narrow passage between the wardrobe and the bathroom to the double bed. He turned her round and dropped her, bum-first, on the mattress. She sagged like a soft toy with barely the strength to keep herself upright. Michael swung her legs up onto the bed and helped lay her head down.

She was a bloody mess. Red, in various stages of coagulation, spread out from her shoulder, down her arm and right side. Looking all the worse against the hotel's pristine white sheets.

The room was probably the same as a thousand other hotel rooms across the country. Walls painted in fresh magnolia, with a bold modern art picture of red, yellow and purple stripes above the bed. Bed of white, fluffed up pillows and duvet. Window with an uninspiring view across the car park estate where Otis had left the car. There was a kettle, white china mugs and sachets for making tea and coffee on the side. There was a small wardrobe with a full length mirror set in the door, a work desk and chair with a complimentary box of tissues. Everything was clean to the point of clinical, with a vague smell of freshly laundered sheets and furniture polish. Until that smell gave way to the body odour of four people on the run.

Jennifer stopped just inside the doorway. The hotel door swung shut automatically behind her.

Otis joined Michael by the bed.

"Perhaps we should have called that ambulance," said Michael, not taking his eyes off Page's wounded body.

"Thought you wanted to get information out of her," said Otis.

"We won't get anything out of her if she dies."

Otis put a reassuring hand on his shoulder. "She's not gonna die, Michael mate."

Michael looked him in the eye. His expression was serious. "If I could perceive you, Otis, would I find out you were just saying that to make me feel better?"

Otis chuckled, not unkindly. "Just as well you're a norm, my friend." He turned away. "I'll put the kettle on."

"We haven't got time for tea!"

"To boil water to sterilise some towels. We need to get her cleaned up. Reduce the risk of infection."

Otis took the kettle and squeezed past Jennifer to get to the bathroom door. She didn't even glance in his direction, so absorbed was she by her reflection in the wardrobe mirror. Her head listed to one side, like an animal confused by its own image.

"Jennifer, why don't you sit down?" said Michael.

She didn't move, she didn't say anything. The only sound was that of a running tap drifting through the open bathroom door.

"Jennifer?" He approached her. "Must have been a hard couple of days, eh?"

He touched her gently on the arm.

She gasped and jumped away from him.

Michael pulled his hand back. "Didn't mean to startle you."

"Michael?" as if she had only just noticed he was there. "I didn't 'ceive you … I meant, I didn't *see* you …" Tears suddenly appeared.

Michael wanted to comfort her. He wanted to hold her in his arms, to tell her everything was okay. But he daren't touch her again.

"Come on, why don't you sit down, eh?"

She nodded.

He pulled the chair out from under the desk and stood back. Her fragile body dropped to the chair, shaking slightly.

He pulled a tissue from the box. As she took it from his hand, her silent tears turned to gentle crying. Like giving her the tissue had given her permission.

Michael perched on the windowsill. He felt hot. The radiator at his legs was blazing. He turned to the window, twisted the handle and swung it open. The cold of approaching winter surged in. Michael stuck his head outside and breathed a lungful.

The room was on the first floor at the back of the hotel. A couple of metres below, a rough bit of tarmac was home to plastic dumpster-style recycling bins which huddled outside the back exit. The door probably led to the kitchens because, standing by the bins, was a man in chef whites puffing on a cigarette.

When he turned back into the room, Page was resting with her eyes closed. The steady rise and fall of her chest showed she was still breathing, still alive.

Jennifer had stopped crying. She still had the tissue Michael had given her and was fiddling with it in her lap.

Otis leant against the wall in the entranceway, having emerged from the bathroom, as the kettle rumbled away next to him.

"Michael?" said Jennifer all of a sudden.

"Yes," he said.

"What's it like to be a norm?"

He shrugged. "I don't know. It's normal, I suppose…"

"How do you know what people are feeling?"

"Well… you don't really. Not for sure."

Jennifer seemed disappointed at the answer. She turned away from him.

Lobotomised was how Otis had described people who had been cured, like a part of their soul had been thrown in the rubbish.

"You use your other senses, I suppose," said Michael, desperate to say or do something to comfort her. "If you look at someone's face you can tell if they're happy or sad. There's body language… and you can tell a lot by what people say."

"But they lie," said Jennifer.

Michael looked up at Otis for some sort of support, but Otis didn't meet his gaze. He stared out ahead, beyond Michael, beyond Jennifer. Because Michael was a norm, he couldn't tell what Otis was thinking. Maybe he was deciding whether to abandon Jennifer like he had done to Jack all those weeks ago.

"It's going to be okay, Jennifer," said Michael. "The human race has been norms for two million years. We seem to have got through all right."

"How can you say that?" She sniffed and wiped her nose with the mangled tissue. "Didn't you say you thought this had happened to you, that they took your perception away?"

Otis snorted a laugh.

The kettle shuddered to the boil. He grabbed it and returned to the bathroom.

"I don't know anymore." Michael shrugged. It had been a theory. Probably a stupid one.

Otis re-emerged from the bathroom with an armful of steaming towels. He dumped them on the bed next to Page. She moaned. Her eyes flickered open.

Otis leant over her. "I need to clean you up, okay?" His words unexpectedly soft and caring.

She let him unbutton her blouse and winced as he peeled back the blood-soaked fabric to reveal the wound. Where the bullet had entered was a dark hole glistening with fresh blood that oozed from her shoulder and down under her armpit. Everything was red; from her once-white bra to the flesh of her chest and arm. Otis wiped at the mess with a steaming wet towel.

She cried out in pain.

She breathed fast and shallow as he touched her. But she let him clean the wound.

Otis was incredibly gentle and patient. He seemed to know what he was doing. First, addressing the front of her shoulder, then asking Michael to lift her up as he cleaned her back. She whimpered and she cried, occasionally shouting with the pain, until Otis laid her back on a clean pillowcase he'd found in the wardrobe.

Blood continued to trickle from the wound. Page's moans got quieter. Her eyes closed for longer periods as she clung to consciousness.

Otis shook his head. "We need to stop this bleeding. Mike, help me sit her up, will you?"

"Isn't she better lying down?"

"We need to elevate the wound. Harder for the heart to push blood up hill," said Otis. "Take her good arm."

Michael went round the other side of the bed. They lifted her nearer the headboard and Otis put a couple of pillows behind her back to prop her up.

"We need a bandage," said Otis. "Michael, see if there's a spare sheet somewhere that you can rip into strips. But wash your hands first. With hot water. Thoroughly."

"How do you know all this stuff?" said Michael.

"First aid badge at scouts."

Michael let out a tiny laugh. "Seriously?" In the middle of their desperate situation it seemed so ironic. "You were a boy scout?"

"I was a lot of things before the world went crazy," said Otis.

They bandaged Page's shoulder. Blood seeped through the cotton strips. But, after a while, the red mark didn't get any bigger and it looked like they had stopped the bleeding.

Otis filled a tea mug with water from the bathroom tap and handed it to Michael. "Get her to sip this. She'll need to replace lost fluids."

Michael took the mug. "What are you going to do?"

"Find some food. She'll need to replace energy too, not to mention the rest of us."

Otis left. The hotel room door clicked shut behind him.

Michael put the mug to Page's lips and, with his other hand supported her head. "Sip this."

She hesitated.

"It's water," he said.

She sipped.

Some of the water spilled from her mouth and ran down her chin. He allowed her head to rest back on the pillow and reached for one of the cotton strips which hadn't been used to bandage her. He wiped her chin.

He helped her sip again.

"Doctor Page …?" said Michael.

"Don't call me that. Call me Rachel."

Calling her by her first name didn't seem right somehow. He brought the mug to her lips again. She took a mouthful.

"Who am I?" he said.

Page coughed. Water spat from her mouth. Michael put the mug on the bedside table and helped her sit forward until the coughing subsided.

"Am I Ransom's son?"

"Michael …"

Frustrated, he reached into the inside pocket of his jacket and pulled out a folded piece of paper; the photograph taken from Ransom's office. It was smashed from the frame, crumpled and creased, but the image of his younger self, Ransom and the woman was still clear.

He held it up in front of Page's face. "Am I Ransom's son?"

She lowered her eyes. "You weren't supposed to know."

"Why not?"

"Because of Cooper."

"Cooper? What does he want from me?"

"He wants you because of who you are." She lowered her eyes. "And because of what he thinks you can do."

"I can't do anything. I'm a norm, I'm …" But he wasn't sure anymore. He remembered the way he felt when he looked into Jack's eyes all those weeks ago in the park. When he saw the blank expression of a cured teenager and related it to his own memory-wiped mind. Otis had laughed at him back then. But now he wondered if his instinct had been right. He turned to look at Jennifer, closed up within herself, sitting quietly at the edge of the room, contemplating the raggedy tissue in her hand. Part of her lost. Like part of Michael was lost.

"Does Cooper think I'm a perceiver?"

"Yes," said Page.

"Because I used to be a perceiver?"

"Yes."

"Because you cured me?"

"Yes."

Michael deflated. His body sagged onto the bed. The realisation weighed heavy. "Why?"

"It was to protect you," said Page.

Michael chuckled. How ironic. And not funny at all. "Like that worked."

"It would've. But you ran away before we could put you somewhere safe. It would have been somewhere secret. Away from Cooper."

The hotel door opened.

Michael stood back from the bed like a child embarrassed at what he'd been doing.

Otis stood in the doorway and surveyed the scene. "Nothing happened while I was away, did it?"

"No, Otis," said Michael.

"We were just chatting," said Page.

Otis raised an eyebrow. "Really?" He walked in and threw what he'd bought onto the bed: a collection of chocolate bars and two packets of different painkillers. He pressed two paracetamol and two ibuprofen out of their blister packs and helped Page swallow them down with more water.

"Help yourself to the chocolate," Otis told the room. "Not exactly healthy, but it'll give you energy," he said.

Page reached out for one of the chocolate bars with her unin- jured arm and brought it to her mouth, where she ripped at the wrapper with her teeth. Jennifer snatched away another for herself. Michael — suddenly desperately hungry — grabbed the first one he came across that didn't include nuts. The glue that sealed the edges of the wrapper resisted him for a moment, then gave way and tore down the edge of the chocolate. He took a large bite. Larger than his mouth really had room for. And he chewed. Flavour overwhelmed his mouth, the smooth chocolate melting into a sensual river of sugar and fat and cocoa.

All too soon, he had crammed the last piece into his mouth and screwed up the empty wrapper.

After a few minutes, only Otis was left eating. He looked less hungry than the others. He'd probably helped himself to one of the bars before he got back to the room. Eventually, all eyes were on Otis. He chewed, slowly and silently until the last mouthful of chocolate and toffee had melted.

He looked across at Page. "So," he said. "Here we are."

Page shifted her back against the pillow. Michael suspected it wasn't her position that made her uncomfortable. It was the way Otis was looking at her. He only had to use his expression to emphasise that he was taller, more muscular and stronger than her, especially in her wounded condition.

"I saved you from Cooper," said Otis. "I patched you up, watered you, fed you. Now I want your end of the bargain. I wanna know about the cure."

"Okay." Page sighed. "What do you want to know?"

"How does it work? And don't give me no skank about injections, 'cos I know they ain't nothing but a sedative."

Page took a moment to compose herself. A hint of a smile formed on her lips. "You lot are quite some detectives, aren't you."

Otis was not smiling. He shuffled his weight from his right foot to his left foot. It was only a tiny movement, but it was enough to emphasise that he was the one in charge.

Page nodded an acknowledgement that it was time to come clean. "You're right about the injection. It helps subdue the patient and wipe their short term memory so they don't know what happened during the procedure. It's a useful cover story for us, but it's not the cure. More of a pre-med, you might say." She smiled again as if she'd made a little joke. No one else in the room was laughing. "Norms can't perform the cure. It has to be done by perceivers. Two, strong perceivers. That's why there are so few clinics. There are not many natural-born, adult perceivers. And the strain of performing them … well, you can't do too many in a short space of time."

"Do what? What is the cure?"

"It's kind of difficult to explain." She paused. Took a breath. "You know when you perceive someone? When you deeply perceive them? You can almost go into their head and feel their mind? Feel that they're a perceiver — like you did with me?"

"Yeah." Otis shrugged. "I suppose."

"We do that with the cure. Except when we feel the perception, we try to contain it. Close it off so the mind can no longer access that part of itself. Like brain surgery without a knife."

"You don't destroy it?" said Otis.

"I don't know if we could," said Page. "Blocking it off is safer. And seems to be effective."

Otis looked thoughtful. His hands fell from his hips. He stepped back and leant on the wall. "Could it be reversed?" he said.

"Unblock the mind and allow it to access the ability to perceive again?" said Page. "We think it's possible. Although, we never tried it."

Otis pushed himself off from the wall. His eyes suddenly bright, reflecting a mind firing with ideas. "Could you do it for Jennifer?"

Jennifer squashed herself up even further against the wall. "No, Otis …" she said.

"Could you?" said Otis again, approaching the bed.

"There needs to be two of us," said Page.

"I'm a perceiver," said Otis. "I can do it."

"You've not even performed a cure before," said Page. "You can't just go into someone's head and perform a procedure. You've not had training."

"Then teach me," said Otis.

"I don't think your girlfriend is keen."

Otis turned towards Jennifer. She looked like a scared little girl. Fragile and vulnerable. "How about it, Jen? You want to perceive again, don't you?"

"Yes, but …"

He walked towards her and put his arms around her. He pulled her close. Her head rested on his chest. He ran his fingers across her hair. She seemed serene.

"You're one of us, Jen." His voice was soft and soothing. Meant just for her, even though in the quiet of the room, Michael could hear every word. "You don't want to be one of them for the rest of your life, a norm."

She burrowed her head deeper into the folds of his shirt. "What if it doesn't work?" she said.

"We have to try. It's our only hope."

"What if it damages me?"

"I'll be with you the whole way," said Otis. "I won't let you get hurt."

"But you don't know!" She pulled back from him. Her face emerged from his chest and she looked up to face him. "You'll be experimenting on me!"

"She's right," said Page.

Otis glared at her.

"Are you sure you want to experiment on your girlfriend's mind?" said Page.

A moment of doubt flickered over Otis's face. A moment for Michael to step in. "Experiment on me," he said.

"No!" said Page.

Michael turned on her. "Why not? You've damaged my mind already. You took away my perception, my memory, my family, my life … You owe me this."

Almost in desperation, Page looked across at Otis for some kind of backup. But Otis seemed excited by the idea.

"It's risky, Michael," said Page.

"I don't care. If it works on me, you can help Jennifer. If it doesn't … well, I've got nothing to lose, have I?"

Page looked at Otis. "I'll have to teach you some techniques."

"Fine."

"You understand, I'll be in charge. You'll have to follow my lead."

"Whatever, lady. Let's do it already."

She turned her attention to Michael again. There was an unspoken question in her expression. *Was he sure? Was he ready?*

He nodded a silent reply.

SIXTEEN

MICHAEL sat cross-legged on the bed facing Page.

"Close your eyes, Michael," she said softly.

He didn't want to. He looked across at Otis. He was sitting on the bed, propped up on a pillow next to Page looking as nervous as hell.

"Look straight ahead," said Page.

Michael did as he was told. His breathing was rapid and unsteady, betraying his unease. He was like a little kid at the head of the queue for the rollercoaster, excited and terrified all at the same time. But she had to know that. She was a perceiver.

"I can't give you an injection of a sedative, so you'll have to try to stay calm and still, okay?"

"Okay."

She looked into his eyes. Deep into his eyes. Like she had done that first time in the clinic, and again in the office. Her green irises with flecks of yellowy brown drew his gaze into her intense, black pupils. As her perception entered his mind.

She lifted the hand from her uninjured left side and touched at his temple. He let out a little gasp at the sensation of unexpectedly cold fingers.

"Relax," she said. "Breathe slow and deep."

Michael tried.

"In … and out … in … and out … That's it. Now, close your eyes."

Spots of red and blue flashed in the darkness of his own eyelids, then settled to a lonely black. He fought to relax, to unfurl his fingers that had clenched into fists and to breathe slow and deep.

He waited. Alone in the darkness of his own mind, the sound of the room amplified to fill the space. Beyond the forced steadiness of his own breathing was the bare whisper of Page's breath centimetres from him. The rustling of the bed sheets as Otis shuffled nervously beside her. An occasional drip of a leaky tap echoing through the open bathroom door. The creak of the chair where Jennifer sat, watching what was going on. Whatever was going on.

Something touched inside of him. Somewhere in his head. He breathed in sharply. His fingers clenched.

Page, suddenly closer. The smell of her sweat, the touch of her fingers, the hint of her body heat. Overwhelmed by the sense of her. He felt … he wasn't sure … her heaviness, a weight on her shoulder. A sharp stab of pain. Her pain. The ache of where a bullet had torn through her flesh was inside of him. More real than any sight or sound or smell. He *perceived* her.

Sensations flowed into his brain. One after another: racing cars whizzing past on a track, a blur of colours.

A wave of anxiety; determined, but uncertain: Otis. He had to be perceiving Otis.

A flash of Jennifer's timidity.

Barriers being knocked down one by one, allowing him greater and greater access to the minds around him.

Concentration, professionalism, love. Distinctively Page. *Was that really love?*

Otis: concern, jealousy, distrust, uncertainty. Big and brash like the man himself.

Jennifer: confusion, fear, anxiety.

All together. Flooding into his mind like rain, like a swollen river.

Something without. Tapping at his old senses. He struggled to clear his head of perception. It was a voice. Female, adult, loud: "Michael? Michael? Are you okay?"

He moved his lips, air passed through them. He tried to say words, but with the cacophony inside his head, he didn't know if any sound came out.

"You can open your eyes now, Michael."

His eyelids flickered. Light stung him. Blinded him. One final sensation on top of a room full of emotions pushed him over the edge. He cried out and clutched his head. Everything swimming inside, all together. Concern and fear and pain and love and worry and confusion. He couldn't distinguish them anymore — even from his own thoughts. A jumble of everyone pressing in on him. Hurting him.

Voices around him.

"Are you all right?"

"Michael?"

"Can you hear me?"

"Did it work?"

"Aarrgghhhh!" His own voice — screaming.

His legs stumbled off the bed. Away from the others. But their emotions got no quieter. His vision: a blur of light and shade. His body hit something hard. The wall. He veered left and struck another wall. He was in the far corner of the room. Trapped with nowhere else to go, the pain of so many sensations crowding in on him.

His legs gave way and he sunk to the floor. Still clutching his aching head. Feeling it about to burst with the thrashing of things that didn't belong inside of it.

"What have you done to him? What have you done?" Jennifer's screeching voice.

Michael tried to focus his sight. The one sense he had relied on the most as a norm. Blurred colours coalesced. Jennifer stood by the window with Otis holding her. Page was still on the bed.

"Is this what it's like?" said Michael through the pain.

"You always were a strong perceiver, Michael," said Page. "You've forgotten how to control it."

He couldn't control it. *It* controlled *him*. Helpless on the floor in the corner.

Another presence pushed into his already crowded mind. At the edge of his perception, but strong. Determined and getting closer.

"There's someone else," said Michael.

"What?" said Otis.

Or more than one. He wasn't sure. The bombardment was so intense. Emotions and thoughts hitting him and swirling around inside him like a whole school full of children screaming for attention. And, in the midst, a strident distant presence concentrating on him. Searching for him.

"He wants me," said Michael in delirium.

The volume of concern from the others increased. They all looked at him: unmoving, unspeaking.

A sound jolted them. The three turned towards the main door. Waves of panic and fear and trepidation crashed through his mind. He cried out with the pain of being made to feel so many things at once.

The sound again. They jolted again. Michael realised it was someone knocking at the door.

Whispered voices. He heard the words, but they were just sounds to his overwhelmed mind. He didn't even know who was saying them.

"Who is it?"

"Well, I don't know."

"Did you order room service?"

"I got chocolate."

"See who it is, Otis."

"Perceive who it is, Otis."

Otis prised himself free of Jennifer's arms which slipped from around his torso. At the door, he laid his palms flat against the wood and leant forward to rest his forehead.

A click of the lock — and the door moved.

Otis — flung backwards — crashed against the wardrobe.

Three men in suits walked in. Three black silhouettes in formation: a desire for Michael spilling from their heads. So loud, his mind burned from the intensity.

Jennifer screamed. She scrambled towards the window.

Otis staggered back from the silhouettes.

Michael squeezed his eyes, willing the shapes to coalesce into people. And, through the squint, he recognised the face of the first man: Cooper.

Jennifer was halfway out the window.

Otis ran towards her. "Jump, Jen!"

Her body disappeared through the opening.

The other two men pushed past Cooper. Otis clambered over the windowsill.

Only one storey to fall, Michael thought — the only thought in his head that belonged to him.

"Leave them!" bellowed Cooper. "They're not important."

The men pulled up short. Otis jumped.

Cooper and his two henchmen stood before Michael and Page.

"Well," said Cooper, "Rachel Page and Michael Ransom. Lucky me."

"How did you find us?" said Page.

"You didn't think I'd let the girl go without putting a tracer on her, did you?"

Page's embarrassment and feeling of stupidity melded with Cooper's smug, self-satisfaction. Michael moaned. He clutched his head and pulled it down into his knees where it was dark. But he couldn't escape the pain of perception.

"Bring him," Cooper ordered.

Hands took Michael's arms, but he barely felt them. They pulled him to his feet; he was powerless to resist him. They took him from the hotel room and he let them.

His head so full of other people, he was unaware of where they were going. Sights, sounds, colours, lights, perceptions blurred into nothing. There was only the pain, the constant pain. Burning in an ever-bubbling cauldron of human emotion and thought.

SEVENTEEN

THEY put him a cell. A grey room only a little longer than the single bed pushed up against one wall. It was narrower than it was long, with a toilet and a basin sticking out of one wall, and a locked door with no handle in the inside set into another.

Michael's body was alone, but his mind was full of other people. He could no longer tell which emotion or thought belonged to whom. It was just noise. All the chatter of everyone's heads jumbled together into one, continuous, unbearably loud cacophony.

Michael curled himself up into a ball on the bed and hugged the pillow to his chest. At first, he was aware he was moaning with the pain. He shifted position and felt the wet patch from where he had drooled on the scratchy blanket. After that, he wasn't aware of what he was doing. There was only the ache in his head.

The cell door must have been opened once or twice because he swore he saw a tray of food on the floor. He let it stay there. He wasn't hungry and he didn't want to move. His head hurt too much. The next time he looked, the tray had gone. Maybe it had been a delusion.

Sleep brought a little relief. He tried to sleep as much as possible, but perceptions kept tugging him awake, bringing back the pain.

HE awoke to the sound of the door opening. A shaft of light entered his cell. He squinted at the doorway and tried to make out the shape that stood in it.

"Michael," said the shape with a deep, authoritative man's voice: sharp and commanding.

Michael continued to squint. He had seen the shape before. The outline of his suit squared him off, but didn't entirely disguise his paunch or his six foot tall stature.

"Michael, stand up when I address you," he ordered.

Michael laughed. He knew that voice from the stairs. He recognised the shape from the hotel room and, inside of him, something familiar touched his mind. It was Cooper.

"Stand up!"

But Michael couldn't stand. He couldn't sit. Anyway, he didn't want to. And, why should he?

The sound of shoes tapping on the tiled floor as Cooper approached the bed.

"What's the matter with you?"

Michael let out a pained moan as Cooper's thoughts rose to prominence in his head: a distaste, a disappointment, a distrust.

Cooper grabbed Michael by the shirt and dragged him to a sitting position against the wall. Michael's body didn't resist, but flopped like an invertebrate.

"Don't resist me, Michael. You'll regret it."

But Michael didn't care. He just wanted the pain in his head to go. He just wanted to lie there. He didn't care if he died.

A blast of anger spilled from Cooper's mind and ripped into Michael. It brought tears to his eyes.

Cooper pushed Michael away from him. Michael struck the wall by the bed and collapsed back on the scratchy blanket. He buried his head into it. His eyes welcomed the dark, but nothing shaded his mind. He became aware he was moaning again.

Cooper's footsteps tapped away. The door shut behind him with a violent clang. Bolts clicked into place. Locked in there, alone, he tried to go back to sleep while a myriad of minds clamoured at his consciousness.

THE man who appeared next at the door was not wearing a suit. His outline was softer. Saggy, even. As he walked forward, the light from the bulb above revealed he wore a patterned black and blue checked jumper and a faded pair of blue jeans.

Michael perceived his presence. But it wasn't harsh like Cooper's. It was closer than the background of other minds, but it didn't stand out from them. It mingled among them, until the man became part of them: indistinct and unreadable.

"Hello, Michael," he said.

Michael squinted harder. There was something about the man that tugged at his memory. Something about the way his black hair with flecks of grey and increasingly greying beard framed his face. Something about his smile.

The clang of the cell door closing made the man jump. He turned round as the bolts secured it shut. Locked in there together alone.

Michael dropped his body back to the bed. He decided he didn't care. Whatever it was, it couldn't be worse than the pain in his head.

His body tilted slightly sideways. He thought it was disorientation. But when hands reached out to touch him, he realised it was the effect of the man's weight sitting on the bed alongside him. Michael shrank away from the hands. But they did not hold him cruelly. They gently lifted him from the blanket and pulled him onto the man's lap. Michael didn't resist. There was something about the way he touched him, something about the aura he gave off — something in the cloud of perception — that encouraged Michael to trust him. His face nuzzled into the softness of the man's jumper. Its washing powder smell, mixed with the faint musk of the man's natural scent, evoked a feeling of security.

It lessened the pain. The sensations in his head seemed weaker. Imperceptible at first — they faded so slowly — but they definitely faded. Like a marching band striding down the road, getting further and further away. Snippets of people's minds outside the cell floated in and out of his consciousness: hunger from someone who had missed lunch; a headache from someone else; a man's boredom; a woman's fatigue. Getting fainter. Dampened. As if wrapped in a blanket.

And, all the while, the man held him. Arms clutched around his upper body, pulling him close into his lap.

"I used to do this when you were small," said the man. "Do you remember?"

"Remember?" Michael mumbled.

"You were always a strong perceiver, Michael. I did this to protect you, to help you learn to control it."

Michael opened his eyes and looked up at the bearded face of the man who held him. He was greyer than his picture. His hair was longer. But Michael still knew who he was. "You're Brian Ransom."

"You used to call me 'Dad'," he said.

Michael played the word over in his head: Dad. It didn't seem right to call the stranger by that name.

"What are you doing?" Michael said. The other minds still whispered — they were there, but they did not hurt anymore. His head throbbed, but it was a normal headache, the remnants of trying to cope with the bombardment of perception.

"I've cocooned your mind," said Ransom. "I've reached out with my perception to shield you. It's a temporary respite to help you regain your strength."

"You're...?" It hurt to think. "You're... a perceiver?"

"You know that, Michael."

"I... don't remember."

He nodded sadly. "Rachel told me. I thought she exaggerated. Unfortunately not."

"Rachel?"

"Rachel Page, my assistant."

"Why didn't it come back? My memory. When she unblocked my perception, why didn't it restore my memory?"

"I don't know," said Ransom. "We think it might have been destroyed for good."

Michael felt tears on his cheeks. Hot, silent tears.

"We didn't anticipate how strong you were. We were going to cure you, hide you somewhere safe — that's all. But you resisted. You broke free in the middle of the treatment. We were pulled out of your mind so fast, it caused some damage."

"Mend it. Give me my memories back."

"Damaged for good, Michael. I'm sorry."

Michael cried out. A long, despairing cry.

Whispers of a dozen minds surged in his head. Their feelings and thoughts suddenly loud; clamouring for attention all at once. Stabbing at him with pain.

Then subsiding. The volume turned back down to a whispering hiss.

There was concentration on Ransom's face. "This is difficult for me," he said. "I can't hold on much longer."

"You're going to put all those minds back in my head? You can't!"

"You have to learn to control it."

"I can't!"

"You did when you were a little boy. You can again."

"I can't! You did this to me. You damaged my brain! You've got to make it stop."

Another wave of other people's minds crowded in on him. The pain was worse than before. He didn't have the strength to bear it.

It subsided a little. Not as much as before. Still loud inside his head.

"I have to withdraw now, Michael."

"No!"

"I'll be back. Be strong now."

He touched Michael on the head. A caring touch like a father might with a sleeping baby. Then he pulled back. His arms withdrew from around Michael's body. The cocoon of protection withdrew from Michael's mind. The cacophony of perception rushed back.

Michael screamed in pain. He writhed on the bed, trying to push the minds away — but they weren't solid, he couldn't touch them. He looked up to Ransom for help, but the man was retreating from him. He turned his back and knocked on the cell door. Unseen hands outside turned the lock. Ransom walked out of the cell and Michael was again alone with the unyielding pain.

EIGHTEEN

RANSOM returned to the cell periodically. There was no window in the enclosed grey room, no daylight to judge the passing of the hours, but Michael suspected he visited once a day. Ransom must have perceived the hatred Michael had for him, but he said nothing about it. He merely cocooned Michael and spoke to him softly, explaining how to control the perceptions that reached his mind.

Michael submitted to his instruction. No matter how much he hated his father for what he had done to him, it was nothing compared to the pain.

Ransom told him how to isolate a single mind from the melee of everything around him. To listen to its tone, categorise it and excise it from his consciousness, until it was possible to ignore it. It was like, he said, a hearing person could block out the background noise of traffic or music playing in a restaurant. Then, after ignoring one mind, he learnt to single out another. And another and another. Eventually,

Ransom said, it would become second nature and the thoughts and feelings in his mind would become his own again.

But it was hard. He was so tired and sleeping was difficult. Ransom gave him some tablets to help him sleep, but they only made him more groggy when he awoke and weakened his ability to control his perception.

On one visit, Cooper accompanied Ransom into the cell.

"When's he going to be ready?" Cooper said.

Cooper's sense of self-superiority had entered the cell with him. The perception of it was loud in Michael's mind.

"He'll be ready when he's ready," said Ransom.

"That's not an answer."

"It's the only one you're going to get."

"Ready for what?" Michael asked. He was more able to function — more able to follow a conversation — now that he'd had several tutorials with Ransom.

Cooper's frustration spilled out of him. Along with a jumble of hatred, distrust and suspicion. "Work quicker, Ransom."

"I told you, this will take as long as it takes," said Ransom. "Michael's making progress, but he's strong and it can't be rushed. Can I suggest, however, that if you want him to work for you when all this is done, you should stop despising him."

Anger joined Cooper's collection of emotions. "What did I say about perceiving me?"

"You're like a foghorn, Bill. Tone it down a bit."

With disgust, Cooper turned and left.

Michael was confused. "He wants me to work for him?"

"Don't worry about it now," said Ransom. He reached out his mind and cocooned Michael in a protective shield. Michael relaxed into the peace and pain-free solace of it and prepared for his next lesson.

DAYS later and Michael's mind was almost clear. The rumble was still inside his head, he still suffered from headaches, but the pain and the bombardment had lessened enough to allow him to think. He thought about where he was: locked in a cell in some unknown place, away from his friends, away from society, and even away from the police and their rules on dealing with prisoners. He'd not been offered a solicitor and he hadn't been read his rights, suggesting that he had none.

Michael flinched at the unexpected turn of the lock of his cell door. He sat up on the bed and held his breath.

The door opened and Cooper took a step inside. Michael was aware enough to notice Cooper had dispensed with his usual black suit to one of dark blue. But there was a day's stubble on his chin and the first shirt button above the belt of his trousers was undone. It gaped to reveal a patch of pale belly and a couple of wiry hairs.

"Ransom says you're well enough for me to talk to you."

Michael drew his knees up to his chest as an instinctive barrier. "Talk to me about what?"

"Shall we go somewhere more comfortable?" said Cooper. "You must be sick of this cell by now."

There was something sinister in the way he said 'more comfortable'. Michael tried to perceive Cooper's intentions, but as soon as he opened his perception, a dozen other minds flooded in and drowned out the man's thoughts.

Cooper gestured to someone outside of the cell. A woman walked in. She was tall and slim, her mousy-blonde hair pulled back tight into a ponytail. Her khaki trousers and perfectly ironed T-shirt had the sense of the military about them.

In her hand by her hip were a pair of handcuffs. The metal jingled as she walked up to Michael.

"Stand up and put your hands behind your back," she ordered.

Michael looked at Cooper for some kind of explanation. He stared back, offering none.

The woman waited a moment, but when it was obvious her order would not be obeyed, she grabbed Michael's arm. Her skinny frame held a hidden strength that yanked Michael off the bed. He tumbled to the floor. She pulled him to his knees so he knelt, as if praying, at the bedside. She twisted his arm behind his back — stretching his ligaments to tearing point — and clasped cold metal around his wrist. He was helpless to resist as she grabbed his other wrist and secured the second cuff.

She pulled him to his feet and turned him round to face Cooper. He was taller than him, larger than him and had the sense of authority about him. The woman was clearly under his command and Michael was of no threat with his hands restrained behind his back.

"Sorry about that." Cooper smiled. "Just a precaution, you understand. Wouldn't want you stabbing me again, would we?"

Cooper turned and walked out. Michael was shoved forward and through the cell door.

He entered a corridor of cells with five metal doors, like the one he had just walked through, in a row down one side. He wondered what lay behind each of them. Maybe more teenagers like himself. But he had little time to speculate because the woman shoved him from behind again. He staggered forward a few steps. It was enough for him to get the hint to follow Cooper.

At the end of the corridor was another door. Solid, white and devoid of features with a security camera looking down on them from above. Cooper swiped a plastic card through a black box attached to a number pad at the side of the door and pressed a series of keys. A flurry of numbers flitted through Michael's head in a whisper he could almost hear. By the time he realised he was overhearing Cooper's thoughts — rehearsing the combination in his head — the moment had passed and the numbers were gone.

With a click, the door sprang open.

A guard was on the other side. Michael recognised him as one who had brought him food on some of the previous days. He nodded an acknowledgement at Cooper.

They were standing in an adjunct where two corridors met. Ahead, magnolia-painted walls and a brown tiled floor led to a set of double doors. But Michael was not to find out what was behind them because Cooper turned to his left. Michael followed him up a second magnolia corridor, with the woman still holding his arm firm.

Past more doors. Not cell doors, but heavy wooden doors that led into other, unseen rooms. Some of them were occupied, others weren't. He knew because, as he passed each one, the perceptions in his head grew or waned with the presences behind them. He couldn't filter out individuals — he was too busy keeping the pain of so many minds blocked out — but he knew they were there.

They reached a set of double doors that partitioned one part of the corridor from another. Cooper swiped his card through the reader at the side and tapped out a number. Michael let his barrier slip a little to listen to Cooper's thoughts. But the number combination was a whisper hidden among the jumble of other minds and he couldn't perceive it.

Behind the doors was yet more magnolia.

A man, dressed in khaki, like the woman, and about the same age as Cooper, but with a better physique, walked towards them.

"Sir," he said to Cooper as he passed them and continued on his way.

Two more security doors and they emerged from the building into the daylight. Michael squinted. He'd been in that cell so long it hurt his eyes to adjust to the sun. The air had a delicious, fresh smell about it. Somewhere above him, a bird tweeted its joy of being free.

They stood beside a perfect circle of neatly trimmed grass as large as a lake. Around the edge, a ring of tarmac linked four roads that snaked off to other buildings. Ahead of them were two metal gates as high as a lorry, guarded by armed soldiers in combat fatigues.

For a moment, he thought he must be in an army base. They were certainly in some kind of secure compound, contained — as it was — within a fence made of steel bars topped with barbed wire. But not everything fitted with that theory. A silver Seat Ibiza passed by, driven by a woman in civilian dress. Some of the people out on foot were dressed in khaki, but others were dressed in smart, ordinary clothes like Cooper. Michael perceived their curiosity as they caught sight of him.

Cooper turned left. Michael and his female keeper followed.

The path led them up a slight slope, past a landscaped area of more perfect grass with neatly trimmed cherry trees planted equidistant along the edge. Behind the fourth tree, were a group of five teenagers dressed in khaki, chatting among themselves. One after another, they stopped talking and turned to stare. Michael perceived their recognition. Five minds, all thinking the same thing. He shivered at the violation. And wondered if they, like him, were perceivers.

At the top of the slope was a two storey office building. Cooper gained access with his swipe card and led them upstairs to an office. Once upon a time, Michael might have described Cooper's office as large and plush. But after sneaking into Ransom's building, it seemed kind of average.

Cooper took up position in a leather padded chair behind his executive wooden desk. Behind him, a window looked out onto the complex below. Michael's female keeper sat him down in a chair opposite. His bum hit the fabric-covered foam seat. He tried to lean back, but his restrained arms were in the way.

The woman stood behind.

Cooper looked at Michael from across the desk. "Would you like a drink?"

Michael stared back at him. He still perceived the background fog of other people and he wasn't sure if he heard him right.

"Well?" said Cooper. "Tea? Coffee?"

He *had* offered him a drink. Odd. As if he were some guest arriving for a dinner party.

Cooper frowned at not getting an answer and turned his attention to the woman. "Get me a coffee, will you? Strong, not too much milk and no sugar. And get lemonade or something for the kid."

"Sir?" said the woman.

"*Now*, thank you."

"Sir." She turned on her heel and exited.

As the door closed politely behind her, Cooper leant across the desk and whispered, "I don't think she approves of leaving me alone with you. Is that what you perceive?"

"I'm trying not to perceive anything," said Michael.

"Strange. After you went to all that trouble to get your perception back."

"I didn't … I didn't know it would be like this."

Michael felt Cooper's doubt leaching across the table at him. He concentrated on blocking it out like Ransom had taught him, but the effort was too much and he settled for having Cooper's feelings nudging at the edge of his mind.

"That Page woman said you suffered some memory loss."

Page. He hadn't thought about her since Ransom mentioned her on that first day. "Is she okay?"

"She's under arrest for shooting at me," said Cooper. "But if you're asking me about her welfare, the doctors say she'll make a full recovery from her shoulder wound."

Michael was relieved. He was very much aware that they could have killed her by allowing Otis to carry out his boy scout's first aid on her instead of calling an ambulance.

His thoughts were interrupted by a polite knock at the door and the sound of someone entering. It was the woman, carrying a mug billowing steam and a glass of clear liquid with a stream of tiny bubbles fizzing to the surface. Michael caught a whiff of Cooper's coffee as the woman carried it past him and placed it on the desk.

She put the glass of lemonade in front of Michael. In order to drink, he would have to lift it to his lips, but his wrists were still handcuffed behind his back.

"Didn't you bring a straw?" said Cooper.

"Sir?"

"A straw for my young friend here."

Michael raised his eyebrows at the concept of being Cooper's 'friend'.

"No, sir."

"Well, go and get one."

"Yes, sir."

The woman left the office again.

"Now, where were we?" said Cooper.

"You were going to tell me what the skank I'm doing here," said Michael.

It was Cooper who raised his eyebrows this time. "Was I, indeed?" He picked up his coffee mug and blew across the top, sending a plume of steam wafting in Michael's direction. He took a sip.

Michael looked at his lemonade, gradually losing its fizz as it sat there unattended.

"Do you know what perceivers have done to this country, Michael? Got it into a right bloody mess, that's what. All thanks to your father and his stupid utopian dream of a world where everyone understands each other. You do realise this all happened because of you, don't you?"

Michael lowered his eyes. He didn't know it, because it wasn't true. He was a victim of the 'bloody mess', not the creator of it.

"I suppose you know you were born as a result of IVF?"

He'd read Ransom and his wife had difficulty in having children, that they'd had fertility treatment. But he hadn't thought until then that he might be the result of it. If he was their son, then he had to have been conceived in a lab. The thought chilled him.

"Perception is the reason he's a successful businessman," Cooper continued. "He'd always win in business deals because he knew what the other guy was thinking. He sought out other perceivers — like that Page woman — to work closely with him. And he wanted his children to be the same, if not better. He invested in secret genetic research to find the key to perception and incorporated that knowledge into his wife's IVF treatment. You're the result."

Michael felt the blood withdraw from his face. He felt nauseous. "He made me this way?" asked Michael, his voice shaking.

"Yes."

"That's why you're punishing me?"

Cooper smiled. An amused smile that turned into a chuckle. "No! Punish you? No." He took a long swig of his coffee. "I want you to work for me."

Michael was confused. After everything he'd gone through, Cooper was offering him a job? It didn't make sense. He risked opening his mind a little. Background perception of people outside the office swelled inside his head. He didn't have the skill to target his perception on one person, but he sensed a little of Cooper's feelings on top of all the others. He perceived honesty.

Michael closed his eyes and forced the perceptions out of his head again. They left a dull thump while the background hum of their presence remained at the edge of his mental barrier.

"Adults are frightened of teenagers because they fear they can perceive all their secrets," said Cooper. "It's destabilised society. They want to stop it, to 'cure' it. I'm all in favour, of course. You can't have a whole generation of people able to spy on everyone else. But that doesn't mean you can't still have a few people with that ability. Think of where perceivers could be useful. Your father used perception to become a successful businessman and make a personal fortune. But you could use it to determine whether a person is guilty of a crime, in negotiations with other nations, even to spy on those nations. I'm gathering together a group of teenagers who will do that."

Michael's mouth hung open. He didn't know what to say or think. He shifted his weight on the chair. He felt the handcuffs digging into his wrists. He couldn't reconcile being a prisoner with being offered a job.

A knock on the door broke the expectant silence. The woman re-entered and dropped a plastic straw into the glass of lemonade. The remaining bubbles lifted it up so it bobbed close to the surface.

"Where have you been?" Cooper asked her.

"The canteen didn't have any straws, sir, so I …"

Cooper waved away her explanation. "Just leave us."

"Sir."

Cooper watched the woman walk back out of his office. When she had closed the door behind him once again, Cooper turned his attention back to Michael.

"What do you say?"

Michael didn't know what to say. It was all so confusing. A job offer seemed so innocent. There had to be a catch. One of his first memories was of stabbing Cooper. Back then — even alone and confused — he instinctively knew he had to get away from him. And Page — whatever her reasons — risked her life to get him away from Cooper.

Michael leant forward and wrapped his lips around the straw. The smell of citrus rose up into his nostrils before he sucked up the liquid and tasted its sweet, artificial tang.

"Your father is set against it, of course," Cooper continued. "Doesn't fit with his utopian ideals. He'd rather take away your perception than let me have access to it. But you know what I think, Michael? I think you're your own man. You can make the decision for yourself. You're a strong perceiver, it'll be an honour to have you work for me."

Michael continued to suck at the lemonade. He opened his mind a little and allowed perceptions of Cooper to filter through. The man was buoyed up on optimism which crowded out almost everything else coming from him. And yet underneath, at the edge, was a sense of insincerity.

NINETEEN

MICHAEL was ready for Ransom when he came to his cell. As soon as the guard opened the peephole in the door and stared through, Michael was off the bed and standing in the centre of the room.

"Right back against the wall," said the guard.

It was a protocol to stop the prisoner rushing at the door while it was open. But Michael had a different plan. He backed up as ordered and felt the cold of plastered brick at his spine.

The cell door opened.

Ransom stood in the doorway. Compared to Cooper, his silhouette appeared unthreatening. Shorter than average height with rounded shoulders and that same open-necked shirt and jumper Michael remembered from when he first cradled him in his arms.

Ransom stepped inside and the cell door closed behind him. A clank of bolts locked them in. Then silence. Just the background perceptions of people outside. Michael eased off on the barriers, as his father had taught him, and sensed Ransom's nervousness.

"This could be the last time Cooper lets me in to see you," said Ransom.

"I went to Cooper's office yesterday," said Michael.

"I heard," said Ransom. "He knows you've gained control."

Control? This was control? Was he never going to get rid of the constant background whisper of so many minds?

"We need to talk," said Ransom. "Why don't you sit down?" He indicated the bed, but Michael had no intention of resting.

"Cooper told me about you," said Michael.

"You shouldn't listen to everything Bill Cooper says. We don't exactly see eye to eye."

"He said you created me in a lab."

Ransom was caught by surprise. Michael perceived confusion and concern from him. "Because Mary conceived you through IVF? That's nothing to be ashamed of. Thousands of babies are born using IVF every year. It's just science helping nature along."

"He said you used IVF to make sure I was a perceiver."

"I wanted the best for you. Perception's helped me succeed in life. I wanted that for my child, I wanted you to be special."

"You did this to me!" Michael looked round his cell. The four, cold walls that enclosed him were a manifestation of everything his father had done to him. His genes were manipulated when he was barely an embryo, setting his fate before he was born.

"It was *Cooper* who did this to you," said Ransom.

Michael shook his head. His emotions were getting the better of him, despite his efforts to keep them under control. "No. You're the one. You made me like this. Then you realised you'd made a mistake, so you went inside my brain and took it away again. But that wasn't enough for you, you had to wipe my memory too."

"Michael, that's what I came here to talk to you about. We haven't got long. Let me explain."

He stepped towards Michael with open arms, innocently offering himself. But Michael moved away, edging sideways along the wall. At the last minute, he remembered to use his perception. Ransom's concern entered his mind, tinged with a little remorse. It made his offer of an explanation seem genuine, but Michael wasn't ready to listen. Having his father's feelings in his head unsettled him and he blocked them out again, building up his barriers and reinforcing them as much as he could.

"Cooper's offered me a job," said Michael.

"He wants to use you," said Ransom.

"And you don't?" said Michael.

"No."

Michael laughed to himself. An ironic laugh. "I don't believe you."

"Then perceive me." That open arm gesture again. "If you perceive me, you'll know I'm telling the truth. I didn't foresee this. Mary — your mum — and I just wanted a baby. And we wanted the best for that baby. When we found out she couldn't have children naturally, we were devastated. You've no idea what it's like to see the woman you love break down in tears like that. After three devastating miscarriages, IVF was our only hope. The procedure took the best part of a year — *a year*, Michael — before she became pregnant. But we did it because we desperately wanted children — we wanted *you*. Yes, I made sure you inherited the gift of perception, but only because I wanted my child to have the same opportunities in life that I had."

"Wanted it so much that you cured me?"

Ransom turned his eyes away from Michael and sighed. He sat down on the bed, his hunched shoulders and saggy body like a half-deflated balloon. "Maybe I shouldn't have."

"Why did you do it?" said Michael.

"I don't know if you've seen what it's like out there, but it's virtually against the law to be a perceiver in this country. When they find out about you, they cure you. Or they keep you on a leash to do their bidding."

"You haven't been cured," said Michael.

"I'm on Cooper's leash," said Ransom. "The government came sniffing when I set up the cure clinics. They found out about me, found out I'd employed perceivers like Rachel Page in key positions in my company. Threatened me, threatened them. I had no choice but to let them take control. But their biggest bargaining chip was you."

"Me?" said Michael.

"Cooper knew you inherited my perception. He was going to conscript you and I couldn't stop him. We thought — Rachel and I — if we cured you then he wouldn't have that leverage anymore."

The facts, so bold and stark, took time to sink into his head. Michael backed away from his father, along the wall, until his knee hit the edge of the toilet bowl. He let his weight drop onto the toilet seat and he sat there, fully clothed, as he tried to match what Ransom was saying to what little memory he had.

"When I found myself in the corridor of your office building, there was a woman calling my name," said Michael. "Was that Page?"

"Yes," said Ransom.

"What happened? What was Cooper doing there?"

"You really don't remember anything before then?" said Ransom.

"No. It's been driving me crazy," said Michael. "I need to know."

"I'm sorry I can't give you your memories back, but maybe I can show you mine."

Michael lifted his head and looked at his father. Interested.

"If we let down our barriers and open our minds to each other."

"Is that possible?" said Michael.

"Not for most perceivers. But for you … it might work. If you've matured enough since Rachel reversed the cure."

"What do I do?"

"Sit next to me," said Ransom.

Michael hesitated. He'd told himself to keep his distance from Ransom, but this was his chance to understand. After a moment, he got off the toilet and sat down next to his father.

"Let go of your nervousness, Michael. It impedes your ability."

He tried. He concentrated on his breathing, forced it to become slow and deep. It helped, a little.

Ransom took his hands and held them in his lap. "Physical contact isn't necessary, but it helps you to focus. Now, look into my eyes."

Michael did so. For the first time since Ransom entered his cell, he saw that his eyes were hazel with flecks of brown and yellow like rays of a sun eclipsed behind the black moons of his pupils.

"Go deeper. Into my mind. See what I see."

Michael willed his consciousness to pass through Ransom's pupils. Ransom's emotions were on the surface: concern, worry, fear, uncertainty.

"Concentrate," came Ransom's voice.

Michael did. His mind swum past the emotions and emerged in a fog of images. Bright lights blurring from a canvas of black. Indistinct and dreamlike. Until he realised the lights represented something real. Yellow street lights, green traffic lights, red tail lights, white headlights. This was a memory. A memory of being in a car at night time …

> … driving through city traffic. A red double decker bus went by. It was London. The speedo edged over thirty miles per hour. A thought passed through his head that he must stick to the limit and the needle dropped below thirty. There was a steering wheel in front of him. He was driving in this memory.
>
> He looked to his left. Next to him in the passenger seat was a teenager, neatly dressed with combed brown hair. On his lap sat a battered rucksack. It took a moment for Michael to realise he was looking at himself. It was Ransom's memory of both of them going somewhere in a car at night.
>
> There was an overwhelming sense of calm and normality inside Ransom's head. So much so that it felt almost artificial.

He explored the feelings and sensed, beneath them, a trace of anxiety that Ransom was trying to mask. As soon as it surfaced from the back of his mind, Ransom fought to subdue it. If Michael perceived it, Ransom thought, he could become suspicious.

"This is the way to your office," said the neater, remembered version of Michael.

"Yes, just need to stop off there for a bit," said Ransom, imbuing his words with a feeling of normality.

"We won't be late for our meeting with Mr Cooper?"

The mention of his name sent a frisson through Ransom and — deliberately — he jerked the steering wheel to the right and swerved into the outside lane. The angry *parp* of a car horn made him shudder. A Land Rover behind flashed its headlights.

Ransom was furious. "Bloody London traffic!"

"Dad?"

He ignored his son and pressed his foot on the accelerator. The car engine roared until the speedo hit forty. He seethed at the driver of the Land Rover, even though deep down he knew he had swerved into its path deliberately. Road rage was a strong emotion, strong enough — he hoped — to deflect Michael's perceptions and stop him probing any further.

The lights on the road outside blurred and the memory shifted...

... They were in the lift at Ransom Incorporated. Watching the display count the number of floors as the mechanism propelled them higher and higher.

Inside Ransom, anxiety was rising. "Damn, bloody lift," he muttered to himself. He remembered all the times he'd cursed the fact that his office was on the top floor. It was another mask. One that he was frightened Michael was starting to see through.

"Dad?"

The display reached 12. Relief. "Ah, here we are."

The lift doors opened to reveal the empty, darkened corridor near to his office. He stepped out. Michael followed.

"Couldn't you access whatever it is from your computer at home?"

"I need to pick up some papers," said Ransom, glad to be on the move. Focussing on striding towards his office.

"Paper? Isn't that a bit last century, Dad? You can store things electronically now, you know."

"Computers are insecure. Besides, they've been talking about the paperless office since the 1970s. If it hasn't happened by now, it isn't ever going to happen."

As Ransom opened the door to his empty assistant's desk, he perceived Rachel's presence. Unmistakable and uneasy, she had not made the effort to mask herself like he had. As he strode through the antechamber into his own, spacious office, he knew without question that she was there and waiting. And if he had perceived it, then so had Michael.

"Is Rachel working late?" said Michael, as he followed him in.

Ransom turned. Page was behind the door with a ball of cotton wool in one hand and hypodermic needle in the other...

… The needle triggered a memory in Michael's own mind. He remembered the hypodermic needle he'd stolen off the nurse's desk and how Doctor Rachel Page had confronted him. The memories were too similar and he was becoming aware of the cell again.

He forced reality from his head. He concentrated — first on his breathing, calming his body — then on his perception. He led himself back inside Ransom's mind, back inside the memory…

… The neater, remembered version of Michael turned to see Rachel Page standing behind the door. Ransom perceived a wave of confusion and fear from his son as Michael dropped his rucksack.

"What's going on?" said Michael. He backed away from Page.

But Ransom was waiting. He grabbed both Michael's arms from behind and felt his son's surprise as he struggled.

Page pushed Michael's shirt sleeve up his arm. She wiped the inside of his elbow with the damp cotton wool and dropped it to the floor. Michael struggled harder. His body writhing as Ransom tried to hold him.

"Brian!" said Page, her eyes appealing to him for help as she held onto the syringe.

Ransom held Michael's bare arm with all his strength to keep him still. Page grabbed Michael's wrist and pulled it so his arm was out straight.

"No! No! No!" screamed Michael. Betrayal and terror screamed in his mind.

Page plunged the needle into his arm and injected.

It was all over in a moment. Ransom released his grip and Michael pulled himself free. With such force, he stumbled backwards towards the office door.

Page was behind him. She pushed the door shut.

Ransom — no need to mask his feelings anymore — let out all of his sorrow and pain. Everything he had been holding back for days. He felt like a tyrant, an evil father who was about to do something unspeakable to his only son. Even though he knew it was necessary.

Michael must have perceived it all because he stood before his father a mess of confusion. He clutched his exposed arm with the other hand at the point the needle had gone in. "You're going to cure me?" he said.

"It's the only way," said Ransom. "We'll set you up with a new life, away from here, away from this mess. You'll be a normal teenager."

"No!" Michael stumbled. Ransom perceived the cloudiness of the sedative taking effect. "I have friends here. I have plans. I'm going to …"

He fell sideways; his legs too weak to hold him anymore. Page stepped forward and caught him before he hit the floor. "It's okay," she whispered.

Ransom perceived a suggestion of her own regret as she propelled Michael to the wall and leant him up against it.

Ransom approached.

"Don't do this," said Michael, his speech slurred from the drug. "Don't treat me like one of those kids you put through the clinics. You said perception was part of me. You said …"

Michael started to slip down the wall. Page helped him sit on the carpet.

Ransom squatted down to face him. "I'm sorry, Michael, I really am." And he meant it.

He lifted his hands and touched his index fingers to Michael's temples.

Realising he was about to witness — about to feel — his own mind being cured, Michael pulled out from the memory.

He blinked open his eyes to see Ransom in front of him. His stomach spasmed like he was about to be sick. He tasted vomit at the back of his throat. He swallowed it down. It was a weird, nauseating reversal. From being Ransom looking at Michael one moment, to being himself looking at Ransom the next.

Ransom let go of one of Michael's hands and touched his shoulder. "Are you all right?"

"Yes," said Michael, shaking his head. He didn't really know if he was all right or not, but it didn't matter because he needed to know more. "Take me back in."

"Are you sure?" said Ransom.

"I have to know."

"Okay." Ransom took Michael's hand again. "I won't take you through the cure procedure. That's uncomfortable for me to remember, but I can show you the rest. Perceive me again."

Michael looked through Ransom's eyes and into his mind…

… He became aware of Ransom's memory. He was sitting on the floor in front of the remembered version of Michael: his hair dishevelled from the struggle with one sleeve still rolled up. His head wavered from side to side under the touch of Ransom's fingers.

He was not deep in the memory. He watched, rather than felt, himself as Ransom with Page beside him while both of them were inside his — Michael's — mind.

In this memory, Ransom was aware that Michael was fighting the cure. Despite the sedative, Michael was not giving in. He shook free from Ransom's hands and pushed him out of his head.

The sudden force of expelling Ransom sent a lightning pain through Ransom which knocked him backwards. Everything went fuzzy and black as Ransom reeled from the shock.

Michael was on his feet, the rucksack in his hand, wild confusion in his eyes.

Rachel was beside him. Unsteady on her feet, but not so incapacitated as Ransom. She took a step towards Michael.

He stepped away. He reached into his rucksack and pulled

out a knife. A kitchen knife with a wide blade of sharpened stainless steel. Ransom recognised it as part of their own set of kitchen knives at home.

Michael pointed it at Page, making sure she kept her distance, then at Ransom, before he turned and ran.

"Michael!" Page called after him.

She turned to Ransom; aghast. All Ransom could do was clutch his head.

A ringing pierced his ears. It was the telephone on his desk.

Page was halfway to the door when she stopped.

"Go after him!" urged Ransom.

"I asked security to call if Cooper came into the building," said Page.

"Shit!" said Ransom to himself. A migraine was descending. He tried — and failed — to close his ears against the ringing telephone …

The memory faded. Michael pulled himself out of Ransom's mind and found himself, once again, sitting in the cell with Ransom holding his hands.

The question he had held in his head for weeks had been answered. His memory loss, as he suspected, had been caused by the cure. He had been too strong, too resistant to it, that he broke free in the middle, damaging part of his brain as he pulled out. He must have made it down a couple of floors of the office building and into a corridor before he passed out.

Michael leant back on the bed and Ransom's fingers fell away. He looked up at his father's face and saw, without having to perceive, the regret in his expression.

"Can you forgive me?" said Ransom.

"I don't know," said Michael.

The background rumble of perceptions started to crowd into Michael's mind. He had little strength left to block them out. Little strength to perceive what Ransom felt now.

A knock on the cell door made him jump.

"Five minutes!" bellowed the guard.

Ransom wiped what might have been the start of a tear from his eye and sniffed to restore his composure. "I have to go," he said. He looked round at the closed cell door as if to check no one was watching. He leant forward and whispered. "Don't succumb to Bill Cooper. He'll own you for the rest of your life. Hang on, Michael. I'm going to get you out of here, I promise."

The sounds of turning locks echoed through the cell. The door opened and revealed the guard.

"You said five minutes," said Ransom.

"Time's up," said the guard.

Ransom backed away towards the open door. He mouthed the words, 'I promise', and followed the guard out of the cell.

As the door closed and keys turned in the locks, Michael reached out his mind to his father. His perceived his sorrow for a moment before he walked away and his mind merged with the myriad perceptions of others. He didn't have the energy to block them out and they rang loud inside his head. In the moment before they overwhelmed him, he wondered if he had the capacity to forgive his father for what he had done to him. Michael wasn't sure he had.

TWENTY

MICHAEL stood and allowed the woman to handcuff him behind his back. He was led out of the cell where Cooper was waiting for him.

"Got something to show you," said Cooper.

At the end of the cell block, Cooper swiped his card. Michael listened with his mind as he tapped the combination on the keypad. Cooper's whispered thought, *5…9…2…0* filtered through. Michael smiled: 5, 9, 2, 0. He would remember.

Cooper led them down the corridor that lay straight ahead. Through the double doors with a swipe and a combination, *3…7…8…2*, and to a continuation of magnolia walls.

Only a few metres beyond that and he stopped beside a door on the left hand side of the corridor. A plaque screwed to the wood at eye level read, *Briefing Room.*

Cooper held open the door for Michael. The woman pushed him forward and, as he stepped inside, he smelt the staleness of dust which suggested the room had neither been aired nor cleaned in a while.

Cooper stayed in the doorway. "Thank you," he said to the woman. "You may wait outside."

"Sir." She nodded.

Cooper let go of the door and it closed with the squeak of rarely used hinges.

The briefing room was dimly lit with painted white, solid walls. A spill of daylight found its way through a series of narrow windows above head height so Michael couldn't see out of them. At the front was a small stage-like platform fronted by a bench-like desk and, on the wall behind it, a white screen that looked out onto racks of seating. Like a classroom or a lecture theatre.

Cooper hopped up onto the platform. "Well, come in, Michael. Come in." He waved his hand in encouragement.

Michael took two wary steps. Ransom's words, that Cooper would own him for the rest of his life, echoed in his mind.

"Are you uncomfortable?" said Cooper.

"No."

Cooper smiled. "Sometimes, you don't have to be a perceiver to tell when someone is lying." He stepped back off the platform and stood in front of Michael. "Turn round."

Goose pimples raised on Michael's arms and down his spine. Turning his back on Cooper while they were alone together in the room felt dangerous. But he did it anyway.

He heard the jingle of keys behind him and felt the warmth of Cooper's fingers on his wrists. With two, brief, metallic clicks, the handcuffs were released. Michael felt the relief of freedom and — rubbing his wrists to encourage circulation to return — he turned back.

Cooper held the handcuffs up to shoulder height. "I don't think we need these anymore, do we?" He dropped them on the bench with a clatter. "We trust each other, don't we?"

Everything he knew about Cooper suggested there was a level of *distrust* between them, but Michael was not about to argue the point.

"Take a pew." Cooper gestured at the front row of seats. Michael took it as an invitation to sit.

Cooper leant back against the bench and folded his arms across his flabby chest. "Thought any more about my offer?"

"Yes."

"And?"

Michael shrugged.

"I heard you spoke to your father yesterday. What did he say about me?"

"Nothing much."

Cooper raised his eyebrows. "From what I know of Brian Ransom, I'm sure it was nothing good."

"He said, if I signed up with you, there would be no going back."

Cooper shrugged. "I'll be honest with you. Soon enough, life outside this complex as a perceiver will be virtually impossible. It's only a matter of time before legislation makes it official. What I'm saying is, Michael, your only choice is to sign up with me."

"Or I could be cured."

"You don't want that," said Cooper.

Michael had thought he didn't want it. But getting his perception back had made his life worse, not better.

"Anyway—" Cooper spun around on his heels and hopped up the small step onto the platform "—I said I wanted to show you something. And so I do."

He touched the top of the bench. There was probably a computer screen or control panel embedded in the wood because, at the behest of his fingers, the screen on the wall flickered and an image appeared. It was a paused video image of a queue of blurry people taken from a vantage point above the entrance of some sort of building. Cooper touched the panel once more. The images started to move.

A woman's voiceover emerged from two speakers on either side of the wall: "This CCTV footage shows everything was normal at the start of the day at the cure clinic in West London." The images showed what looked to be parents and their teenage children, some of which looked barely thirteen, standing on a pathway.

"Nobody knows what happened, but something sparked the teenagers into violence."

The image changed to shaky eye-level footage of angry teenagers throwing bottles. "This footage was posted anonymously to a pro-perceivers website. Although we've been unable to verify its source, witnesses say it's an accurate reflection of what happened." A woman in a white coat was dragged by her hair out of the building and into the shade of a tree where she was kicked by a boy of about fourteen years old while an older girl urged him on.

The image then changed to show a dozen teenagers — their backs to the camera — pounding fists into the air. Chanting: "We won't be cured! We won't be cured!"

"A doctor was taken to hospital where she was treated for minor injuries," said the voiceover. "Damage to the building was superficial, but staff and visitors to the clinic have told us they were frightened for their lives."

The images became steady, sharp and professional. They were taken from outside the grounds of the building which was surrounded by the yellow tape of a police cordon. Uniformed officers stood on guard with no sign of the teenagers. This, it seemed, was the aftermath.

The camera panned to show the reporter at the scene, a suited woman in a warm coat with a scarf round her neck: the same one who provided the voiceover. "It's thought what happened here today was organised by those opposed to the normalisation of our teenagers," she said, looking directly into

Michael looked at the heavy-set older teenager with shocking blond hair and a shiver of recognition passed through him.

"I think we know who this person is, don't we?" said Cooper.

Michael shrugged.

"Oh, come on. Don't you recognise your friend? It's Oliver Smith, isn't it? The one who abandoned you in the hotel room by jumping out of the window."

"He didn't abandon me," said Michael.

"If you say so. The news report is interesting, though, don't you think?"

"Are you threatening me?" said Michael. He could be using Otis as a bargaining chip, just as he used Michael as a bargaining chip with his father.

"It's no threat, Michael. It's just more information so you can make a decision. I wanted you to realise what the world's like outside. Some perceivers — like your friend Smith — want to plunge us into civil war. I want to prevent that. Either way, perceivers will be caught in the middle. There will be no place for your kind in society, whether they're cured or arrested. What I'm offering you is a chance to avoid all of that, to serve your country."

Michael didn't want to serve a country that forced its teenagers to be 'cured' of something that wasn't a disease. He didn't want to spend the rest of his life in a cell either. Or to allow someone to get inside his mind and destroy his perception, along with whatever else of his brain in the process. He wanted another choice. He *needed* another choice.

"Why me?" said Michael.

Cooper smiled. "I thought you might ask that. Why am I wasting my time with you when there are thousands of other perceivers out there? Because you're special, Michael. If there's one thing I agree with your father about, then it's that. Have you heard of other teenagers crying out in pain when they first experience perception?"

Cooper waited, allowing Michael to consider his question.

"You haven't heard of it," said Cooper, "because it doesn't happen. Do others say they can perceive the minds of others around them all the time? That the whispers are always there in the background? They don't say it because they don't experience it. You're strong, Michael. Stronger than anyone else. Your father knew what he was doing when he created you. You can be more valuable to me than anyone else. You can perceive more than anyone else. That's why I want to find a role for you."

Michael closed his eyes. He heard the whispers inside of him. They pushed him into believing Cooper. The man he had fought so hard to run away from.

"If it matters so much to you," said Michael, "why don't you just force me?"

"I need you to do this willingly," said Cooper. "I need you to trust me and for me to trust you."

"I don't trust you," said Michael.

"But I'm telling you the truth, you must have perceived that."

Michael lowered his barrier and perceived the man who stood before him once again. Not deeply — he couldn't control his perception enough for that yet — but enough to tell he wasn't lying.

"Think about it," said Cooper. "But don't take too long or I'll have to make the decision for you."

Cooper stepped off the platform and picked the handcuffs up from the bench. "Sorry Michael, but we have to put on a show for everyone else."

Michael looked at the cuffs with disdain, a symbol of how he was locked into a choice between two unpalatable options.

"Stand up and turn around."

Michael did as he was told. He felt the metal encase his wrists.

Cooper led him back into the corridor where the woman in khaki was waiting. "Take him back to his cell."

The woman gripped Michael's arm and obeyed his order.

In his cell, he stood passively with his face towards the wall while she unlocked the restraints. As she did so, he felt something being pressed into his hand. Small, almost imperceptible. She closed his fingers around it.

He turned to face her. Instinctively, he looked beyond her eyes, into her mind. He perceived her feelings — sorry for him, but frightened and desperate for him not to react.

He said nothing and made no movement as she turned and left the cell. He waited for the sound of the guard locking the door, then sat on the bed. He opened his fist to reveal a small, scrunched up piece of paper. He unravelled it. Barely five centimetres square with torn edges, it contained a series of numbers written in blue biro:

5 9 2 0

6 4 9 1

8 7 6 4

3 0 5 5

He read them over and over again and wondered if the numbers meant what he thought they meant.

TWENTY-ONE

MICHAEL woke to the sound of his cell door being unlocked.

With sleepy eyes, he blinked into the gloom to see a hunched figure creep in.

He perceived him before he recognised him. It was Ransom.

A bundle of cloth hit him in the face.

"Put those on," whispered Ransom.

They were a pair of khaki trousers and T-shirt, like he'd seen others in the complex wear.

"I said I'd get you out of here," said Ransom. "It's time to act on that promise."

Michael stumbled out of bed and put on the clothes. He didn't have time to scramble around for a pair of underpants, so he went without.

"I thought Cooper wasn't going to let you back in here," said Michael.

"I called in some favours," said Ransom. "Now, less talking, more speed."

"What about the guard? The cameras?" said Michael.

"They were really big favours. You got the security codes?"

Michael looked at him for a moment, his mind still foggy.

"You should have a piece of paper with numbers on it," said Ransom.

Of course. Michael reached under his pillow where he had stashed the tiny scrap. He held it in his hand, not sure of what to do.

"You trust me, don't you, Michael?"

"I don't know."

"Perceive me." He opened his arms in the same gesture Michael had seen before.

Michael looked into his father's eyes. Beyond his hazel irises, deep and penetrating. A cocktail of emotions flowed from him. Anxiety, sorrow and a touch of fear — all hovering on an undercurrent of love.

Michael withdrew. He shivered. He had no love for his father — not after what he had done to him — and he had no desire to feel his father's affection for him.

"Now, would you prefer to stay in this cell, or did you want to escape?"

"Escape."

"Good man," said Ransom. "Follow me. Be quiet. And forheavensake stop looking like a nervous wreck."

Ransom peered out of the cell door, then exited into the corridor. Michael followed.

At the security door, Ransom produced a swipe card from his pocket. He grinned at Michael, then swiped it through the reader.

"Number?" said Ransom.

"Oh." Michael unfurled the scrap of paper in his hand. He tapped the first number from the list onto the pad: *5, 9, 2, 0.*

The door clicked open.

There was no guard in the corridor outside. There was no one at all. The lights were dimmed to a night time glow. They turned left. Ransom swiped the card at the next security door and Michael tapped in the second number from the scrap of paper.

The same at the next door.

At the last door, Ransom stopped. "I can't go any further."

"What do you mean?" said Michael.

"A teenager alone, dressed in those clothes, is far less conspicuous than taking me with you."

Michael looked down at the khaki he was wearing.

"There's a car," said Ransom. "Parked at the back of the building on the other side of the roundabout. A white Renault Laguna. It's unlocked. Get into the boot. Someone will drive you out through the security gates."

"Then what?"

"Then you're free to do what you want." Ransom took both of Michael's shoulders in his hands and looked him direct in the eye. The earnest anxiety coming from him was difficult to block. "But Michael, please take my advice and run. Run as far away as you can from this place. From Cooper, from your friends, from the country if you have to. I can't escape from this mess, but you can. You must."

"And you?" said Michael.

"I'm on Cooper's leash. I can't leave."

Ransom reached forward and swiped the card through the reader by the security door. Michael looked down at the list of numbers. Then back up at his father.

He hated his father. For all the things he had done to him. But he was still his father, the only link he had to his past. Suddenly, he didn't want to leave him.

Ransom must have perceived it because he said, "You need to go. Now."

"There's so many things I need to ask you," said Michael.

"No time."

Michael glanced back the way they had come. Back towards his cell. He didn't want to go back there, but if he ran, he may never know the answers to his questions — and he needed those answers.

He pushed Ransom against the wall — so fast, the man had no time to perceive him. In his surprise, Ransom's mental barrier slipped. Enough to let Michael through: beyond his eyes and into his mind.

"Show me your memories," said Michael.

"Whaa—?"

"How you created me," he insisted.

A flash:

> Ransom in his office. Younger. In shirt and tie. Sitting at his desk, silhouetted against the window. Another man stood beside him.

Flash out again. To the corridor, in the present.

Ransom resisted.

Michael pushed.

He looked deeper. He had to believe what Cooper had told him, that he was strong. Strong enough to break his father's resistance and pull the memories from his head.

"*Show me.*"

> The man standing next to Ransom's desk — unkempt with straggly hair — wedged his hands deep into his trouser pockets. "We've actually done it, Brian."
>
> "You're sure?" said the younger Ransom.
>
> "Oh yes. We've found the gene that causes perception."
>
> "Will my children be perceivers?"
>
> "You carry the gene. There's a fifty per cent chance. If the donor egg comes from a perceiver too, then I'd say, Brian, it's pretty likely…"

The memory dissolved.

"Show me more." Michael concentrated harder, deeper.

The same unkempt man, but at a later time in his life when he had shorter hair, in an armchair in someone's house. Ransom sat opposite him. In Ransom's memory was the bitter smell of black coffee that drifted up from the mug in his hands.

"You sure you want to do this?" said the man, who Ransom remembered was called Lockwood.

"Think of a world where everyone can perceive each other," said Ransom. "Think how people would understand each other. Conflict would be reduced. People would be happier."

"Sounds too good to be true," said Lockwood.

"I know. But you can't deny that life's been better for us with perception." Ransom sipped his coffee. It was hot. It scalded his lip.

"Sure. I applaud what you're doing, Brian, you know that. There's just a little bit of me that's frightened we're trying too hard to play God."

"God or fate or evolution gave us this gift," said Ransom. "We were born with it. You've got to remember, what we have is a natural genetic mutation which is already spreading among the population. All we're doing is helping evolution along a bit."

"By triggering the change in children who would otherwise have been born normal," said Lockwood.

"Right." Ransom blew steam from his coffee and took another tentative mouthful. "I have no regrets. I made sure I gave this gift to my child, didn't I?"

The memory dissolved.

Then re-formed.

Ransom squinted into bright lights as camera lenses stared at him and an array of microphones pointed at him. A gallery of journalists in suits watched him, all looking silly in the hairnets the regulations insisted they wore.

Ransom — also suited — stood in a factory. Behind him were stilled machines and operatives in white coats and hygiene hats. Next to him was a heavily pregnant woman beside him.

Michael's own memory flashed in — this was the press conference he had seen on Otis's phone, the one where Ransom announced his plan to give away free vitamins to pregnant women. Except he was seeing it from Ransom's perspective, not that of the news camera. He also realised that the pregnant woman had to be his mother and, inside her bump, was the baby version of himself.

Ransom remembered his feelings of overwhelming love and pride. For the woman at his side, for the child she was carrying, and for the produce of the factory behind him.

"When Mary and I—" he gave his wife a little squeeze "— embarked on the adventure of having a baby, we were lucky. We had money to buy the best care and the best doctors. Not everyone has that opportunity, so I wanted to do my bit to help. That's why — today — I am offering pregnant women across the country free vitamin supplements. In itself, this small gesture cannot ensure optimum health for mother and baby, but it is my way of helping them towards that goal."

He stood aside to reveal two plastic buttons — one red, one green — set into the metal framework of the nearest machine and protected behind a transparent plastic box. Ransom opened the box, reached inside and put his hand on the green button. He turned to look at the cameras and journalists. He made an effort to smile in the glare of the lights and pushed.

The factory came to life. The machines whirred and shuffled as they launched into their automated motions and began to churn out little orange pills.

Ransom stepped aside and allowed the journalists to take it all in. And, out of the glare of the cameras, he kissed his wife gently on the cheek. A swell of love, care and protection welled inside of him. "I'll meet you in the reception area, okay?"

Mary smiled. "See you in a minute."

As she departed, leaning back slightly to balance the weight of her pregnant body, a seriousness came over Ransom. He looked up as Rachel Page approached him from behind the reporter throng. Like the factory workers, she wore a white coat and hat with a net holding her hair at the back.

"You did it, Brian," she said.

"Guess so," said Ransom.

"You're really going to change the world."

"For the better, I hope," he said.

Michael pulled himself out of the memory.

He was back in the corridor. He let go of Ransom and stepped back. He perceived the man's violation, but Michael didn't care. He'd got the information he wanted.

"It's true," Michael said. "Your vitamin pills caused perception."

Ransom said nothing. His embarrassment and shame said it all for him.

"You created all this!" He gestured to indicate the complex they were in. "It's all your fault."

"I didn't know it was going to be like this," said Ransom. "I swear."

Michael turned away from him in disgust.

"I perceive what you think of me, Michael. But I can't change it. Lord! If I could go back in time … All I can do is try to make amends now."

"Is that what the cure clinics are?"

Ransom's regret filled the corridor. "You need to go, Michael. A lot of people took risks so I could get you out of here. I perceive you don't care what happens to me, but — for their sake, if not your own — get out of here."

Ransom swiped the card on the reader.

Michael wasn't ready to let go the feeling of disgust.

"Please," said Ransom. His eyes went down to the scrap of paper in Michael's hand. Michael's eyes followed. He read the last number on the list — 3, 0, 5, 5 — and tapped it onto the number pad. The door clicked and he opened it.

He took one last look at Ransom — his father; violated, ashamed and pathetic — and stepped outside.

TWENTY-TWO

THE dark of night brought an eerie quiet to the complex. Four street lights around the edge of the grass roundabout covered everything in a yellow glow. The roads were without cars, the paths were without people and the swish of wind rustling through the trees was without birdsong. Michael opened his perception. Even the minds around him were quiet. And distant. He was almost alone, apart from the two soldiers standing guard with their rifles at the gate.

Michael leant back into the protection of the doorway. A chasm lay between him and the building across the grass. There was no way to get there other than walking out into the open. He thought about running or trying to skulk undetected. But he remembered his father's words, that a teenager dressed like him would be unlikely to raise suspicion. So he walked with confidence, out of the doorway, onto the tarmac and around to the other side of the roundabout.

All the time, he kept his perception open for danger.

A path led around the back of the building to a small car park with painted markings showing spaces for six cars. Only one car was actually parked there: an estate car with Renault Laguna written on its back bumper and white bodywork which was clearly visible in the night.

Michael clicked the catch on the boot. As promised, it was unlocked. He opened it to its full height and revealed a space big enough for him to crawl inside.

He clambered in and curled his knees up before reaching to pull the hatch down. He suddenly thought — if Ransom's plan went wrong, he wouldn't be able to get out. There was no handle on the inside. Once the hatch was closed, it would remain closed until someone on the outside opened it again.

Michael swallowed his fear. He pulled the hatch and it slammed shut, locking him in the dark hole just big enough for his body. He hoped hadn't traded one cell for another.

IT could have been ten minutes, it could have been half an hour, that he waited huddled in the darkness. Lying on the thin mat that covered the metal chassis of the car, he got progressively colder. The mat had the faint smell of sour milk which, he imagined, had got spilt there on the way back from the supermarket one day and never properly washed out of the carpet.

A click sent a subtle vibration through the body of the car. It was a car door opening. The floor moved with a gentle bounce as the suspension adjusted to someone getting into the car. The door closed again with a clunk that sent more vibrations through the metal.

The engine started up — shaking the whole compartment — then settled to a steady rumble. Wheels propelled the machine from beneath. He felt each gear change, and each turn of direction as the car headed — he hoped — for freedom.

He reached out to perceive the driver. It wasn't easy to sense whoever it was. Whether it was because he couldn't see them or because they were further away, he wasn't sure. All he sensed was a hint of their concentration and a little anxiety.

The car stopped. The engine died and the chassis stilled.

Michael's own nervousness welled in his stomach. They hadn't gone far enough to be out of the complex, he was sure.

The volume on the driver's anxiety dialled up a notch. And there were other presences outside. Tired ones, trying to stay awake and alert, but still too distant from him to get a clear picture.

He heard voices. He listened hard, but couldn't make out the words. Just the pitch of a man and a woman. Conversing calmly.

A click of a car door opening.

Nervous waiting.

The door slammed shut, the car rocked, he jumped.

Another door opened. *What was going on?*

The voices neared. He heard the odd word. "Working late … yeah … not long … the boot."

Michael tensed. The minds were close now. The nervous driver was the closest. A woman's voice: "… can look if you like."

A loud, terrifying click close to his ear. The boot — open a crack — opening wider.

Michael stared into the night, waiting for the trigger which would tell him to run.

The opening hatch revealed a tall woman standing at the back of the car. Michael recognised her instantly as the woman who'd handcuffed him, the same one who had slipped him the piece of paper. The nervousness was coming from her, *she* was the driver.

She shot a warning glance at him and the words 'stay there' reached his mind.

She looked away from Michael — towards someone else he couldn't see — with a fake smile. "There really is nothing in here."

Michael crunched himself up as small as he could.

"Yeah, yeah," said a bored man's voice. "Off you go." He didn't even look!

Slam.

The boot closed. Michael was shut back in his tiny cell again. Safe.

He let out a long breath he didn't know he was holding and perceived the driver's relief.

The engine shuddered to life again and they were driving.

Through — Michael imagined — the gate at the complex and away from the two bored soldiers with rifles who were too tired to properly check an outgoing vehicle.

After a while, the car settled down to a steady rumble with no gear changes and few turns. For what could have been half an hour. Until it slowed, came to a halt and the engine stilled.

The boot opened.

The woman stood before him. Nervousness still seeping from her. "Get out," she whispered, beckoning him with her hand.

Michael unfurled himself and stepped out of the car. He shivered at the cold and stretched his stiff muscles.

They were alone. Parked on a strip of rough ground at the side of a quiet road.

The woman reached into the back pocket of her trousers and pulled out a brown, sealed envelope. "Here."

Michael took the package. It was light and slim.

"Money," said the woman. "Enough to get you away from here."

"Where?"

"Not my department. I agreed to get you out. That's all." She slammed the boot shut and went back to the driver's seat.

"Wait!" said Michael.

He headed after her, but she was already inside.

He put his body between her and the car door so she couldn't close it. "Why are you doing this?" he asked.

"You don't need to know that," she said.

But Michael perceived a flash of something. An image of a girl, about Jennifer's age, in school uniform. "Your daughter? She's a perceiver?"

"She was." A sadness in her voice and her mind. "Please move, I need to go before I'm missed."

Michael stepped back. She closed the driver's door and started the engine. As she moved off, he realised he hadn't thanked her. He ran after the car. "Thank you!" he said. But she was gone.

He watched the red of her tail lights until they disappeared around a corner at the end of the road. Then he was truly alone. He couldn't perceive anybody. It was gloriously quiet. He savoured the feeling. It reminded him of what it had been like to be a norm. He felt a twinge of nostalgia.

But he wasn't a norm anymore. And he couldn't stay on that road forever.

To his right, glowed the lights of a town. He didn't know what he was going to do, but he had to start somewhere. He started by walking towards the town.

TWENTY-THREE

MICHAEL reached the outskirts of the town as night turned to dawn. It was called Ruislip, according to the sign he passed on the outskirts. A place not far from London and, judging by the length of the car journey, not that far from the complex either. Cooper was most likely to start looking for him there. He had probably less than an hour before his escape was discovered and maybe another one or two hours before he needed to be out of Ruislip.

Up ahead, two people waiting at a bus shelter leant out towards the traffic and waved. A bus, with West Ruislip illuminated in red letters above the windscreen, blinked its left indicator and slowed to a stop beside them. Michael ran and got to the bus just as the second person flashed their travel card at the driver and moved inside to try to find a seat among the crowd.

"Single please," Michael said, breathless, as he clambered on board.

"Where to?" said the driver, a gaunt man whose bus company tie was skewed sideways with the knot half under the flap of his collar.

Michael hadn't thought where he was going. Anywhere and fast were his only criteria. "To the end of the line," he said. He pulled the cash the woman had given him from his pocket.

The driver gave Michael a hard stare as he took the twenty pound note. He fiddled with getting the change which he slammed down on the tray in front of him. *Bloody teenagers*, he seemed to say, although he didn't open his mouth.

Michael squeezed his way down the aisle of the bus, past several people standing in the way. Each with a resentment that he, a teenager, should be polluting their territory. There was one free seat about two thirds of the way down, next to a woman with bold make-up. As he closed in on it, she lifted the rucksack from her lap and put it on the empty seat. He stopped. She glared at him — resolute — with tight, dark red lips. He reached for the metal pole beside him and held onto it as the bus jerked forward.

He turned his back on the woman, but he still perceived her. That determination she had to stop him sitting down had turned to self-satisfaction. Michael concentrated on blocking her out, and the hatred from every commuter on that bus who didn't want to share their journey with a teenager.

The end of the line was West Ruislip train station. Michael got off and stood beside a busy dual carriageway while the other passengers filed past him. Most walked up the street to a pedestrian crossing where they could get to the station opposite. Michael realised he'd stumbled on the right place for a quick getaway and followed them.

By the look of it, West Ruislip was little more than an outpost of the British rail network. The station was no bigger than a shop and contained a few ticket barriers, ticket desk and kiosk. It was far too small for the number of suited commuters flowing through its doors. Few stopped to buy tickets, they just pulled their season pass out of their pockets, waved it across a sensor by the barrier which opened with a double flap of doors and allowed the commuter through.

Hardly any of them spoke to each other, which meant the hubbub of the station was a mix of shuffling feet and flapping ticket barriers.

A smell stirred Michael's stomach. He sniffed the air. Bacon, sausage and fried onions. The kiosk he was standing next to — with its display of newspapers, chocolates and fridge containing sandwiches and fizzy drinks — was cooking breakfast baps. His stomach grumbled.

Michael fingered the cash in his pocket. He had enough to spend on breakfast. He bought a bap with sausage, onions and tomato sauce. The anticipation of food was so great, that by the time he took a bite, his mouth and stomach had prepared themselves with saliva and gastric juices. The taste didn't disappoint, with the primal pleasure of cooked, fatty meat with the bite of onion and the tang of sauce. He had barely swallowed before he took another bite.

In front of the kiosk, still eating, with juice running down his hand, he looked up at the display board which hung from the ceiling and perused its choice of destinations.

He remembered what Ransom had said, to get as far away as he could. But he also remembered his friends and what they had sacrificed for him. Especially Jennifer. He wanted to see Jennifer again more than anything. So he searched for a train that would take him back into London.

He saw something that froze his stomach mid-digestion. In the upper corner of the station, staring down, was a CCTV camera. His eyes flashed around. He saw no others, but where there was one, there would be more. They were watching him; had probably been watching him from the moment he stepped off the street.

How stupid!

He'd walked straight into one of the most likely of places to have surveillance. If Cooper's men came looking for him there — and surely they would — they would find him on the digital recording: a teenager in T-shirt and trouser fatigues standing in a sea of suited commuters, looking up at the camera like an idiot.

He checked the departure board again. There was a service head-ing for Princes Risborough in ten minutes. If he hurried, he could get on it.

There were several machines lined up along the right hand side, but he ignored them. Instead, he queued at the ticket booth where a ginger-haired man in his twenties (who knew how to tie his tie straight) took an extortionate amount of money for a one-way fare to Princes Risborough.

Queuing took longer than he hoped and left him with only two minutes to catch the train. He ran to the platform and hopped on board. As he caught his breath, he saw he was one of only half a dozen people in the carriage, representatives of a rare breed of traveller who commuted out of London for work. Michael took a seat close to the door and waited.

About thirty seconds later, a warning bleep rang out, the doors slid shut and the train eased itself out of the station.

It wasn't like the bus. The other passengers were wrapped up in their own business and took no notice of Michael. It did nothing to ease his nerves. He was fully aware he couldn't rely on the train to do his running away for him. He had to keep one step ahead of Cooper.

His eye was on a suited man at the end of the carriage where the aisle narrowed to make room for a toilet cubicle. The man sat by the window, sharing his attention between the polluted buildings outside and the phone on his knee. He'd taken off his suit jacket and thrown it across the seat next to him.

Michael stood and sauntered up the aisle towards the toilet. On the way — lightly, without drawing attention — he rested his hand on the man's jacket. He swiped it off the seat as he passed and dis-appeared into the toilet.

He locked the door and breathed a sigh of relief. He heard no shouts or cries, no commotion from the carriage. The man probably hadn't even noticed his jacket was missing.

Michael tried it on. He looked at his reflection in the scuffed mirror above the sink where someone had left a ball of soggy toilet paper. The jacket hung off his shoulders and the arms reached down to below his wrists, but it disguised his khaki T-shirt and that's all he needed.

The train slowed as it approached a station. Michael unlocked the toilet door and emerged back into the narrow corridor. Behind him was the carriage he'd left and, in front, a rubber floor and two connecting doors. He went through into the adjoining carriage as the train stopped. The doors opened, he jumped out of the carriage and onto the platform. Part of him wanted to turn round to see that man's face staring out of the window as the train departed, watching his jacket disappear from view.

But Michael needed to act with stealth, not bravado.

He walked down the steps, off the platform, where a sign facing him revealed he was at Denham train station. Beside it was a ticket machine. Michael used it to buy a ticket to London, then made his way across to the other platform.

As he boarded the train going in the opposite direction, he allowed himself a smile. He hoped Cooper had assumed Michael would use public transport to get out of Ruislip. That he would have seen him on the CCTV at the train station buying a ticket at the booth. That he would interview the man there and discover Michael had bought a ticket to Princes Risborough. His men would then be dispatched to Princes Risborough station in order to catch Michael as he arrived. Except, he would never arrive. Because he never had any intention of going all the way to Princes Risborough. And no one was looking for a teenager in an oversize black jacket heading into London.

LONDON was a big place. A very large haystack in which to search for Jennifer and Otis needles. Michael didn't know where to start looking and ended up on a bus heading for the street where they used to live. It was foolish to think Jennifer and Otis would have gone back there. The likelihood was Cooper had known about it and searched it, but he had to check. He'd heard Otis say once, decent squats were like gold dust. As soon as one lot of squatters moved out, another lot moved in. Maybe that had happened in their old flat. Maybe the new tenants had information on where the old tenants had gone.

After perceiving no one was keeping watch on the flat, Michael arrived to find a group of workmen stripping it bare. He watched from across the road as the sofa he once slept on was manhandled out of the entrance of the block and thrown into a skip parked outside. It was only a bit of old, lumpy furniture, but it made him feel sad.

"What's going on?" Michael asked one of the workmen.

"Bunch of squatters've been living in there. Place is bloody disgusting. Landlord's doing it up to sell."

If there'd been any clues in the flat as to where Otis and Jennifer had gone, they'd already been torn to shreds and thrown away.

BY the end of the day, Michael's reservoir of money had dwindled. A combination of takeaway food plus train, tube and bus fares had eaten into it badly. He could spend more on a hotel overnight, but continue like that and he'd have nothing left to eat with.

So he opted for a park bench. He'd slept rough before, he could do it again.

He'd forgotten the cold and the damp. And, with winter closing in, the temperature dropped off sharply overnight. Then there was the fear. That he'd be attacked or mugged or found by one of Cooper's men. So, although he lay down and closed his eyes, he didn't sleep.

In the morning, he used some of his precious cash to buy a phone. He chose a second hand device which he recognised as the same model Jennifer used to have. He remembered the thing being easy to use, but without all her settings programmed into it, he struggled to get the information he wanted. He suspected he would have been good at that sort of thing before his memories were destroyed, but now he felt like a caveman trying to program a computer.

He wanted to get on the perceivers network. But it was, by its nature, a secretive group which not only had to stay ahead of the internet police trying to shut it down, but also was picky about who it let in. Add to that Michael's ineptitude with the phone, and it equalled a lot of frustration.

In the end he gave up and used the phone to call Sian Jones, Jennifer's reporter friend at *The Daily News*. *The Daily News* had a website with the main number on it, so he didn't have to use much cunning to get put through to her desk. Within the hour, he was sitting in the same American-style diner where they had first met and using a fork to pick cubes of ice out of his Coke before dropping them into the empty serviette holder.

Sian arrived looking hassled. She spotted Michael and gave him a wave of acknowledgement before dashing over towards him, her bulbous handbag suspended from her elbow and bouncing off her hip as she walked.

She sat opposite him with a heavy sigh. She threw out her arm to a passing waitress — as if hailing a bus — and ordered tea.

Sian sighed a second time and sat back in her seat. "Glad you called. It's mad at the office."

"I didn't pull you away from anything important, did I?" said Michael.

She waved away his concern. "Oh, only a meeting I wanted to get out of. So, what's up?"

A lot of things. But only one that he'd come to talk to her about. "Jennifer."

"Oh, how is she? I wondered how she was getting on."

"I don't know, that's the thing." Michael took a self-conscious sip of his Coke. "She's gone missing."

"If I remember correctly, wasn't she already officially classed as missing?"

"Not a missing person. Jennifer…" Michael paused. "Jennifer… Well, a little while ago, Jennifer was cured and now I can't find her."

"Oh." The waitress brought over Sian's tea and placed it in front of her. Sian didn't seem to notice. "You surprise me. Jennifer doesn't strike me as the sort of girl who'd want to take the cure."

"It wasn't voluntary," said Michael.

"I see."

"I don't know where else to look. I thought — you being a journalist and everything — you might have some ideas."

Sian shrugged. "I know a few tricks."

She reached into her bag and began rummaging. From the bottom she pulled out a tablet computer. She scrolled through a number of screens using the fingers of her right hand, while her left picked up a spoon and stirred her tea with the teabag still in it.

"Hmm," she said, eventually.

"Hmm what?" said Michael.

"She's not listed."

Michael's confusion must have shown on his face, because she turned the screen around and pushed it across the table for him to see.

It was a website detailing a list of missing persons. Name after name after name. Michael's gaze drifted down them, not really reading, not really understanding.

"Just 'cos she's not listed as missing, doesn't mean she's not missing," he said.

"Ah, but it might." Sian squeezed the teabag against the side of the mug and dropped it into the serviette holder where the steaming ball quickened the melting of Michael's shrinking ice cubes.

"Look," said Sian. "We already know Jennifer ran away from home, right?"

"Yeah."

"I found out because her parents listed her as missing on this website." Sian reached over and tapped the screen with her fingernail. She inadvertently hit one of the names on the list and the details of a missing teenager named Ed Gishtari filled the screen.

"But she's not listed there anymore?"

"Right."

Michael thought over what she said, trying to piece together the clues. "You think she's gone back home?"

"That would be my guess," said Sian. "If she ran away from home because of her perception, makes sense she might return home after being cured."

"I suppose…"

It was hard to think of Jennifer at home with a family of her own. Michael pushed Sian's tablet back across her side of the table. "Do you have her home address?"

"I should think so," said Sian. She took a gulp of her tea and resumed pulling up webpages on the screen. By the time she lifted the mug to her lips again, Michael perceived a sense of triumph within her. "There, that was easy."

"So, where is she?" Michael said.

"Hmm," said Sian. "You know what I'm thinking?"

Michael did to a certain extent. He couldn't hear her thoughts as such, like he had with the bus driver, but he perceived something devious going on in her mind. Sian had only agreed to their first meeting on condition she got information out of Jennifer. Michael got the feeling this time was going to be no different.

"I'm thinking this could be a story," said Sian.

"Jennifer's not a story," said Michael, "she's my friend."

"My editor might be interested in a teenager who didn't want the cure, but is now living with the consequences of being normal," said

Sian. "The media's full of how fantastic this cure is and how it's going to save the world, etc etc. It's about time we put the other side of the story, don't you think?"

TWENTY-FOUR

MICHAEL didn't want to go with the journalist. He wanted to see Jennifer alone. But the word 'no' was just another way of saying 'yes' in Sian Jones's vocabulary and she wouldn't listen to argument. So, half an hour after meeting her in the diner, he was sitting in the passenger seat of her car, taking a drive out to Hemel Hempstead where Jennifer's parents lived.

They stopped in a residential street of terraced houses, romantically called Jupiter Drive, and parked outside a house with a little grass front garden and a neatly trimmed bush under the front window. He found it difficult to imagine Jennifer living inside. It was so different to the untidy squat he associated her with.

Sian turned off the engine and unclipped her seatbelt. "Ready?"

Suddenly he wasn't ready at all. *What if Jennifer didn't want to see him? What if Jennifer's mother answered the door?*

Sian was already out of the car and heading up the path. Michael unclipped his seatbelt and jumped after her. She'd rung the doorbell before Michael joined her at the head of the garden path. He stood up straight and tried to look presentable. He brushed down the stolen oversize jacket he still wore and hoped it was enough to create a good impression.

A woman, rubbing damp hands on a blue and white striped tea towel, teased open the door and stuck her head between the gap.

"Yes?"

The woman was old enough to be in her forties, with grey streaks through her brown hair.

"Mrs Price?" said Sian.

"Yes?" She opened the door a little further.

"My name's Sian Jones. I'm from *The Daily News*. I don't know if you remember, but Jennifer helped me out when she did work experience at the paper."

"Oh yes," said Mrs Price. The door opened fully. She relaxed.

"And this is Michael, a friend of Jennifer's."

Michael attempted a friendly smile. "Hi," he said, somewhat pathetically.

"I wondered …" Sian continued talking, but Michael stopped hearing her words.

His mind perceived something familiar. A presence that he had never felt before, yet instantly knew. He peered beyond the woman into the darkness of her hallway. There, clutching onto the end of the banister at the bottom of the stairs like a shy five-year-old, was Jennifer. Her sleek, brown skin, black skirt and T-shirt camouflaged her against the shadows.

"Jennifer?" His words interrupted the women's conversation. They turned to look at him.

Jennifer took a step further into the hall. A stream of light from the open doorway fell across her face. He perceived her hope and disbelief and, in that moment, knew it was her.

"Michael?" Her eyes brightened with recognition. Joy flooded out of her in such a rush it almost knocked him over.

She ran to the front door, squeezed herself through the gap between her mother and the doorframe and out onto the garden path. She flung her arms around him. "Michael, you're alive! You're alive!"

Her emotion was so powerful, Michael had to raise his blocks against her. Physically, she overwhelmed him with a hug incredibly strong for such a skinny teenager.

"Of course I'm alive." He pulled her away from him and looked her in the face. Tears fell silently from her eyes, down her cheeks and to the corners of her smiling mouth. But beyond the emotion of the moment, she looked unwell. Her complexion had lost some of its natural iridescence and he could see the angle of her bones beneath the skin of her already-thin body.

"Why didn't you call me?" said Jennifer.

"I didn't have your number," said Michael.

"But you found my house."

"Sian found it, really."

Jennifer turned to her mother. "Mum, can Michael come in?"

"I don't see why not," said her mother.

Jennifer took Michael's hand and pulled him inside with child-like excitement. Behind them, he heard Mrs Price inviting Sian inside.

Jennifer led Michael through the hall and up the stairs. It was such a relief to see her. He'd been so worried. His body responded to being close to a beautiful girl he had liked for a long time. It was automatic, embarrassing, he couldn't control it. He tried to hide his embarrassment as she took him into her bedroom.

The room had the essence of her. That same smell that filled his nostrils when she was close, that made him want to get even closer. A subtle scent that hung unobtrusively in the air. But, to look at it, the room was like a little girl's bedroom.

It was bright, with early afternoon sun streaming through the window, past the pastel curtains with their pink rose pattern, and alighting on the painted yellow walls. A child-size desk with a computer, yellowed by age, sat on the top, along with a jumble of random things: a book wedged open by a pair of sunglasses, a hairbrush and a make-up bag with a mascara and lipstick sticking out of it. Her single bed, clothed also in yellow, stuck out in the middle of the room with the headboard pressed against the wall. Sitting on the pillow, with its legs splayed out in an unnatural position was a cuddly giraffe.

Once inside with the door shut, Jennifer opened out her hand. "Give me your phone."

Michael passed it over.

Jennifer tapped something into the device and handed it back. "Now you have my number."

"Thanks."

She went over to the computer. "I want to show you what I've been doing."

"Can't that wait?" said Michael.

She tapped a couple of keys on the keyboard and the screen came to life. "I've been in touch with the network, we're getting organised, we're—"

"Jennifer …"

"—really taking a stand now. More and more people are getting in touch with us."

"Jennifer, can you leave that for a moment?"

She turned back, blinking at him, uncomprehending.

Michael stepped backwards and sat slowly on the bed. The springs, made for a smaller person than him, gave way under his weight. "Sit down."

"Michael, don't you want to see?"

"In a minute."

She paused. "Okay."

She sat.

"Are you okay?" said Michael.

"Why wouldn't I be?"

"Because of what Cooper did to you."

He perceived the pain she was trying to hide from him. She averted her eyes.

"Look at me."

She kept her eyes fixed on the patch of duvet that lay between them.

"Please." His fingers touched her soft chin and eased her face back towards him. "I was worried about you. Are you sure you're all right?"

"Of course!" A false smile. It hid the sadness in her expression, but Michael perceived her repressed emotion building inside of her.

"Let me see." He looked into her eyes.

"No, Michael."

"I'll be gentle," he whispered.

He looked into her. Like she once did to him, so long ago. Beyond the surface of her face, past the iris and into the pupil of her eyes. He opened his perception and took in everything that was her. He felt the same fear she felt. Understood her vulnerability. Saw what it was like to be a perceiver stripped of her perception: lost in a world where sight, sound, smell and touch were pale senses. The teenager she once was, was only a memory. She was like a child again, protected against the world in the comfort of her childhood home, with a mother to look after her and a toy giraffe to cuddle at night.

Michael pulled back. He didn't want to probe deeper. He didn't need to. All her feelings were just under the surface.

"Did you …?" Tears were welling in her eyes again. "Were you perceiving me just then?"

"Yes."

The tears fell slowly from her cheeks. "It's weird."

"What is?"

"I couldn't feel you at all."

"You don't mind, do you?"

She shrugged. "I don't know."

"I only did it because I'm worried about you."

"I'm fine. I said I'm fine."

"You came back home. I didn't ever think you would do that."

"I only left because they wanted me to have the cure," said Jennifer. "After … well, after what happened, there wasn't any reason to stay away anymore."

"Your mum seems nice," said Michael, trying to be more cheery.

Jennifer rolled her eyes. "Yeah."

"And your dad …"

"At work. He's nice too. It's like they're walking on eggshells, though. Don't want to do or say the wrong thing. It's driving Janey mad."

"Janey?"

"My sister."

"Oh."

"She's at school."

"I see."

There was so much Michael wanted to say to her, but he didn't have the words. "Have you seen Otis?" he said, eventually.

"A couple of times," she said. "He's in London, so it's difficult."

Michael nodded. His eye caught the bright colours of the webpage on the computer screen. "You said there was something you wanted to show me?"

"Yes!" Jennifer got off the bed, her mood suddenly brighter, and went to the computer. "We've been arranging protests at cure clinics."

"I saw the news report — that was you?"

She nodded with pride. With a click, the screen displayed a page listing all of the cure clinic protests. There were more than Michael expected. About ten over the past couple of weeks. In Manchester, London, Liverpool, Guildford, Belfast and others, where clinics had to be closed for a day or where people were arrested.

"I thought the government kept shutting down your websites," said Michael.

"We've got a computer whizz who's a perceiver. He keeps the site one step ahead of the authorities."

"Jennifer …?" he asked.

"Yes?" Her eyes still bright with enthusiasm that poured, unrestrained, out of her. If she saw his doubtful expression, she didn't register it. After a lifetime of perception, she probably didn't know how to read the signs.

"On the news," said Michael, "the report I saw … it was — well, it wasn't very favourable. Teenagers throwing bottles and attacking doctors."

"We're making a stand, Michael. At last. We're showing them we're not going to lie down and take it."

"The news report made perceivers look like terrorists. Like the quicker they round us all up and cure us, the better."

"They're taking away what we are, Michael! Can't you see?" Tears formed in her eyes again. Tears of anger and frustration. "We have to stop them. Whatever way we can."

In the tense silence that followed, Jennifer's mother called from downstairs. "Jennifer? Are you all right up there?"

"Yeah!" she shouted back.

"I've made some tea, why don't you come down?"

"In a minute," shouted Jennifer.

"Okay, but don't let it get cold."

Michael felt the edge of her anger subside. The red of her cheeks faded and her breath returned to its normal steady rhythm.

"If you're going to win this war, you need to convince people," he said. "Not just other perceivers, but adults. I know you want to fight back, but violence will turn people against you."

Jennifer threw her arms up in the air in despair and flopped down on the bed. Her volatile emotions turned to regret. "It wasn't my idea to hurt the doctors. I wanted our protest to be loud, to make a fuss, not to be violent. But a lot of the kids are angry."

Michael sat beside her. He took her hand and cradled it in his own. Her skin was soft, it felt nice to touch her. "I understand," he said.

"I haven't told you about Monday!" She was suddenly excited again.

"Monday?"

"Yes! We're gonna hold a massive protest in London. Every perceiver we can get in touch with is going to be there. We're going to march on Parliament."

"Won't most teenagers be at school?" said Michael.

"Not on Monday. They're going to skip school and come into London. A whole mass of people telling the government we haven't got some horrible disease, that we don't want to be cured of who we are."

Her eyes bright. Expectant, waiting for Michael's approval.

A shout from downstairs: "Jennifer! Tea's getting cold."

She ignored it. "Well?"

"Sounds like they're going to have to listen to you."

She smiled. "I think so. But it's a secret. You can't tell anyone. Only 'ceivers."

"Sure," he said.

"Promise?"

"Scout's honour." He lifted two fingers to his temple in salute.

"Were you a scout?" she said.

"I can't remember," said Michael.

She laughed. A delicate, beautiful laugh. She turned to the bedroom door and shouted, "Coming, Mum!" She took Michael's hand and led him back down the stairs.

SIAN'S car bumbled down the M1 back towards London. Her mind was alive with excitement. She was more buzzed about her newspaper article than she had been when she first offered to drive Michael to Hemel Hempstead to find Jennifer. He couldn't figure out why.

A thought … *could be big* … drifted over from Sian's mind.

He hadn't been eavesdropping, but it intrigued him, so he concentrated: *Need to call Mark... he perceived. ... Hands free kit's in my bag... Wish I didn't have this damn kid in the car...*

Michael stared across at her. Outwardly, she appeared not to care he was sitting next to her in the passenger seat. Her eyes were on the road with one hand drumming on the steering wheel and the other clutching the gear leaver. Inwardly, something was festering. A frustration at the traffic and a resentment at Michael being there.

Mark's going to go for it... He's got to... Thank God Ted's on holiday... If I get home before six — God, don't say I'm going to hit the rush hour — then I can... Mark will go for it, I know he will...

He pulled his phone from his pocket and awoke the screen with a touch of his finger. The contacts page was still active where Jennifer had typed in her number. Michael texted: 'S v. excited bout story. What did U tell her?'

They turned off the M1 onto the North Circular and hit stop-start London traffic.

"Who's Mark?" Michael asked.

"What?" Sian woke from her driver's daze.

"Who's Mark? You mentioned him back at the house," he lied.

"I did?" Annoyance at his question. "I don't remember."

"Yeah, you said you needed to call him about something."

"Oh, did I?" It was a reasonable explanation of how he'd heard the name. Although untrue, she accepted it and became less defensive. "Mark's my editor. Acting editor, really. He's stepping up while Ted's on holiday."

"Is that bad?" said Michael.

"Good," said Sian. "Ted didn't like me bringing perceiver stories to him. I think he was under government pressure to toe the official line, not as if I ever had any proof. But Mark... well, he's got two weeks while Ted's in the Maldives — or wherever he is — to make his mark, so to speak."

"And that's why you have to call him?"

"Got to tell the editor what story you're working on."

"Feature," corrected Michael.

"What?"

"Feature. You said 'story'."

"Story/feature — same thing," said Sian.

But it wasn't, if he perceived her correctly. Michael reached for his phone: 'Don't think S is writing "feature". Text me.' He hit send.

Damn this traffic … she kept thinking … gotta get the kid out of the car … gotta ring Mark … he'll need to bump the lead and it's getting late …

As they turned off the North Circular onto the Hendon Way, Sian turned apologetically to Michael. "I'm running really late. I'm not going to be able to take you all the way into town. I'll drop you at Cricklewood train station. It's hardly centre of the universe, but there's a quick service into St Pancras and you can get where you need to go from there."

"Okay," said Michael.

Up ahead a road sign indicated it was only a mile to Cricklewood. He hadn't got much more time to find out the story in her head.

"What are you running late for?" he asked.

"Deadlines," said Sian. "Always deadlines."

"You're going to write up the stuff about Jennifer tonight?"

"While it's fresh," she said.

"I thought, with a feature, there wouldn't be so much urgency."

Bloody children and their bloody questions. "No urgency."

Michael looked at his phone. He brushed a finger across the screen to wake it up. Still nothing from Jennifer. 'Where R U?'

A few minutes more and Sian turned right. Ahead of them loomed Cricklewood train station.

"Nearly here," said Sian, with relief.

"Thanks for the lift," said Michael.

"No problem," she said, even though her feelings said different.

"So you think Mark will be happy to run the story then?" he prompted.

"I would think so." *I got an exclusive, he better bloody run it.*

"What angle are you going with?"

"Angle? It's a feature, there is no angle." *Demonstration to bring London to a standstill… schoolchildren planning to abandon their classrooms…*

And Michael had his answer. She knew about the planned demonstration, the one Jennifer said was secret.

They pulled up at the taxi rank at the front of the station. "There isn't going to be a feature, is there?" said Michael.

A pleasant, puzzled smile masked her lying face. "You think I'd drive all the way to Hemel Hempstead and back for nothing?" she said.

"Don't run the story," said Michael.

Anger boiling within her. *How does he know? Does he just suspect?* "You need to get out now, Michael, I'm not supposed to park here."

Michael gave her a hard stare. There was nothing inside her that seemed ashamed at what she had done. He punched at the clasp holding the seatbelt. It leapt out of the holster. "Jennifer wouldn't want you to run it." He got out of the car.

The forecourt of the station smelt of the exhaust of half a dozen running taxi engines. Dirty and polluting, like the journalist.

He was about to close the passenger door when Sian leant across the seat. "It'll be fine, Michael. The publicity will be good for Jennifer, you'll see."

He perceived she meant what she said. She had no remorse.

Michael slammed the door and watched her drive off.

He dialled Jennifer's number on his phone.

It rang for a long time before someone answered. "Hello?"

He put a finger in his other ear and turned away from the noisy road. "Jennifer?"

"Yeah."

"It's Michael. Where have you been? I've been texting you."

"Sorry. I was at dinner. Mum's banned phones from the table."

"Did you tell Sian about the demonstration?"

"What?"

Louder: "Did you tell Sian about the demonstration?"

"The journalist? No! Are you a skank?"

"She knows."

"It's supposed to be a secret," said Jennifer.

"I didn't tell her!" said Michael.

"Then, how—"

"I was thinking, maybe your mum …?"

Silence on the other end of the phone. A strange nothingness in his head — he couldn't perceive Jennifer at such a distance, even though her voice had been right there in his ear.

Jennifer swore. "I told her not to say anything."

"You mean you told her? Why on earth …?"

"She kept going on about how I needed to do something with my life," said Jennifer. "I thought it would shut her up."

"It seems to have done the opposite."

"Yeah," she said.

"I rang to tell you because I think Sian's going to publish it."

"She can't."

"I don't think she cares," he said.

An audible sigh down the phone line. "What do I do?"

"I don't know. I just thought I should tell you."

"I'll ring Sian," she said.

"I don't think it'll help."

"Then I'll get onto the network." A pause. "Are you sure about this, Michael?"

"I'm sure."

"Skankin' hell," she said. "What a skankin' disaster."

TWENTY-FIVE

PERCEIVERS PROTEST TO PARALYSE LONDON
By Sian Jones, staff reporter

Teenagers are planning to flock to London on Monday in a secret plan to bring the capital to a standstill, The Daily News has learnt. Thousands of perceivers who oppose the government's plan to return normality to our streets have been organising behind the scenes to stage an illegal march on Parliament.

"We've been told to go down to the clinic to get the cure for our perception like it's a flu shot," said organiser Jennifer Price. "But what we have isn't a disease, it's part of us and we should have a say in whether it's taken away."

Underground websites are urging teenagers to leave their classrooms to join the demonstration. "Don't tell your parents or your teachers, don't tell your brothers and sisters," proclaimed one site. "Just get up in the morning and join us. Sneak out of the house in your school uniform if you have to, but make sure your voice is heard."

That site has since been shut down by officials, but the viral nature of the internet means the information continues to spread. Regional groups of perceivers are believed to be organising transport to get into London on the Monday. There are fears classrooms could be emptied and teenagers will spill out onto the roads and stop traffic. There's even concern young tempers could flare and violence could break out in what is planned to be an illegal protest.

The Metropolitan Police confirms no group has applied for a march or demonstration permit in the controlled zone around Parliament. But a source within the security services admitted they have been following what they call 'internet chatter'. "We're not concerned," the source told The Daily News. "We believe this is an isolated group of teenagers with delusions of grandeur. We foresee no public disorder occurring in the capital or elsewhere on Monday. We are, however, keeping an eye on the situation and liaising with our colleagues at the Met to ensure public safety is not put at risk."

TWENTY-SIX

JENNIFER sat in a dark corner of the coffee shop, her trademark large coat wrapped around her and a paper copy of *The Daily News* in her hand. Her attention was consumed by it. She didn't notice Michael walk up to her.

"Got your message," said Michael.

She looked up from her curled up position on the low coffee-house sofa. Her eyes were red and the dim lights picked up the remains of tears underneath. "You were right," she said. She threw the paper down on the coffee table with disgust. The headline looked darker and uglier on paper than it had done on the tiny screen of his phone. Underneath, her picture in younger happier times in her school uniform, was the only one smiling.

"You want coffee?" he asked.

"That'd be great."

He noticed, then, she already had a full cup on the table. He went to the counter anyway. After all Jennifer had done for him back in the past, the least he could do was buy her a coffee.

The place was full, despite it being one of three coffee shops in the street, and Michael had to queue. Businessmen and women in suits holding relaxed meetings with each other, casually dressed customers on phones and laptops, a jogger with a fruit smoothie; and noise everywhere. Conversations that merged into one and bounced off the walls, mixed with the grinding of coffee beans and the frothing of milk. Jennifer had chosen a good place to meet. It was somewhere where they could be anonymous. Just another couple of coffee drinkers.

Jennifer's coffee smelt bitter as he carried it back to the table. Amazing how its pungency overcame the background smell of everyone else's coffee in the building. He'd paid far too much for a bottle of orange juice for himself and a bagel which made his stomach rumble when he looked at it.

He put Jennifer's coffee on the table next to the one she had hardly touched and sat next to her. She was staring at the paper again.

"How many times have you read that?" he said.

She tapped the paper with her index finger. "Teenagers with a sense of grandeur!" she quoted.

"I know," said Michael.

"How could she do this?"

"I don't know. She's a journalist, I suppose, it's what she does."

"My skankin' mother! She was 'so proud' of me that she just 'had to tell' the 'lovely lady' all about the 'little thing' I was planning in London. You'd think she was old enough to understand the meaning of 'secret.'"

Jennifer was wobbling in the way people do when they are fighting emotion. In her case, a mixture of betrayal, anger and despair. Michael reached across and held her hand. He didn't know what else to do.

She sniffed and got control of herself. "I shouldn't've told her in the first place. It was stupid."

Jennifer looked up. She whisked her hand away from Michael's. He followed her gaze to see a familiar figure with shocking blond hair approach their table.

Michael stood up. "Otis!"

"Michael mate!" Otis put out his hand for Michael to shake, then changed his mind and put his arms round him in a bear hug. "You're okay. You're really okay. I thought, after the hotel room, y'know …"

He let go of his embrace and Michael got a chance to have a good look at him. He looked just the same. But it was the first time he was able to perceive him. There was a confidence about him. A friendliness that hid a sense of wariness beneath.

"Hey, Jen, how ya doin'?" he said as he sat down next to her. He put his arm around her shoulders and she sank into his body. Michael perceived how he — more than any other — was able to comfort her. Michael tried not to be jealous. Otis was a perceiver and would know.

Jennifer sniffed again. "I'm okay."

"I tried to call you to say I was running late," said Otis, "but I couldn't get through."

"I turned off my phone," said Jennifer. "Journalists kept calling me."

"Ah," said Otis. He picked up the paper and frowned at the headline. He chucked it dismissively back on the table. "I'm going to get some coffee," he said. "Anyone else?"

"Have this one," said Michael. Jennifer was never going to drink both coffees, he realised, and passed the one he'd just bought across to Otis.

"Cheers."

"I heard you'd been arrested," said Michael.

"Got community service," said Otis. "It was my first offence, so they went easy on me."

"Did they make you …?" Michael began.

Otis finished his sentence with a whisper. "… have the cure?" He gave a mischievous grin. "They gave me an appointment as part of my release conditions. Of course, I didn't actually turn up, so I suppose I'm a fugitive."

Michael smiled. "Join the club."

Jennifer banged her fist loud on the table. For an instant, the whole coffee shop went quiet. Heads turned in her direction. She turned her face into the shadows. The other customers realised nothing interesting was going on and went back to their conversations. But it got Michael and Otis's attention.

"This is serious," she said. "What are we supposed to do now?"

"Maybe it's not that bad," suggested Otis.

"It's on the front cover of the skankin' newspaper," she said. "It's all over the net, every media outlet from here to Timbuktu's been calling me …"

"You want this demo to be big, right?" said Otis. He wasn't just trying to cheer Jennifer up. Michael perceived he was excited about something.

"Well … yeah," said Jennifer.

"Then this is great publicity," he said.

"But it's illegal, Otis. And I'm quoted as the organiser. I'll probably be arrested or worse."

"Don't be so pessimistic, Jen. You're cured already, you can afford to be the public face of perceivers."

"Public face?" she said.

"Hear me out," said Otis. "You said this story is everywhere, that journalists are calling you. Fantastic! Speak to them. Put our opinion out there. If you want this demonstration to show what teenagers feel, then this is your opportunity to do that."

Michael was sandwiched between Otis's excitement and Jennifer's reticence.

"I don't know," she said.

But Michael thought Otis had a point. And he remembered Sian's words at the train station, 'the publicity will be good for Jennifer'. "I think you should do it," said Michael.

"Really?" said Jennifer.

"Tell them what it's like to be a perceiver," he continued, "what it's like to be cured against your will. If you don't tell the truth, who else is going to?"

Jennifer thought about it and Michael perceived she was warming to the idea. He turned to Otis. Otis perceived it too.

"Turn your phone back on," said Otis. "Start returning those journalists' calls."

TWENTY-SEVEN

Natasha Hill looked up from her computer screen and turned to the camera: "Some news just in: we're getting reports that a counter demonstration is planned against the teenage perceivers in London. With more, I'm joined by our Home Affairs Correspondent, Frank Maplefield…"

The image changed to a wide shot which showed Frank, in hastily tied blue tie clashing with his cream suit, sitting across the desk from the newsreader.

"Frank, what more do we know?"

"News is just coming in, as you say, Natasha, but it seems a demonstration is being organised in London at the same time as the teenage perceivers plan to march on Parliament. The announcement's been made by Action Against Mind Invasion, who — as we know — are very much in favour of the normalisation of the teenage population."

"Do we know what form this demonstration will take?" said Natasha.

"Not as yet, but it seems the AAMI want to show how much support there is for their side of the argument—"

"Can I just stop you there, Frank?" Natasha pressed her earpiece closer into her ear. *"I think we can go to a statement from the AAMI now …"*

The shot changed to somewhere outside and a close-up of a suburban front door. It was painted yellow with a number 27 in black lettering above the letterbox. The door opened.

Mrs Angelheart, in floral dress and thick make-up, emerged on the doorstep. "Thank you for coming," she announced. She stepped onto her garden path. The microphones, photographers and old timers with trusty pen and paper rushed towards her, getting into the edge of shot. "I would like to confirm that Action Against Mind Invasion will be demonstrating its opposition to the rogue element of teenage perceivers who plan to gather in London on Monday—"

A caption rolled out across the bottom of the screen: Claudia Angelheart, President AAMI.

"—It is imperative that we show that the nation as a whole believes the cure is the right way to ensure harmony between the generations of this country. As such, I would encourage every parent, every teacher, every person who cares about the future to join with us as we petition Parliament. Thank you, ladies and gentlemen. There will be more details on our website, AAMI dot …"

FROM her position high on top of the Queen Victoria Memorial, the gilded statue of Victory looked down upon the teenagers. There were many, many of them: all around the monument and spilling out across the rusty red of the tarmac that surrounded her and onto the green of St James's Park. At the side, forming a human barrier between the crowd and the gold-topped railings of Buckingham Palace, a line of uniformed police officers in stab vests watched them.

The blanket of teenagers stretched up the avenue that led away from the monument; stopping halfway in a wobbly line, like runners clustered at the start of the London Marathon. At the head of them was Jennifer Price, talking to a collection of journalists, TV cameras and fluffy microphones.

Several rows back, Michael hid behind a couple of taller teenagers. He had no intention of getting his face on the news. It was enough to be part of the crowd and soak up the feeling of so many people gathered together in a single cause. There was so much excitement, anticipation, trepidation and every other possible emotion, he couldn't possibly block everything out. And so the melee of minds continued to buzz at the edge of his perception.

A couple of girls behind him started a chant: "*What do we abhor? We abhor the cure*" As they repeated it, more joined in, including Michael, who answered the question with all his heart, "*we abhor the cure*". It was an amazing feeling, like he was truly part of something. The adrenaline as he shouted the same thing with everyone around him — magnified by a shared perception of their feelings — was unbelievably empowering.

As the chants continued, a portion of the crowd became out of synch. Some teenagers started to giggle. Others blew whistles in time to the rhythm, until it broke down in a cacophony of noise. It didn't diminish their spirit. If anything, it enhanced it. They clapped and cheered and the whistles continued to blow.

Michael felt a tap on his shoulder. He turned to see Otis standing next to him.

"It's like a carnival!" shouted Otis over the noise.

"Where have you been?" said Michael.

A morning of difficulties were expressed in one single frown. "Police diverted the bus, I had to come round a different way."

Otis had his phone in his palm displaying a news site. Michael craned his neck to see: *Thousands of Perceivers Gather for Demo*, said the headline. It was remarkable to think only a few days ago, perceivers who feared the cure had hidden their identity from others. Now they were standing together with one voice for everyone to see.

Some of them started to chant: "*Ten … nine … eight …*"

"What's going on?" Michael shouted over the noise.

"We're setting off at one," said Otis. He showed Michael his phone, its clock counting down the seconds. Otis joined in: "*Five … four …*"

Michael too — and everyone around him: "*Three … two … ONE!*"

Cheers erupted. Those at the head of the crowd started to move forward. Like a ripple on the water played in slow motion, the movement flowed back through the assembled mass. Space opened up in front of them and they were walking — marching — away from St James's Park, around to Birdcage Walk and towards Parliament Square.

Ahead, Michael could see Jennifer's long sleek hair and the thin body. She thrust her fist in the air as she cried out: "*What do we want?*"

The crowd replied: "*We want a choice!*"

'*What do we want to be?*'

In unison, fists punching: "*We want to be ourselves!*"

Even from behind, she looked magnificent. She was out on her own now. The press had disappeared, off to file their stories, ring their editors or whatever it is the press do. The police kept a respectful distance at the sides of the marchers, walking like sheepdogs keeping an eye on their flock.

Michael and Otis made their way through the crowd to meet Jennifer at the front.

"Otis!" she cried with glee as soon as she saw him.

"Look what you did!" said Otis, waving his arm out behind to indicate all her followers.

"It's amazing," she said.

Otis looked at his phone. "Police say we've got two thousand here — that's a lie, there must be at least four."

"What about the other demo?"

Otis ran his finger over his phone. "Pretty big turnout for Mrs Devilkidney's lot," he said.

Jennifer giggled. "Angelheart," she corrected and peered across at the news site on his phone. "Do you think their protest takes away from what we're doing?"

"No skankin' way," said Otis. He pocketed his phone and raised his fist: "*What do we want?*"

Jennifer smiled: "We want a choice!" she shouted, along with everyone around her.

"*What do we want to be?*"

"*We want to be ourselves!*"

They kept walking. Stretched out down the path, with the traffic of Birdcage Walk to their right, the leafless winter trees stretching up to the sky to their left, and the spacious green of the park beyond. On normal days it must be a tranquil place to walk through. But not that Monday. Any tranquillity it had was chased away by the noise of thousands of teenagers' footsteps, voices and whistles.

As they approached the end of Birdcage Walk, the iconic tower of Westminster, with its gold-edged clock face housing Big Ben, appeared from behind the buildings on the right of the street. Jennifer strode forward towards the target with renewed confidence.

But Otis was hesitant. He nudged Michael's elbow and pointed ahead. "What's that?"

Where the line of trees stopped, the park ended and the road led into the bustle of Westminster, stood a line of figures in black and white.

"Police," said Michael.

Officers in black stab vests over white shirts lined up to block their path. Behind them, risen up on horseback, were half a dozen mounted police.

Jennifer slowed her pace. "What's going on?" she asked Otis.

He ran his fingers over his phone. He shook his head. "Dunno."

Behind him, loud worried conversations broke out.

"We need to stop them," she said. And, without missing a beat, she jumped out in front of the crowd and raised her hands aloft. "Stop!" she cried.

Her single voice was virtually lost among the noise of several thousand people, but a few at the front — already uneasy — came to a halt.

Otis — his body bigger and more impressive — also jumped out in front of the crowd. "Stop!" He went up and down the line urging everyone to stay where they were.

The marchers bunched up into a huddle. A policeman broke free from the line and walked towards them. Jennifer met him halfway.

They talked.

Michael wanted to perceive them, but with so many people around, it was impossible to filter them out. He couldn't hear them either and so was reduced to looking at their body language which suggested a fierce discussion was going on.

Jennifer ran back to join the marchers. People clustered around her. "They're not letting us into Parliament Square," she said.

"What?" said Otis.

"I thought you agreed the route with them," said Michael.

"So did I," said Jennifer. "The AAMI demo's gone off the agreed route. The police want to divert us up Horse Guards Road."

Otis consulted his phone and pulled up a road map of the area. "That's basically a walk around the edge of the park. No way. Jen, you gotta tell 'em, there's no way."

"What do you think I've been doing?!" she said.

Otis typed something on his phone.

Michael put his hand between Otis's fingers and the screen. "What are you doing?"

"Posting to the group," he said.

"Otis, no," said Jennifer. "Police don't want trouble."

"That's exactly what they're gonna get if people don't know why we've stopped," said Otis.

Michael removed his hand and Otis sent his message. Within minutes, everyone knew. Knowledge spread through the crowd in a hail of bleeping phones and raised voices. The buzz at the edge of Michael's perception turned to disquiet. It was an uncomfortable feeling.

Otis tapped Michael on the shoulder. He showed him a live newsfeed being streamed to his phone. Video of Mrs Angelheart, in a vibrant red coat, leading a swarm of adults across Westminster Bridge played on the screen. *AAMI diverts from agreed demonstration route* … read the words scrolling along the bottom … *Marchers now heading for Parliament Square: clash with rival perceivers demo feared* …

The video switched to a graphic of a map. It showed that Mrs Angelheart and her gang of vigilante followers had — instead of turning to walk along the embankment of the River Thames after crossing the bridge — continued straight down Bridge Street, which took them directly into Parliament Square.

Michael grabbed the phone to look closer. The site was being updated as he read … *unconfirmed reports say sympathisers within the police may have allowed them to take the detour, forcing colleagues to stop the perceivers in their tracks* …

The tension around him was building. Most of the teenagers were probably looking up the same news site.

A couple of perceivers broke out from the ranks. Followed — spontaneously — by another dozen. Charging like hooligans towards the police line. The police officers who had quietly flanked them since leaving the park rushed in to stop them getting as far as the cordon. They caught a couple of protestors: one by the arms, pulling him back so his limbs flailed helplessly; another by the hood of her top, swinging her round; another slipping from the officer's grasp and running free.

As many as ten made it and ran head-long towards the police cordon.

Jennifer turned — panicked — "You've got to post for everyone to be calm."

Otis instantly typed, but the time for appeals had passed.

From somewhere Michael didn't see, the police pulled riot shields. They formed a plastic barricade between them and the protestors. The ten who'd made it through, bounced off the riot shields like tiny children bouncing off the wall of an inflatable castle.

Others ran to join them. Suddenly Jennifer, Otis and Michael were standing in a sea of running and shouting teenagers. Some rushing towards the cordon, others simply trying to get out of the way.

"What do we do?" said Jennifer, still panicking.

Otis clutched his phone, scrolling through screen after screen. "This is bad."

"What?" Jennifer grabbed it off him. She read. Michael didn't need to perceive her to know she agreed with Otis's assessment. Her face turned ashen. She let the phone hang limp. Michael took it from her.

Anonymous posts urged people to rush the police line. Several others suggested possible ways round the cordon.

"We need to go," said Otis.

He didn't wait for an answer from Jennifer. He ran back the way they had come and, within seconds, he was lost in the crowd.

"Should we follow him?" said Jennifer.

In that moment, she looked like a little girl again. Her magnificence destroyed by the same crowd who had given it to her.

Michael shrugged. "Probably not, but let's do it anyway."

They charged into the crowd. Dodging the other protestors, until they saw a mop of shocking blond hair bobbing in and out of view. They followed.

The crowd thickened and, steadily, Otis's pace slowed. The teenagers had formed a bottleneck at a turning where at least a hundred of them were trying to get through a gap capable of taking no more than half a dozen at a time. Michael clasped Jennifer's hand and pushed his way through. He trod on somebody's foot.

"Ow!"

"Sorry."

But kept pushing until they were up alongside Otis. "What's going on?" Michael asked him.

Otis shouted over the excited voices of the crowd: "We're going to march on Parliament whether the police want us to or not!"

"*Yeah! Yeah!*" cheered the crowd in reply. They were carried along by the pressure of bodies pushing against them as Michael perceived a confusion of emotions: the thrill of out-smarting the police, the unity of acting all together, the anxiety and excitement of knowing they were breaking the law, and the panic of some stuck in the middle.

Eventually, the bottleneck widened out into Old Queen's Street. Teenagers spilled out over the paths and the road. A car behind them bibbed its horn, but no one got out of the way. There was the sense of determination now.

Tens of posts on Otis's phone had worked out the same route: turn right at the end, down Storey's Gate, left onto Victoria Street and all the way up to Parliament Square.

They were marching again. From somewhere in the midst of the crowd, a couple of people started off the chant again. "*What do we abhor?*"

Michael joined in: "We abhor the cure!"

The chant continued, but Michael saw Otis and Jennifer weren't taking part. Otis passed his phone to Jennifer.

"What's up?" said Michael.

"The AAMI—" His voice was drowned out.

'*We abhor the cure!*'

"What?"

"Angelheart's lot," Otis shouted above the noise. "They're already in Parliament Square."

"*What do we want? … We want a choice!*" rang out as they walked past the gothic carved stone of Westminster Abbey.

"*What do want to be? … We want to be ourselves.*"

Visible ahead was the majesty of the Palace of Westminster — the heart of Parliament. The minute hand of the clock face marked half past one and the deep tones of the quarter bells sounded underneath the chanting.

Pressure pushed in on Michael's mind. He staggered sideways and knocked into Otis.

"You all right?"

"Can you perceive that?" said Michael.

"What?"

Michael put his hand to his head. So many minds. So disparate. So much anger and hatred. He'd been concentrating for more than an hour to keep the crowds out of his head and he was starting to fatigue. He looked around. None of the others seemed to be affected. "It's so strong."

"What are you talking about?" said Otis.

"Forget it," said Michael. He remembered his father in the cell, the cocoon of his perception surrounding and protecting him. Michael tried to draw on some of that strength to ward off the migraine that tore at his consciousness.

The marchers stopped. Coming to a halt like a row of traffic braking at the approach to an accident.

"What's going on?" said Jennifer. Her words echoed by the mumbles of confused voices around them.

Otis took his phone back from her and scrolled through screen after screen. "Dunno. No one's posting."

"It's Angelheart and the AAMI," said Michael. "I can perceive it."

"You can't possibly perceive that!" said Otis.

But Michael could, he just didn't want to explain to Otis it was because he was stronger than him. "They're in Parliament Square," he said. "Thousands of them."

"Let's find out the old-fashioned way," said Jennifer. "Let's go see."

She ducked under elbows and slid through tiny gaps between teenagers to weasel her way through the crowd towards the front. It was harder for Michael — and especially Otis — who weren't as lithe as her and had to push their way through. As they neared the front, the sound of an amplified female voice rumbled through the air, her words indistinct.

Michael scrambled through the last of the teenage protestors to join Jennifer at the head of the crowd. Otis emerged moments later. They were faced with another line of police officers; standing shoulder to shoulder at the entrance to Parliament Square. Behind them, a wide circular road humming with traffic — mostly taxis — enclosed a mass of adults. The adults stood on a large square of grass, overlooked by the historic buildings which had been the home to the rulers of Britain for centuries.

Most were looking ahead, towards the sound of the amplified voice, others stared at the teenagers. Even through Michael's mental barriers, he could feel them and their hatred. It was horrific to have hundreds of people standing in front of them, feeling how they despised people like him.

"What now?" said Michael.

Jennifer and Otis didn't get a chance to answer before a teenager shouted: "Get out the way!" towards the police.

"Let us through!" came another try.

It turned into a chant. "*Let us through! Let us through!*" Hundreds of young voices together. "*Let us through! Let us through!*"

Michael leant towards Jennifer and shouted to make himself heard. "You need to talk to the police. Make them do something."

"Do what?" she said, as a bottle was lobbed from behind. It sailed over their heads and landed centimetres from the police in a smash of glass splinters.

A police officer at the end of the line lifted his radio to his mouth and said something into it. Tension built in the crowd. The buzz in Michael's head increased its intensity. The chant collapsed into a mix of out of sync voices. As it died, it was replaced by frustrated conversations. The amplified voice in the square had ceased and more of the adults watched the teenagers.

A lone teenage voice rose from the crowd: "The police can't stop us all. Charge!"

It was what the angry crowd wanted to hear: "*Charge! Charge! Charge!*" cried the teenagers.

"No!" screamed Jennifer. But hardly anybody heard her.

Everyone behind them surged forward. Michael was pushed aside. Jennifer grabbed onto Otis to stop herself being knocked over.

In seconds the teenagers had overwhelmed the police and were pouring into the square. Car horns sounded all around them as they swarmed across the road. Alarmed cries and several women's screams erupted from the adults on the grass.

Michael, Otis and Jennifer stood among the few who hadn't surged. The police officers who'd made up the line re-appeared from the left and from the right. Michael got the awful feeling they were going to be arrested — easy pickings for a constable desperate to have something to show from the fiasco.

Otis and Jennifer ran.

Michael ran.

He ran into the square and joined the huddled teenagers at the edge of the grass, berating the adults who were penned in like worried sheep.

"*We want to be ourselves! We want to be ourselves!*" Fists jabbing the air.

At the near end of the square, where the grass stopped and a pavement began, steps led up to a raised area half a metre high. In the centre — between two bronze statues on stone plinths — was Mrs Angelheart in her red coat. She spoke into the microphone in her hand and her voice — straining to be heard above the teenagers — boomed out of two speakers either side of her.

"This is the sort of behaviour we've come to expect from perceivers!" said her amplified voice. Cheers and shouts of approval from the norms. "Not content with invading our minds, they want to invade our democratic right to free speech."

At that, a girl not much older than fifteen with red streaks in her hair, jumped up onto the raised area and launched herself at Angelheart. Clunk went the speakers as the microphone was knocked from her hand, struck the hard pavement — and, with a screech of feedback — died.

Mrs Angelheart went down after the microphone, the girl on top of her, mauling at her like an enraged animal. Two men appeared from the side. They tried to pull her off. She resisted and struck one in the face with her elbow.

The square was sudden pandemonium.

Panic from the norms.

Teenagers charging at every adult.

Fights breaking out everywhere.

Anger, pain, violence.

Police officers wading in, too few to make much impact.

A TV news crew getting pictures of it from a safe distance.

The emotions of hundreds of people around him clawed at Michael's mind. He whirled around, not knowing what to do. He couldn't see Jennifer. He couldn't see Otis. He was in the middle of a flash of flying fists. Shouting people. Running people. He needed a way out. But police were streaming in from all sides. The only way to escape from the square was into another jail cell.

Something hit him in the back. He lurched forward. It was a man — with ginger hair, ugly freckles and a cut on his cheek — who'd been pushed hard by a teenager. He emitted a flash of anger so loud, Michael couldn't help but perceive it. The man's assailant — a boy with wire-rimmed glasses — took fright and dashed off into the crowd.

The ginger man turned on Michael. "Perceiver!" he shouted.

"No!" said Michael, backing away. Not a denial of who he was, but a plea not to be beaten up.

He brought his hands to his face to protect himself. Ginger rammed a hard fist into his stomach. Every last bit of breath was knocked out of his lungs. He clutched his belly, but had hardly registered the pain before a second fist struck his face. The force of the punch propelled him backwards. His foot stood on a discarded water bottle and he lost his balance.

He screamed as he fell.

His head struck the ground with the hideous sound of bone on pavement.

Vision, sound, sensation, perception collapsed.

His consciousness fell into a deep hole and the world went dark.

TWENTY-EIGHT

THE world was lit by blobs of misty colour that blinked in and out of the blackness. Pain throbbed through his head, amplified by the violent thoughts of hundreds of people he perceived around him.

"Michael? Michael?" a woman's voice called to him.

He squinted open his eyes. The light stung him. Adding to the pain in his head. He groaned.

He saw a familiar face through the veil of his eyelashes and the still-blinking coloured blobs.

A hand took his and pulled him to his feet. He felt dizzy. He gripped the hand tighter for support as nausea rose from his stomach. His nose hurt — he touched it and winced. It could be broken or, at the very least, badly bruised. It was too painful to wiggle it to find out. He took his hand away and brought his fingers down in front of his eyes. They were covered with blood.

"We need to get you out of here," said the woman.

He turned and focussed on the familiar face. "Doctor Page?"

"Rachel," she corrected him.

He looked around the square. Things had changed in the however-long-it-was he was unconscious. There were fewer people, many of them in groups scattered on the grass, still fighting. Fists, feet, missiles flying in a mess of flesh and blood. A man dressed in jacket and tie — looking more like a headmaster than a protestor — ran past them clutching his forearm, dripping blood from a gash just below the elbow. Others hadn't been so lucky. A kid, several years younger than Michael, lay on the ground under the statue of Nelson Mandela, groaning from a wound in his side. An adult — a woman — knelt at his side, her smart white coat smeared with the boy's blood. She held his hand and gently wiped his forehead. In all the craziness, a norm had found compassion enough to tend to a perceiver.

"We have to get you out of here," said Page.

"Where's Jennifer and Otis?" said Michael.

"Who knows? Gone, probably."

"I'm not leaving without them."

"Michael, it's not safe."

"I'm not leaving without them."

She must have perceived he meant it because she sighed as if she knew she wasn't going to win the argument. "They could be anywhere. They could've been arrested. They could have been taken to hospital." *They could be dead.*

Michael pretended he hadn't perceived her thought. He strode out across the square, calling: "Jennifer! Otis!"

Page reluctantly followed.

Police in riot gear — helmets with visors down; truncheons drawn — waded into a fight in front of them. They pulled a fighting teenager off an adult. Both were forced to the ground and handcuffed.

"Jennifer! Otis!"

"Michael, this is a waste of time," Page called after him.

He didn't hear her. He didn't want to hear her.

Sirens wailed close by. A girl barely old enough to be in her teenage years sat on the grass with her knees pulled up close to her chest, crying.

He walked by the statues of former prime ministers, dukes and lords. All of them, had they been still alive, would probably be sickened by what was happening in front of them.

"Michael!" cried a voice from the left. He turned.

Jennifer ran out from behind the stone plinth where the bronze figure of Sir Winston Churchill gazed out towards the Houses of Parliament. Michael hugged her. She squeezed him. The warmth of her body melded with the warmth of the feelings he perceived from her.

"Thank God," she said. Her eyes narrowed as she looked at him. "You're bleeding."

"Yeah." Michael touched his sore nose again and felt the stickiness of his own blood. "Took a bit of a bump."

"He was knocked out," said Page. "He'll need to see a doctor, he might have concussion."

Jennifer looked up at Page as if noticing her for the first time. "It's you."

"Never mind about that," said Page. "We need to go."

"Where's Otis?" said Michael.

Otis emerged from behind Churchill's plinth. His shirt was torn and his hair was messier than usual, but he appeared uninjured. He looked directly at Page. "You again."

"I think we've established that," she said. "Can we go now?"

Otis shook his head. "We tried. Police have sealed off all the exits."

"Why?" said Michael. "Are they trying to keep everybody in here until they kill each other?"

"That's one theory."

Screams behind them caused them to turn. A police car — lights flashing — mounted the grass square and drove into the middle. Teenagers and adults, perceivers and norms, scattered out of its way.

Smoking canisters dropped from its windows on either side. They billowed fumes as they rolled across the grass.

"Tear gas!" said Page.

The few near the police car started to cough. They staggered away from it like they couldn't see.

"Hey!" a voice shouted. A young Asian man with smart hair, smart shirt and garish jumper stood near them, a broken off wooden chair leg in his hand. "Perceiver bitch!" he shouted at Jennifer. He lifted the chair leg, warrior-style, and rushed at her.

Otis charged — his head bent like a bull in a bullring — and struck the man in the chest. Both went sprawling onto the ground. They wrestled.

"People recognise me because of all those interviews I did," said Jennifer. "Otis, be careful!"

Michael blinked his eyes several times. They were stinging. Everything became blurry.

"We need to get away from the gas," said Page. She'd lifted the top of her blouse to cover her nose and mouth, but tears still streamed from her eyes.

Otis and the man fought on the ground, but half the time their punches and kicks weren't hitting each other. They had to be affected by the gas.

"Otis, leave it!" shouted Michael.

Otis either didn't hear or didn't pay attention. Michael stepped forward. His vision was blurred, but he could see enough to distinguish between blond and black hair. He grabbed hold of Otis's shirt. At the same time, Page weighed in and, between them, they separated the fighters.

With a hard shove, Page threw the man towards the tear gas. Disoriented, he staggered a few steps, giving the four of them enough time to hide behind Winston Churchill.

"Skankin' hell," said Otis rubbing his eyes. "My eyes hurt like skank."

"We need to get out of here," said Page. "My car's parked not too far away, if we can get out of the square, we can get to it."

Michael peeked around the side of Churchill's plinth. Blinking, trying to focus — even though it hurt — he saw police vans encroach from all sides. They mounted the grass. Doors opened and uniformed officers in gas masks poured out. Confused adults and teenagers stumbled away from them.

He ducked back behind the plinth. On his next breath, he took in a mouthful of gas. He coughed and wheezed. "Which way?" he said through a rasping throat.

"Up Parliament Street," said Page.

"Come on," said Michael.

He ran out onto the road and headed towards Big Ben's clock tower. The others followed him, zigzagging through stranded cars with their engines off. A taxi driver and his female passenger looked fearfully through the windows at them as they passed. Onto the pavement where two teenagers leant against the railings, their arms round each other, sharing a tissue to wipe their streaming red eyes.

Michael dodged a police van, its back doors wide open, a gaping invitation for arrested prey. Back on the square behind him, officers in gas masks rounded up demonstrators, perceiver and norm alike.

They made it to Parliament Street. Page took over the lead and broke into a run, her blouse still over her nose and mouth. The others followed, their lungs wheezing at the after effects of the gas.

It was further than she'd made out and, at the end of Whitehall, they slowed to a walk. They'd put some distance between themselves and the fighting and, besides, four running people drew the attention of others on the street.

Eventually, they made it to the NCP where Page had parked her car. They went down the steps of the pedestrian entrance, with its piss-stench, to where she'd left her Peugeot on the underground floor.

She pointed her electronic key. The car responded with a bleep and flash of yellow indicators. "Get in."

Michael reached for the handle on the passenger side. But there he stopped. "Why should I?"

"Don't you trust me?" she said.

"No," he said.

"You can perceive I mean you no harm."

"Come on, Michael mate," said Otis. "There's three of us and one of her — what's she gonna do?"

He perceived Otis was tired. Both he and Jennifer.

"Don't you want to know what she was doing at the demo?" said Michael. "Why she came for us?"

"Not really," said Otis.

Page tapped the roof of her car with her fingertips. "Can we have this conversation in the car?"

"No," said Michael. "We make our decision here. Once we're inside and you're at the wheel, you're in charge."

Page slammed the driver's door shut again and marched to the other side of the car. "What do you want to do? Deep perceive me now?"

"Tell me why you're helping us," said Michael.

"I'm your father's employee," said Page. "He wants you safe."

"So he sends his assistant into a riot to pull me out?" The idea was so incredulous. "My 'father' is under Cooper's thumb. And you — Cooper said you'd been arrested."

"Lucky for me, I can afford good lawyers."

"Tell me straight you're not working for him," said Michael.

Page took a deep breath. She spoke slowly. "I'm not working for Cooper."

Michael concentrated hard, looking for a shred of evidence that she was lying. He perceived she was not, but he still found it difficult to believe.

"She's telling the truth, Mike," said Otis.

"If this was Cooper's doing," said Page, "it would be easier for him to have you arrested and collect you from the police."

Michael thought about it. It made sense, except … "Are you telling me Ransom sent you to rescue me?"

"Yes," said Page.

"Doesn't he have security people to do that sort of thing?"

Jennifer opened the back door. "Michael, will you get in the skankin' car?" she said. "I want to go home." She got in the back seat and sat down definitively. It had been a long day for her. An emotional ride of hope plummeting to despair and Michael had perceived every moment of it.

Otis opened the door on the opposite side and joined Jennifer on the back seat.

"Are you going to join your friends?" said Page.

Michael looked through the rear window at the two of them. "You're taking me to my father aren't you?"

Yes. The one word in her mind leaked from behind her mental barrier.

She must have figured it out — perceived it, probably — because she became defensive. "He cares for you, Michael."

Her words made one statement, but her thoughts betrayed another. It was a perception so marginal he might have missed it a week ago.

"It's *you* who cares for me," he said to Page.

"Of course I care. I've known your father since before you were born."

It triggered a memory inside Michael. A memory of his father's memories. Of wanting a child with perception, of getting a perceiver to donate her eggs for the IVF treatment to make sure the child was a strong perceiver. "Are you …?" His mouth was suddenly dry. He cleared his throat. "Are you my biological mother?"

Page smiled. She tried to laugh it off. "Michael! What a question!"

He perceived the answer, but he wanted to hear it from her. "Are you?"

The smile disappeared from her face. She became more serious than he had ever seen her. "If I tell you the truth, will you get in the car?"

Michael nodded.

"Yes," said Page. "I am your biological mother."

TWENTY-NINE

MICHAEL sat in the front seat of Page's car, his head still throbbing. And not just from being knocked onto the pavement. He looked across at Page. Really looked, at every curve of her face, at every aspect of her body. He had the same brown hair as her. And her nose — not especially large, not especially small — but with a wide bridge that made wearing some sunglasses difficult.

"Please don't stare at me, Michael, you're making me feel uncomfortable."

He turned away and craned his neck to see his reflection in the rear-view mirror. He looked nothing like her, he decided. Even accounting for the swelling of his bloody nose.

The mirror also showed Otis and Jennifer together in the back seat. She had her head rested lightly on his shoulder. Michael subdued his feelings of jealousy. They were both just tired, he told himself.

A quietness descended on the car as they headed out of London. There was only the sound of the engine and passing traffic. Michael rested his head against the window. The rumble from the road travelled through the body of the car until it vibrated Michael's skull. It did nothing for his headache, but the glass was cool on his skin and so he rested his head there and closed his eyes.

He may have dozed off a few times because the next time he opened his eyes, they were on the M40, with acres of green fields rushing by the window.

"Did I know?" Michael asked all of a sudden. "Before, I mean?"

The question pulled Page out of her driver's haze. "Sorry?"

"Did I know about you before I lost my memory?"

"You may have suspected, but nobody told you. Your father asked me not to."

"So you disobeyed him."

"A lot's changed, Michael."

He wondered how it made him feel, knowing it now. He didn't love her, he was sure of that. But did he care for her? Could he summon up any feelings for her at all?

Page flicked the indicator at the side of the steering column and the gentle tick-tock revealed to the occupants they were about to leave the motorway. The sign at the side of the road said they were heading towards Beaconsfield.

"Why are we coming all the way out here?" asked Michael.

"I'll let Brian — your father — explain," said Page.

They travelled another ten minutes or so. Onto a dual carriageway. Then a major A road, followed by a residential street and a cul-de-sac lined with tall trees. Page slowed the car as they approached a gap between two leylandii. She turned into the driveway and the tyres scrunched on the gravel beneath as the car drove towards the large house at the end. It was quaint-looking, built of brick with leaded windows and flowering climbers that intertwined through wooden trellis on either side of the front door.

The car came to a halt at the end of the drive and Page turned off the engine. All four got out, creating loud crunching noises on the gravel. Michael breathed in the fresh air, full of oxygen from the trees, shrubs and plants around them. It contrasted with the dull thump in his aching head. He wished he had some painkillers.

Otis groaned.

"What's up?" said Michael.

Jennifer rolled her eyes. "He's been whining about his stomach hurting."

"It doesn't hurt," said Michael.

"How do you know?" said Otis.

"I'm a perceiver now, remember?"

"You can feel my pain?" said Otis.

"And it's nowhere near as bad as my head," said Michael. "So give it a rest will you?"

A ringing sound from inside attracted their attention. Page removed her finger from the doorbell and stepped a polite distance back from the doorstep.

Michael felt inexplicably nervous.

Otis, standing next to him, leant over and whispered. "We ran like skank to get away from this guy's office once. Are you sure this is a good idea?"

"No," said Michael.

Ransom opened the door. He looked more or less the same as he had all those times Michael saw him in the cell: the same style jeans, shirt and jumper. Only, he looked older. His face was grey and drained, he was stooped over more and he rested more of his weight on the door than a fit person might. He let out a breath that sounded as if he'd been holding it in all day. "Michael," he breathed. He stepped across the doorstep and took his son in his arms.

Michael felt his body being squeezed against the synthetic wool of his jumper until most of the breath had been wrung out of him. He perceived his father's love, but like a dessert made with too much sugar, it tasted sickly sweet. Ransom pulled back, Michael filled his lungs and felt the disappointment inside his father. After what happened on their last meeting, what else did he expect?

"I thought I told you to get the hell away from all this mess," said Ransom.

"I've done enough running away," said Michael.

"Hmm," said Ransom. His attention turned to Jennifer. "And you, Miss Price, I've seen you on television. Looks like you've made this mess worse."

"I didn't—"

Ransom waved away her explanation. He turned and went back inside the house.

The four of them — Page included — stayed uncertainly on the other side of the threshold.

"Well, come on in if you're coming," Ransom called after them.

Ransom's home, like his office, was amazingly plush. The hallway alone was the size of the living room from their old squat, with stairs leading up to the left and internal doors on every other side.

Stepping into the lounge was like stepping into a cathedral. Light filtered through net curtains at the front windows and sun shone in through patio doors at the back. Polished wooden sideboards lined the walls to the left and the right, one holding a candelabra and the other a vase of fresh lilies that wafted their perfume throughout the room. Three cream leather sofas were placed around a patterned rug in the centre of the room. And yet there was still space.

The television was set to the BBC news channel which was covering the events at Parliament Square. It showed a boy of maybe thirteen being carried into an ambulance, people scrambling away from a billowing cloud of tear gas, police charging at rioters, rioters charging at police. Screaming adults and teenagers — some of them no more than children.

"Bloody mess," said Ransom. "Bloody, bloody mess."

They stared at the television. No one said anything.

"At least five dead," said Ransom. "God knows how many injured. The hospitals are overflowing." He turned to Jennifer. "Got what you wanted did you?"

"No," she said.

"I saw you on the TV telling perceivers to come out onto the streets of London," he said. "What did you expect the population to do, stand by and do nothing?"

"I wanted a peaceful protest," said Jennifer. "To show to the country how strongly we feel."

Ransom gestured at the television. "Well, the whole damn country certainly knows about it now."

Michael perceived his words were getting to her. The whole day was getting to her. Inside, her whole body was distressed. She was having trouble holding onto her composure.

Otis's anger flared in an instant. "How dare you!" He jabbed an accusing finger in Ransom's direction. "We didn't create this skankin' mess. You're the one behind the cure clinics. Those kids wouldn't be out there if it weren't for you."

Otis's words wounded Ransom. Knocked the wind out of him so he couldn't reply. He turned to Page. "Who is this person?"

"He's Miss Price's boyfriend," she said.

Michael felt a pang of jealousy. Strong and unguarded, it was picked up by every perceiver in the room. That was everyone except Jennifer. He felt his cheeks go red.

Jennifer burst into tears. The emotion of it was all of a sudden too much. "I didn't mean for this to happen," she sobbed. "I wanted … I only wanted …" The rest of her words were obscured by her tears.

Page snatched a tissue from a box on a nearby table. "Here." She handed it to her. Jennifer took it blindly and wiped the tears from her cheeks.

Page led her to one of the sofas. "Sit down. It's all right. It's going to be all right."

The men looked at each other — embarrassed.

It was Michael who spoke first. "Why did you get Page to bring us here?"

"To sort out this mess," said Ransom.

"How?" Michael glanced at the television. The news was running the picture of the teenager being taken into the ambulance again.

"*Try* to sort it out," Ransom corrected. "I've asked someone to meet us here."

"Who?" said Michael.

The door at the far end of the lounge opened. Ransom turned. The others looked up. It was a woman. In her forties, dressed casually and wearing blue fluffy slippers. Michael recognised her but, for the moment, couldn't think where from.

She recognised him too. "Michael? My God, Michael." She looked accusingly at Ransom. "Why didn't you tell me he was here?"

"He just got here, Mary."

She rushed towards him. In the time it took her to walk the metre or so of carpet, Michael realised who she was. She was older than her picture, her dyed blonde hair showing its grey roots at the parting. But that, and a bit of extra weight aside, she was the same woman he'd seen in the family photo he'd found in Ransom's office.

She embraced him. Her love was so strong it blocked out every other emotion in the room — even his own. "I've missed you, I've missed you, I've missed you," she said over and over as he felt her tears of joy soak into the shoulder of his T-shirt.

When she finally let him go and stood back, he was able to take a proper look at her face. He recognised nothing of himself in it. She was his mother, but genetically he had inherited nothing from her. She had brought him up, but his mind had been wiped of every memory of her. He perceived her love, but he felt nothing for her. She was a stranger.

He looked at Page. He felt nothing for her either. He was in a room with the two women who helped create him — the one who donated her genetic material and the one who had given birth to him. He wished he could return the love that he perceived in them. He wished he could know what it was like to be part of a family. But his father and his biological mother had conspired to take that from him.

"Rachel," said Ransom, cutting through the moment, "why don't you get our guests some water?"

"Sure," said Page.

She went out of the same door they'd come through, presumably to go to the kitchen.

"What happened to your nose?" said Mrs Ransom.

The question surprised him. "Oh," said Michael. "Someone hit me."

"You're bleeding," said Mrs Ransom.

"Yeah."

"You might need stitches. You should see a doctor. Brian—" she turned to her husband "—did you call the doctor?"

The chimes of a doorbell rang in the hallway.

"Saved by the bell," said Ransom. "Excuse me."

He left the room.

"How have you been, Michael?" said Mrs Ransom. "Brian kept telling me you were okay, but when I didn't hear from you …"

Otis butted in, ignoring the woman. "We should go," he said to Michael and Jennifer. "Get out now."

"Go where?" said Jennifer. She blew her nose on the tissue.

"Who cares? Out of here. Away."

"Wait," said Michael. He perceived other minds who were not in the room. Many minds — and they weren't Ransom or Page.

"What?" said Otis.

"Can't you perceive that?" he said.

"The person at the door?" said Otis. "They're peripheral. Why? Can you 'ceive who it is?"

"Not *it*," said Michael. "*Them*. I perceive … ten people?"

The lounge door opened to reveal Ransom with a whole gaggle of men and women in suits behind him. He held the door open for the man at the head of the queue. It was John Pankhurst, the Prime Minister.

THIRTY

"**S**KANKIN' hell," said Otis.

It may not have been the correct thing to say when the Prime Minister walked into the room, but it was what they were all thinking.

Michael stared. Prime Minister John Pankhurst was a man who appeared on the television, not a man who rings the doorbell and casually walks into someone's living room.

"Mr Pankhurst, you know my wife of course," said Ransom. He stepped aside so he had a clear view of her.

"Mary, of course," said Pankhurst, leaning forward and shaking her hand.

"I don't believe you've met my son, Michael." Ransom opened his arm as an invitation to greet Michael.

Pankhurst held out his hand. Michael shook it dutifully. It seemed the thing to do.

The Prime Minister's entourage filtered through the door to fill the room. Several of the suited men had curly bits of translucent wire coming out of one ear and a certain gun-shaped bulge under their jackets.

"What is all this about, Brian?" asked Pankhurst.

Ransom was about to answer when he was distracted by Page's voice coming from outside in the hallway. "Excuse me … Sorry … Thank you."

The two security men at the door gave her a suspicious glance, but parted to let her through. She carried a tray with four glasses of rattling water. She placed it on the table.

"Our guests are here, I see," she said.

"Yes," said Ransom. "Rachel, could you do me a favour and keep Pankhurst's … um … 'friends' entertained in the other room?"

"Sure," said Page with the professionalism of a personal assistant. "I'll put some coffee on. Gentlemen, if you'd like to follow me."

Page walked back the way she had come.

The men with curly wires, and the men and women without, looked to the Prime Minister for their cue.

Pankhurst turned to Ransom. "Brian, my security people get a bit edgy if I send them away."

"You and I have known each other a long time," said Ransom. "You trust me, don't you?"

Pankhurst took a moment. He nodded in an *I suppose it'll be all right* kind of way and waved his entourage away.

"Why did you drag me all the way out here to your house, Brian?" said Pankhurst. "What's wrong with coming to Downing Street?"

"I can't," said Ransom. "I'm under house arrest."

Pankhurst chuckled. It was odd to see a man who's normally so serious actually be a human being.

"No, really," said Ransom. He grabbed the material of his trouser leg and pulled it up, revealing a wide black strap around his ankle with a black box the size of a child's fist attached to it. A red light at the corner blinked on and off.

"What's that?" said Pankhurst.

Otis leant forward on his chair. "It's an electronic tag."

Pankhurst looked at Otis, then looked at Ransom.

"The boy's right," he said. "I'm not allowed to leave Beaconsfield. If I do, all manner of alarms go off, or so I'm told."

Michael perceived Pankhurst's disbelief. The man let out a sigh and sat down. "I think my security team might be a bit concerned to know I'm consorting with a criminal. What did you do? Why are you wearing that thing? Because if you're asking for a Prime Ministerial pardon for something, I don't know if I can — I mean, it would be seen to be doing a favour for a friend…"

Ransom waved his concerns away. "William Cooper gave me the tag, but that's not why I asked you here, John."

"Cooper," considered Pankhurst, "the head of the Perceiver Task Force. Is this about the perception thing? You know my government's very grateful for all the work you put in at the cure clinics…"

Pankhurst trailed off as he caught sight of Jennifer sitting on the sofa across from him.

Jennifer went red.

"You're Jennifer Price," said Pankhurst.

"Yes, sir."

Pankhurst turned — accusing — to Ransom. "You called me out here to meet with this girl?" Anger was inside of him. It manifested in his strong words, an echo of all the stern speeches he'd made down the years. Except, this time, Michael not only heard his anger, he perceived it.

Pankhurst stood up. "I can't be seen talking to her. Have you seen the news today? Kids like her are killing people right now in London. Five are dead. God knows what the death toll's going to be when the day's over."

"Sit down," said Ransom.

"No." Pankhurst fastened the button of his jacket as if making to leave. "I agreed to come to see you, Brian, because we're old friends; because you gave generously to my campaign at the last election and because you've been good to my government. But I will not sit down in a room with the perpetrators of violence. I can see myself out."

With two long strides, he was at the door.

"At least hear what she has to say," Ransom called after him, getting out of his chair and rushing — far quicker than it looked like his body would manage — towards the door.

Ransom gripped the door handle and stopped Pankhurst reaching for it. "You're here now," said Ransom. "At least listen to us."

Pankhurst frowned and looked at his watch. "I'll give you ten minutes," he said.

"Thank you, Prime Minister."

"But Brian, if this was anyone else…"

"I understand, Prime Minister. Please sit down." Ransom led Pankhurst back to the sofas. They sat. Tension grew between them. The friendliness of those first handshakes had evaporated.

Michael, Otis and Jennifer watched. Mary Ransom stood clutching and unclutching her fingers. She tried to pretend not to be staring at Michael.

Ransom cleared his throat. "Mary, why don't you see if Rachel can spare us any of that coffee?"

"Of course," said Mrs Ransom. "Milk, cream, sugar…?"

"Just bring a tray of everything," said Ransom.

"Of course." She took the hint and left the lounge.

Ransom leant over and picked up two glasses of water left on a table by the side. He passed one to Pankhurst. "You can't win this war, you know," said Ransom.

"I don't negotiate with people who incite others to riot," said Pankhurst. He shot an accusing glance at Jennifer.

"I didn't," she protested. "I wanted a peaceful—"

Ransom put up his hand and silenced her. "This is a bigger issue than today. You're not going to get rid of perception."

Pankhurst looked at him sideways, trying to figure him out. "You were the one who invented the cure."

"So," said Ransom, "would it surprise you to know that I'm a perceiver?"

Pankhurst gagged on his water. He coughed and spat. The glass in his hand shook with the spasms. Ransom took it away from him. Pankhurst continued to cough. He pulled a handkerchief from his pocket and put it over his mouth until the spasms subsided and he breathed without wheezing.

"Cooper didn't tell you then?"

"Brian, you're not serious."

"Very much so. My son is also a perceiver."

Pankhurst glared at Michael.

"The young man here—"

"Otis," said Otis.

"—is a perceiver," said Ransom. "And, as you probably know—"

"I used to be a perceiver," said Jennifer, "but I was cured against my will."

Pankhurst looked round the room like a victim backed into a corner. "I'm in a room with three people who can read my mind?"

Ransom smiled. "We don't read minds. That's a common misconception. Well, perhaps my son can a little bit." Pankhurst stared at Michael again. There was an anxiety coming from him this time. Pankhurst stood. "Theo!" he shouted.

Michael stepped towards Pankhurst, concentrating hard, perceiving everything he could from him. "You're scared," he said. "You think a man like you who has national secrets in his head shouldn't be in the room with a group of perceivers."

The lounge door burst open and a man in a suit rushed in. "Prime Minister?" he said, his face red with urgency.

"I need to leave, Theo," said Pankhurst. "Right now."

"Sir."

Pankhurst walked towards the safety of his security guard.

Michael called after him. "I'm only reading your emotions. I couldn't go into your head and pull out national secrets if I wanted to."

Pankhurst was at the door. Michael glanced across at Ransom, knowing their chance for influence was walking away from them. "My father's right — perceivers are here, you're not going to get rid of us!"

Theo opened the door for Pankhurst to walk through.

Michael ran. He followed them out into the hallway. "I'm like him because I inherited perception from him," he said. "You think you're going to get rid of perception by curing one generation of teenagers? It won't work."

The rest of the entourage emerged from another room. They crowded in on him. Someone opened the front door. Through the bodies suddenly in front of him, Michael saw Pankhurst's head disappearing through the doorway. "What happens to the teenagers when they grow up and have babies?" said Michael.

Michael tried to go after him, but the large body of a man with a curly wire hanging from his ear blocked the way. "Prime Minister?" called Michael, but he was gone.

He watched the rest of the suited gaggle depart from the house. All of them, apart from the one blocking Michael's way, filed out neatly. Then the large man stepped backwards, keeping his eye on Michael, until he was out of the house and had closed the front door behind him.

Michael swore.

He went back into the lounge. He saw the expectant faces of Jennifer, Otis and Ransom. It took only a moment for Otis and Ransom to perceive Michael had been wasting his breath.

Jennifer, however, was still optimistic. "Well?"

"He's not going to listen, Jennifer. He's a norm. He's scared of us."

Michael stepped further inside and flopped on the sofa next to Ransom.

His father put a reassuring hand on his knee. "You can't blame me for trying, son."

Michael shrugged. It seemed pointless. The whole skanking thing was pointless: the demonstration, the ride out to Beaconsfield, the whole skanking lot.

The rattling of cups roused Michael from his despair. Mrs Ransom was returning with the promised tray of coffee.

"'Fraid you missed the Prime Minister," Otis noted, ironically.

"That was rather the point, wasn't it?" she said.

"What are you talking about, Mary?" said Ransom.

"I've been married to you long enough to know that when you ask me to make coffee, it's because you want me out of the room."

"It's not like that, Mary."

"It is, Brian. But that's okay."

The doorbell rang.

"I'll get it," said Mrs Ransom, putting the tray down on the table.

Jennifer's face lit up. "Perhaps Pankhurst's changed his mind? Perhaps he wants to talk."

Otis tutted. "Perhaps one of them left their gun in the bathroom."

A perception touched the edge of Michael's mind. Like a familiar smell far away. He sat up and concentrated. He knew what it was, but he couldn't put a name to it. Like recognising a voice on the radio and not knowing who it belongs to.

Through the open lounge door, he heard Mrs Ransom. "Of course, come in." The presence became stronger.

"Shit," said Michael.

"What?" said Jennifer.

"Cooper."

"Here?" she said.

Otis looked accusingly at Ransom. "Did you call him?"

"No."

Michael got up. He looked to his father. "Is there a back way out of here?"

Before there was time for an answer, Cooper walked into the lounge.

Michael bolted for the other door, the one Mrs Ransom had used.

Through it, confronted by stairs leading up, he hesitated. No way out. But no way back either. He didn't need to look behind him, he perceived Cooper getting closer.

He scrambled up the stairs.

His breath and his pumping heart were loud in his ears.

At the top of the stairs was a landing and other doors. Maybe there was a bedroom window he could get out of.

Something grabbed his foot.

Michael pulled it back. He felt his shoe slip from his sock.

He kept going.

Another tug at the bottom of his trouser leg. He tried to take the next step, but the hand had him firm this time. He slipped. He missed the step entirely and fell on his face. His hands scratched at the stair carpet, but they couldn't get a grip. He bumped down from step to step — bashing his elbow, bashing his knee, clunking his head — until he reached the bottom. His body stopped and he felt the sting of a dozen bruises.

He turned himself round. Standing above him was Cooper. "We meet on the stairs again," he said.

THIRTY-ONE

MICHAEL was back in the cell.

It all seemed pointless. The escape, finding Jennifer, the march — they'd all led back to where he'd started. He lay on the bed, looked at the four walls of his cell and didn't care if they were the only thing he would ever see for the rest of his life.

The rhythmic clunks and clicks of the cell door being unlocked caused him to shift position and prop himself up on one elbow. He perceived who it was before the door was opened.

Cooper stood in the doorway. He was the same slightly chubby man, except he'd smartened himself up a bit. The cut of his suit hid the paunch of his belly. He had shaved. He was wearing a tie. His mood, however, was still its usual smug.

"Morning, Michael, how are you today?"

"Like you care."

"I do actually," said Cooper.

"Am I supposed to be grateful?"

"If you like." He put his hands in his trouser pockets and slumped. "Thought any more about my job offer?"

"Working for the government who wants to screw all perceivers?" He pursed his lips in a mock thinking expression. "That's a tough one …"

"We can talk about that later," said Cooper. "Stand up, I'm taking you for a walk."

Cooper called in the guard from outside. The guard handcuffed Michael's wrists behind his back and led him out of the cell.

The three of them left the cell block and went across the complex to the building that housed Cooper's office. He was led upstairs and along the corridor and, as they got closer, he perceived a presence he recognised. He was still trying to place it when Cooper stopped outside the door of his own office and knocked.

"Come!" said a voice inside.

Cooper opened the door. And there, sitting in the executive chair, behind the executive desk, was John Pankhurst. The Prime Minister, with trademark bright tie of orange and blue stripes, beckoned them forward. "Come in, come in."

Michael wasn't aware he was standing with his mouth open until the guard shoved him forward.

Cooper stood awkwardly to attention. "Michael Ransom, sir."

"So I see," said Pankhurst. "Do take a seat, Mr Ransom."

It took a second for Michael to realise the Prime Minister was talking to him. With tentative steps, he moved away from the guard and put his bum in the seat on the near side of the desk. It was awkward to sit with his arms behind his back, so he perched on the edge of the chair.

"Bill, we don't need those cuffs, do we?" said Pankhurst to Cooper.

"Sir?"

"I mean, I'm in no danger from the boy, am I?"

"With respect, sir, he did once stab me in the stomach."

The Prime Minister looked across the desk at Michael. "You're not going to stab me, are you?"

It took a moment for Michael to realise he was supposed to reply. "No, Prime Minister." He hastily added, "Sir."

"There you are, then," said Pankhurst.

"If you're sure, sir," said Cooper.

"Oh for heaven's sake, Bill. As I understand it, it's his mind that's the real threat to me, not his arms."

"Yes, sir."

Cooper ordered the guard to remove the cuffs. Michael felt the relief of his wrists being free of the metal and his back being able to rest firmly on the chair.

"Thank you, Bill. You can leave us now."

"Sir?"

Michael perceived Cooper's unease at being ordered about in his own office. And being ordered to do something he didn't want to do, at that.

"Is there a problem with your ability to understand English today? It's a simple request. Go away."

"But, sir—"

"You can post a guard outside the door if it'll make you feel any better. I promise I'll yell if the young fellow tries to stab me."

Rankled, Cooper nodded and departed.

The door closed. Michael was left to face the Prime Minister. He concentrated on the man. There was none of the fear he had possessed back at Ransom's house. He was confident, in control, at ease. His thoughts, though, were strange. Tuneful, even: *I was strolling in the park one day, in the merry merry month of May ...*

He was singing in his head.

"I'm told," said Pankhurst, "if I think about nonsense, like having a song playing in my head, it can block your perception."

"Well," said Michael. "Perceivers occasionally pick up strong surface thoughts. If the song is the thing you're thinking about ..."

"Quite so. But you are different. Bill Cooper tells me you're stronger than most."

"He tells me that too," said Michael.

A smile from the Prime Minister. "You can pick up more than thoughts on the surface?"

"Surface thoughts are easy for me. Going deeper is … hard."

"But you can — go deeper, I mean?"

"I suppose."

"That's what worries me." The Prime Minister stood from the chair, turned and looked out of the window. "Come and look at this."

Michael didn't move. It didn't seem right somehow. The whole meeting was kinda surreal.

"Well, come on," said Pankhurst. "I'm not going to throw you out from the first floor."

Michael did as he was told. It meant he stood next to the Prime Minister, so close he could smell his aftershave.

"Look at those people."

Michael looked out at the complex below. A group of four teenagers in khaki left the building opposite and turned right; two men with rifles slung over their shoulders stood guard at the gate; a woman driving a red car headed towards the car park.

"They have many things on their minds," said Pankhurst. "They're wondering how they can get through the day without upsetting the boss, what they're going to cook their children for tea, how they're going to pay the mortgage this month." He pointed to the woman getting out of the red car. "Perhaps she's wondering how she's going to tell her husband she's pregnant." He pointed to one of the guards at the gate. "He might be wondering how he can get through the day with a hangover, his colleague might be thinking about how he hates guard duty.

"But you can tell none of this from looking at them," Pankhurst continued. "It's private to them. The thought that other people might be able to see what's in their head — it scares them."

"Why are you telling me this?" said Michael. "Are you trying to convince me all perceivers should be cured?"

"Maybe I'm trying to convince myself." The Prime Minister, suddenly reflective, turned away from the window and leant back against the glass. "You said some things at your father's house that made me think. All this time, I've listened to people like Bill Cooper and my advisors and … well, I only listened to adults, really. I never listened to people like you."

Michael perceived the man was being genuine. He'd really come to listen. Michael stepped back from the window and hopped up to sit on Cooper's desk so the two of them faced each other again.

"You should speak to Jennifer," said Michael. "She's the voice of perceivers."

"Yes, well, Jennifer Price's profile is a little public at the moment. If I met with her, it'd be all over the press. Whereas I can come to this facility and no one blinks an eye. Even my own staff think I'm in a private meeting with Bill Cooper."

Pankhurst shifted his position against the window and self-consciously fiddled with his tie. "It was one of my staff who called him, by the way; when I was at your father's house. He recognised you or Jennifer. Sorry about that."

Michael had wondered how Cooper had known he was there. Not as if it mattered now. He was more interested in why the Prime Minister had come to see him. "There was something I said that made you think?" prompted Michael.

"Hmm," considered Pankhurst. "You said, 'what happens to the teenagers when they grow up and have babies?' In all the briefings I've had, it was never a question I asked. I wish I had now."

The man was worried, and he made no attempt to hide it. There was no song in his head, just the thought that he'd screwed up. That, in offering a solution to the problem of perceivers, he'd made the situation worse. That 'the cure' was no cure at all. That all it did was sweep the issue under the carpet. And it would taint his legacy forever.

"You're thinking the problem won't go away," said Michael.

Pankhurst frowned. "I'm thinking you should stop perceiving me and answer your own question: what happens to the teenagers when they grow up and have babies?"

"I don't know the science of it, all I know is that there were perceivers out there, like my father, before all this fuss about teenagers started. You didn't know about it because they hid it from everyone. I inherited it from my parents, I don't know if teenage perceivers will pass it onto their kids."

"But the cure—"

"Doesn't cure anything," said Michael. "It blocks perception. It doesn't take away the genetic trait that made them perceivers in the first place."

"So curing teenagers won't solve the problem long term," said the Prime Minister, thinking aloud.

"I don't know what's going to happen," said Michael. "But that's not really the point. The point is, the cure isn't a solution. We haven't got a disease. What we have is another sense, like hearing or seeing. It's normal for us. It's like—" Michael tried to think of an example "—it's like how they used to treat disabled people: lock them up in an institution and forget about them, keep them out of sight because they're not 'normal'. Don't let half the population vote because they're women. Don't sit next to that man on the bus because he's a different colour. I thought we'd moved on from that."

"Are you accusing me of being a bigot?" The thought appalled the Prime Minister.

"You thought you were doing the right thing," said Michael, trying to be conciliatory.

But Pankhurst wasn't ready to give up the argument, not yet. "Some teenagers want to be cured, you can't deny that."

"It's like Jennifer said," explained Michael. "You need to give people a choice. Don't force them to have the cure. It's not just 'a little injection' like they say on the advert, you know. It goes into our heads and stops part of our brain from working. It takes away one of our senses — like someone had poked you in the eyes and blinded you.”

The Prime Minister was taken aback. “It’s not that bad.”

“Have you seen it happen to one of your friends?”

No. Pankhurst allowed the thought to betray him. *I can’t imagine.*

“Jennifer isn’t the same person I used to know,” said Michael. “I don’t think she ever will be.”

A ringing burst from Pankhurst’s jacket. “Blasted hell!” He delved into his inside pocket and pulled out his phone. “Yep?” he said, putting it to his ear. “Just finishing up … No, no, I’ll see you over there … Right … Five minutes.”

He hung up. “I need to go, otherwise I’ll be late for my next appointment, or so they tell me. Thanks for our little chat.”

“What are you going to do?” asked Michael.

The Prime Minister didn’t know. He didn’t say it, but he didn’t need to. He pushed away from the window and strolled over to the door. He poked his head outside. “You can take him back now.”

The guard came in brandishing the handcuffs. Michael’s esteem fell. One minute he was being treated as a personal advisor to the Prime Minister of the United Kingdom, the next he was being treated as a common criminal. The guard forced Michael’s hands behind his back and secured the cuffs to his wrists in front of Pankhurst, adding to his humiliation.

The guard led Michael to the door.

“Wait a minute,” said Pankhurst.

The guard halted. Michael turned round.

“I understand Bill has offered you a job.”

“Yeah,” said Michael.

“You should take it.”

Michael had no intention of taking Cooper’s skanking job.

Pankhurst smiled. “If perceivers are here to stay, like you suggest, then we’ll need people like you. Strong perceivers who can put their skills to good use, to help the country.”

"I told Cooper I'd think about it." He'd told Cooper no such thing, but it sounded like the sort of thing he should say to the Prime Minister.

"Then think about saying yes," said Pankhurst. "I don't know you at all, Michael, but I know your father. The idiot may have lied to me about being a perceiver, but he's been a friend to me in the past. So I can only assume the best of you. And, I have to say, Michael, this is no life for you."

"What choice do I have?"

"You can take the job. From where I'm standing, it's the best choice."

THIRTY-TWO

MICHAEL was overwhelmed by the vastness of Westminster Hall. Its stone walls were as high as ten men standing on each other's shoulders and reached up to a vaulted wooden ceiling. So spacious, it was like being in a shopping mall, except it was built in medieval times, centuries before the word 'shopping' was invented. At the other end were stone steps that spanned the width of the hall and climbed the two metres to the next level, where a most magnificent stained glass window sparkled with coloured light. Not so much a window, more a wall — floor to ceiling — of thousands of blue, yellow, green, red and purple glass pieces radiating in the sunlight behind. With such majesty that it made Michael realise what a small, insignificant human being he was.

Just, he suspected, as the craftsmen who made it had intended.

Michael walked the length of the hall and climbed the stone steps. At the next level, he turned left to where two policemen in shirt sleeves stood guard at a stone archway that led into a different room. He perceived no animosity from them. They nodded and he walked through.

The buzz of other minds greeted him. Curious, awed and a few excited — but all unthreatening. He shut out their thoughts — some of them in German, others in Japanese — and continued walking. A souvenir shop on the left offered to take his money in return for little trinkets, but its lure was nothing to the history all around him. Oversize stone statues of historic figures in the wigs and breeches of times past stood watching from the sides. Giant paintings depicting the scenes of ancient battles and long-dead aristocracy filled the walls. All of it illuminated by stained glass above, and the electric bulbs of half a dozen chandeliers.

A tour guide surrounded by a group of schoolchildren was explaining, "…when King Henry VIII moved out of here in the sixteenth century…"

Michael walked on into the central lobby. After the vastness of Westminster Hall, and the opulence of St Stephen's Hall, it seemed oddly small. He walked across its floor of patterned tiles to where a man in a frock coat greeted him. The man looked entirely at home in his traditional outfit of white stiff-collared shirt, white bow tie and black waistcoat with a golden seal resting where his belly button was.

Michael showed him his ticket.

"This way, sir." He opened an ornate door of solid wood for him to pass through.

Inside, it was plain and functional, like some kind of servants' entrance. Stone stairs, covered in modern carpet, led up to a younger man in a frock coat who directed him to a cloakroom area. Michael handed over his rucksack to a similarly dressed woman, who placed it in a pigeonhole behind her and, in return, gave him a round plastic tag with the number 45 on it.

He was directed through another door, and another corridor, into a gallery of green padded benches overlooking the debating chamber of the House of Commons.

Jennifer sat in the front row, watching the MPs file into their seats below. Her hair was as sleek and black as ever, and her body disguised beneath her large coat. Michael made his way towards her. As he did so, a face topped with shocking blond hair peered out from the other side. It was Otis. He smiled at Michael — perceived him coming, probably — and gave Jennifer a little nudge.

"Michael!" she said, her voice uninhibited.

"Shh," went an adult behind.

Jennifer hugged him, bringing him close enough to smell the perfume of her shampoo mixed with the essence of her. While, at the same time, he perceived her delight at seeing him. She lowered her voice to a whisper. "Michael, what are you doing here?"

"Same thing you are," he said.

Otis reached round and offered his hand. They shook in a manly fashion. "Michael mate, how ya doin'?"

Jennifer nudged them both. "It's starting."

MPs had filled the benches of the chamber to the point where latecomers had to stand just inside the entrance. In the middle of one of the front benches down the side sat John Pankhurst, clutching a folder of notes. He'd even changed his usual bright tie for a serious grey one.

At the far end, the Speaker — a black robe slung over his regular suit, and sitting on a throne-like chair — announced to the House: "The Prime Minister."

John Pankhurst rose from his seat and placed his folder of printed notes on the dispatch box. The shuffling and hubbub from the assembled MPs settled down.

"It can have escaped no one's attention that just over three weeks ago, two factions of our society clashed in Parliament Square," said Pankhurst, his voice amplified by a microphone in front of him. "As I expressed to the House at the time, I was appalled at the loss of life and injuries that resulted."

Murmurs of, "Hear, hear," from the benches.

"But that one incident was merely the latest to explode from the increasing tensions that have been building since we first learnt of the existence of perceivers. It is clear to me that we cannot ignore this tension any longer. I fear to do so would lead to more clashes within society and possible further loss of life. In short, something has to be done."

Michael perceived a glimmer of hope inside Jennifer—

"I stand by the work being done by the cure clinics," said Pankhurst. "They are doing an excellent job of restoring many of our teenagers to normality."

—only for it to wither again.

"But it is not enough. And it is not the right solution for everyone. Over the past weeks, I have consulted with many people. Many suggestions for a way forward have been considered. But I believe the following is the best hope for bringing peace and tranquillity to our streets again."

He paused for dramatic effect and looked at his notes before looking back up at the crammed chamber. "Perceivers will be given a choice over whether or not to take the cure—"

Jeers from the benches opposite interrupted him as MPs waved their order papers in disapproval.

"At last," said Jennifer under her breath.

"Yes, yes, a choice," said Pankhurst over the noise. "Just as we — as members of a free society — are free to express choices in many other aspects of our lives."

"Shame!" shouted a grey-haired man with glasses, sitting on the back row.

The Prime Minister continued regardless. "Perceivers who decide not to take the cure will receive education to help them control their perceptions so the majority of the population can live without fear. And we shall educate the wider community to understand that perceivers are not mind invaders, but merely ordinary people with a sixth sense who want to go about their ordinary lives.

"Furthermore, it will become an offence to discriminate against perceivers."

Michael closed his eyes and leant back against the bench. "Yes," he said to himself. Such a relief.

Beneath him, uproar broke out among the MPs. So many people shouting at once, it was difficult to hear anything more than a collective rabble. They waved their order papers in the air, fluttering like a flock of white birds. Michael perceived only a few of them were actually angry, it was mostly bluster.

"Order!" cried the Speaker.

None of the politicians paid any attention. The jeerers kept jeering. Loyalists around the Prime Minister shouted back for them to be quiet.

"Order!"

The jeers subsided a little.

"No longer will it be allowed…" Pankhurst shouted across the House, just about managing to be heard. "No longer will our teenagers have to worry they won't be allowed into a certain school or sports club because they are perceivers. No longer will taunts in the playground or in the streets be tolerated. And, when they reach working age, it will be illegal to refuse to give them a job because they are a perceiver."

MPs opposite were still jeering like badly behaved schoolboys. Pankhurst diverted from his prepared speech and looked across the floor. "I think honourable members on the other side of the House forget what sort of society we're trying to build in this country. Once upon a time, it was acceptable to discriminate against someone because they were a different colour, a different religion, the 'fairer sex', in a wheelchair…"

"We don't need a history lesson!" shouted a buxom woman in a powder blue suit from the back. Laughter rose up around her, filling the chamber.

"I think the honourable lady does indeed need a history lesson," said Pankhurst. "Until 1918, not only would it have not been permitted for her to sit on that bench as a Member of Parliament, she wouldn't have been allowed to vote to decide which man would be sitting on that bench. Because she is a woman. I think she will agree we've grown as a nation since then and we rightly see those laws as barbaric and discriminatory. Perceivers are the new minority in this country. It is right that they be allowed to live like any other person. Therefore, my government will be outlawing discrimination against perceivers and I call on every member of this House to do their bit to encourage integration into society."

He closed his folder and sat back down on the bench behind with finality. There was uproar from the chamber.

Jennifer could hold back her excitement no longer. She stood up and cheered. She grabbed Otis round the neck and hugged him. Then she turned and hugged Michael. MPs below looked up to see what the kerfuffle was. Adults in the gallery gave the teenagers a stern look and mumbled disapprovingly.

A frock-coated man approached them. "Guests are required to sit down and be quiet," he said, "or you will be asked to leave."

Back in the chamber beneath, the Speaker was calling the MPs to order again. "Questions for the Prime Minister," his amplified voice announced. He nodded at an opposition backbencher. "Douglas Pendleton."

A plain-looking man with thick-rimmed glasses stood. "In my constituency, many of the local shopkeepers have had to close their doors because of high business rates. Would the Prime Minister agree…?"

Otis turned away from the proceedings. "Let's go," he said.

"Yeah," said Jennifer, grinning widely. "I don't want to stay somewhere where I have to sit and be quiet. I want to celebrate!"

Jennifer and Otis joined Michael as he retraced his steps to the cloakroom and headed back downstairs.

"Can you believe it?" Jennifer was saying, her voice echoing up and down the stone staircase.

"Only because I heard it with my own ears," said Otis. "Michael, did you perceive him? Did Pankhurst mean it?"

"He meant it," said Michael. He hadn't made the effort to filter out Pankhurst's emotions from the crowd of jeering Members of Parliament, but he knew from their previous meeting that the man was sincere.

Once in the central lobby, they were directed back into St Stephen's Hall where the tourist throng hung around the historic paintings and statues.

"I'm going to get a souvenir!" said Jennifer. Michael and Otis followed as she rushed over to the gift shop.

"What about a pen?" She pulled a biro from a display of pencils, rulers and bookmarks. It was green with the words House of Commons and a picture of a crowned portcullis on it, embossed in gold. She picked up a packet with a picture of the Big Ben clock tower on it. "Hey look, they do the thing where you cut out cardboard to make your own Big Ben." She looked around again. "Ooh, House of Commons chocolate."

"Jen, you're behaving like a five-year-old," said Otis.

"Who cares?" she said. "We won!" Jennifer added the chocolate to the rest of the stuff in her arms and went off to the till.

Michael watched her, amused. "All this — today — wouldn't have happened if it wasn't for Jennifer," he said.

"Organising the demonstration?" said Otis.

"Yeah."

"I think your father inviting the PM to his house might have had something to do with it."

Michael shrugged it off. "Maybe."

"I didn't think I'd see you again after that day," said Otis. "What happened?"

"With Cooper?" said Michael.

"With Cooper," said Otis.

"He offered me a job."

Otis looked at him, perceived him. "You're being serious."

"Yeah."

"You took it?"

"Yeah," said Michael.

"I thought…" Otis faltered, trying to figure it out. "Wasn't he the guy you were running away from?"

"Yeah."

"But—"

Michael interrupted. "I had no choice."

"You have a choice," said Otis. "We heard the Prime Minister say so."

"There's no choice, not for me. Jennifer's gone back to her family and you don't live in the squat anymore. I don't know anyone else. The only thing I know about my family is the despicable things my father did. I have a mother — well, two mothers, really — but I don't remember them, I don't love them. I can't remember anything about my old life and I never will."

"So, what are you going to do?" said Otis. "In this job, I mean?"

"Do what perceivers do. Look into other people's minds."

Jennifer returned from the till with a House of Commons bag full of stuff.

"Michael's going to be a spy," Otis told her.

"I'm not going to be a spy," he said.

"What else would you call it?" said Otis.

Michael didn't want to call it anything. He didn't want to talk about it anymore. "Are we going or what?" he said.

They made their way out through the throng of tourists, down the steps into Westminster Hall and towards the visitors' exit. Otis spotted a sign to the toilets and dashed off, leaving Michael and Jennifer together in the ancient space.

"You and Otis are together then?" Michael asked.

"Not really," said Jennifer. "With him in London and me back home, it's difficult."

Michael thought about telling her, then, how he felt about her. That he thought she was fantastic, that it was wonderful to see the light in her eyes again. But he perceived a sadness about her when she thought of Otis. When she thought of Michael, she felt nothing more than a warm friendship.

"The thing is, Michael," said Jennifer, "I'm not a 'ceiver anymore."

"That doesn't matter," he said.

Emotion welled within her as she tried to keep it under control. "Me and Otis, we used to be …" She sighed. "How do I explain it? When we used to kiss … it was a lovely feeling. His lips ignited a fire within me and I knew mine did the same for him because I could perceive it. It was as if we became the same person, enhancing each other's feelings as we 'ceived each other. Now when we kiss, it's nice but …"

"You could get your perception back, you know," said Michael.

Jennifer shook her head. "No."

"We know it can be reversed. It was done to me. Why not?"

"I'm getting used to it," said Jennifer. "My mum's so thrilled to have me back home, she's making plans to redecorate my bedroom and wanting to know what subjects I'm going to study in college."

"You can do all those things as a perceiver," said Michael. "You heard the Prime Minister. We won, remember?"

"I don't know … And anyway, I think Otis has moved on."

"He hasn't," said Michael.

"Are you saying that to make me feel better or have you perceived it from him?"

Michael thought back to his perceptions of Otis that morning. He cared for Jennifer, but there wasn't love there. Perhaps she was right, perhaps a norm — as Jennifer now was — wasn't suited to be with a perceiver. Not when they knew how it used to be before Jennifer was cured.

Otis came back from the toilets wiping the palms of his hands on the back of his jeans and they made their way out to the busy streets of Westminster. Just over the road was Parliament Square, now full of tourists wandering around looking at the statues. They didn't seem to know or care that, just three weeks ago, five people had been killed there.

Jennifer's pocket bleeped. It bleeped again. She pulled her phone from her bag — still bleeping — and looked at it. "I've got ten messages!"

"Have you got a new boyfriend you've not told me about?" joked Otis.

Jennifer scrolled. "It's from journalists."

Just as she said that, there was some shouting from down the road. Michael looked where it was coming from and saw a host of people, cameras and microphones swarm in their direction. "Miss Price! Miss Price! Miss Price!" they called.

Suddenly, Jennifer was standing on the street in front of the Houses of Parliament, with TV lights and camera flashbulbs going off in her face. "What's your reaction to the Prime Minister's statement?" asked a pushy woman at the front.

Jennifer, caught unawares, pulled her composure from somewhere. "This is a great day for us, for all perceivers…" she told them.

Michael backed away. He had no desire to be in the middle of a media scrum.

He watched Jennifer from a distance with admiration, and a little regret that he would not be seeing so much of her anymore.

A man was suddenly at his shoulder. It was Hodges, a retired soldier in his fifties and Michael's driver. "The car's waiting," he said.

Michael watched Jennifer for a moment longer. She would be giving interviews for a long time, he suspected, and he wouldn't get a chance to say goodbye to her. Otis had also disappeared somewhere, either lost in the crowd or run away from all the attention.

"Mr Cooper wants you back at the complex as soon as possible," said Hodges.

"I know," said Michael.

"Shall we go then, sir?"

Michael smiled. It felt strange being called 'sir', but he supposed he would get used to it.

Goodbye Jennifer, Michael said in his head. Even if she had still been a perceiver, she probably wouldn't have heard him. He thought it anyway.

He paused for a while, but there was nothing else to say and nothing else to do. So he turned, joined Hodges on the walk back to the car and went back to his new job.

~ END ~

A note from the author…

Thank you for reading *Mind Secrets*. If you're not already signed up to my newsletter, you're missing out on the latest news, details of new releases, special offers and *free* stuff!

Come and join in at:

janekillick.com

Find out what happens next to Michael when a mission to look into the mind of a terrorist leads him to uncover a conspiracy more terrifying than he could have imagined, in:

Mind Control: Perceivers #2

The Perceivers series:

Mind Secrets
Mind Control
Mind Evolution
Mind Power